IN THE
BLOOD

Lindsay Woodward

For Mark, my Scientist.

PROLOGUE

Her eyes opened as she gasped. That was the raunchiest dream yet. Where was she getting these thoughts from?

Just as her lips started to curl a smile as she recalled the touch of his hands, the sound of her husband lying next to her pulled Loppy fiercely back to reality. It was the middle of the night and the visions of that gorgeous man were nothing but visions. Just a wonderful fantasy she was playing out night by night.

They weren't just tantalising her sleep though, these thoughts were increasingly seeping into her daydreams too. Every time she closed her eyes, there was that man, that handsome man, dancing through her mind.

Loppy Fox turned to her husband who was facing her, snoring, with his mouth gaping open. Should she feel guilty that night after night she was dreaming about another man? It wasn't as if he was real. She didn't know where her mind had concocted him from.

She tried to lie back and return to her fantasy but now all she could focus on was her husband's snoring. It was really irritating.

With an aggravated sigh, she got up. She threw her dressing gown over her flannelette pyjamas and headed downstairs. She made her way through their small but cosy home and into the kitchen, with some vague idea of making a cup of tea. She walked past the window and peeked through the blinds. Snow was due and she half expected a blanket of white. It just looked cold and windy, though. Typical mid-January weather.

She couldn't help it - an image of her dream man wrapping his warm, sensual arms around her slipped into her mind. David Royall. He was gorgeous, tall and well-toned. Of course he was, he was her fantasy.

As she reached for the kettle and filled it with water, her thoughts became more serious. What if he wasn't just a silly fantasy? What if he was a symbol? Like something her subconscious had invented because deep down she wasn't satisfied.

She had a lovely home, a husband who looked after her, a close-knit family and a good job. What more was there to want in life? She couldn't actually say that she wanted anything else; not specifically. But she also knew, being absolutely honest, that she wasn't happy.

Thoughts of David filled her head. The first time he'd come to her was on Christmas night. A simple dream of her going to the pub and meeting a lovely man. She'd woken up happy, but she'd expected the dream to fade away with the light of dawn. Quite the opposite had happened though, and her fantasy was getting more intense with every passing second.

Not that Loppy saw it as a problem. She welcomed it. She'd smiled more in the past few weeks than she had done in the last few years. In fact she couldn't ever remember feeling so alive. David truly excited her; even if it was all in her head.

She walked over to the dining table in the open plan space and knocked the laptop awake to see the time. It was just after three thirty am. She really should go back to bed. She really did want to get back to that dream. Just thinking about it brought a smile to her face.

She bit her lip as she recalled the adventures they'd been on together. No matter what they did in her mind, it always ended up with sex. And not just any sex. If she was ever to even utter to her husband some of those antics she'd imagined, he would probably die of embarrassment. She was surprised by how creative her subconscious seemed to be.

She brushed her fingers across the keys of the laptop and a yearning suddenly pulled in her stomach. She knew David. She knew everything about him. In her dreams she'd made him completely real. He lived in London and he was head of a scientific research facility. He didn't really have any friends to speak of. He was a very private man. He'd been waiting for Loppy to come into his life; to give him something more than just his work. But she needed him just as much.

She tinkered with the keys below her fingers and an idea starting forming in her mind. What if she was to take her fantasy and immortalise it forever? Just the idea made her heart flutter. She took a few deep breaths and sat down. She had to think of her heart condition.

She knew they wouldn't approve of her writing a book. She'd have to write about sex. She'd want to write about all the things in her head that she could never talk about otherwise.

Her heart fluttered again with the thrill of what she was considering. She took some more deep breaths and reached into her pocket for her pills. She didn't normally have her tablet until breakfast but she needed to steady her heart now more than ever.

She stood up and poured herself a glass of water, the boiled kettle long forgotten about. She knocked back the small white tablet and then sat back down in front of the laptop, glaring at it with anticipation.

Before she knew it, she'd opened up Word and a plan was developing in her head.

She wasn't a writer though, she was a PA. She loved

reading, but it was a whole different thing writing a novel.

Everything in her body was telling her to give it a go. She couldn't ignore that. It was as if, at that very moment, she'd tapped into the one thing she'd wanted to do all her life.

It would be so easy. She could start it that night. Just for half an hour. Then she could email it to herself at the office and delete it from the laptop. Her husband would never know. She could work on it when he was asleep, stay late at work, draft chapters in her lunch hour. No one would ever need to know. This would be her exciting little secret.

She typed out the words "David Royall" in the middle of the page. Then under it she typed "By Loppy Fox".

She hated that. She hated Loppy. Why did her stupid family always insist on calling her Loppy? Why did everyone call her it? It wasn't even her real name.

Loppy would never write this. Loppy wasn't a writer. Loppy was a silly, naïve girl who had never done anything.

If she was going to be serious about this then she'd have to use her proper name. Her full name. Her true identity. She would need to become the person she'd always longed to be but was too afraid to set free.

She typed out the letters P E N E L O P E in the middle of the page. This was it.

Penelope Fox. The author.

PART ONE

PENELOPE FOX

1. THE LIFE CHANGING EMAIL

I'm still staring at it. I keep re-reading it in case I've missed something important. What if there's something I haven't noticed, like I actually need to read between the lines to see what the email is really telling me?

Whereas she appears, in black and white, to say that she wants to meet with me to discuss my manuscript, she could actually, subtly be saying that she hates the novel I sent to her and I should be taking a long, hard look at myself for even considering it. This could all be a joke and she's mocking my amateur status; my wannabe author skills. This could be the literary world's way of cruelly telling me that I have no place trying to get my debut novel noticed.

I take a deep breath. I have to get a grip. The few words that make up her email can, in no way, possibly be misunderstood. An agent wants to meet with me!

I hadn't written my story originally with any thoughts of it being published, but when I'd finished it I couldn't leave it there. I wanted someone to read it. I wanted to share David Royall - my gorgeous, talented lead character - with the world. I'd written the story to bring him to life, but then it felt like the words alone weren't enough. I would only be bringing David to life if someone actually read about him.

So I took to an online search to find out how I'd go about getting my book published. My exploratory journey led me to the website of the Royall Literary Agency. How could I ignore that? It was calling out to me.

I sent them my first three chapters, as instructed, and within a few weeks a lovely lady called Suzanne had replied asking me to send the whole manuscript. So, of course, I did. Then this morning I received an email from Suzanne asking me if I'd meet with her as she wanted to discuss my book further. In London. Tomorrow. What?

'You look like you've seen a ghost.' The chirpy voice of my friend at work, Siobhan, snaps me from my thoughts. She's hovering in the doorway of my office looking all tall, slim and well-groomed, as always. I'd hate her if she wasn't one of the nicest people I'd ever met.

'Just tackling a pesky spreadsheet,' I lie.

As it stands, the only two people in the whole world that know about me and David Royall are myself and this, wonderful, Suzanne. No one else can know. They'd try to stop me. I know it probably isn't good for my health, starting a new exciting adventure, but what's the point in staying alive if you can't live your life? That's what writing this book has taught me.

'Cuppa?' Siobhan dangles her mug emblazoned with "World's Best Girlfriend" in the air as if to demonstrate what she's asking.

'If you're making one,' a male voice suddenly purrs. That's my boss. My horrid boss. 'I'm yet to taste anything those skillful fingers have created.' He attempts to dazzle Siobhan with his smile. It makes my skin crawl.

She forces a smile back and then looks at her mug. We both know she's very single and has no desire for a boyfriend to mess her about. The mug is there to keep the sleazy Managing Director at bay.

'Isn't that what you have a PA for?' Siobhan notes. I flash her my deadliest glare but I can't blame her for deflecting. The PA that she's referring to is me and making this horrible man coffee is one of my many awe-inspiring tasks.

'Would you like a cup of coffee, Wesley?' I ask.

He looks across at me as if the world's most boring wallpaper has been hung up in front of him. 'No, I'm just bringing this back,' he says, dumping a file on my desk that I'd given to him earlier to sign.

'Thank you.'

'Coffee for one, then,' Siobhan mumbles before darting off as quickly as she can.

I can't blame Siobhan for a very good reason. Wesley Parker, our glorious leader, is about as slimy as a boss could possibly be and no one could be blamed for wanting to get away from him. He's a total flirt who chats up just about every female he comes across. Well, every female except for me. Never me. So when Siobhan deflects it's because I'm a very safe option.

My monitor flicks into sleep mode as I haven't done any work now in quite a while, and I catch a vague glimpse of myself in the reflection. The plain, boring sight in front of me is a depressing reminder of why I'm of so little interest to the biggest flirt on the planet. I don't wear make-up - in fact I wouldn't even know where to start - and my hair hangs freely across my shoulders as if a brush has never seen it. It has, but I don't blow-dry my hair or treat it in any special way. It all seems like far too much effort.

I look down at my baggy jumper, comfortable trousers and sensible shoes. I'm hardly a sex symbol. But why do I need to be for a stupid job where I sit behind a desk for most of the day not speaking to anyone?

I can't say the rumours haven't hurt me, but I am what I am. The gossip seems to believe that the only reason I got the job was because I'm not attractive enough for him to chat up and so I make a more practical PA. The truth is my sister's friend works in the sales department and she got me the job. I needed a job and, like every other woman in this place, my sister's friend has the MD wrapped around her little finger. It's good to know what people think though, and I won't be sending the guilty party any Christmas cards this year, that's for sure.

'Did you send those emails out, Loppy?' Wesley asks, swiping his hand through his dark blond hair. I inwardly smile. He definitely thinks he's more attractive than he is. Far from the tall, Greek God he no doubt believes himself to be, he's actually about five foot five with pointy features and skinny limbs. He also definitely looks post forty, which I know he is. He's not ugly, but he's far from gorgeous.

I'd love to know what goes on in his head when he looks in the mirror. It can't be anything that reflects reality with the way he swaggers around this place. I don't know how he gets away with it. You'd think in the twenty-first century men like him would have been sacked years ago, but he has this charm about him that seems to win people over. The average worker around here forgives him anything. Thank goodness I have friends like Siobhan who can see right through his façade.

'Yes, I sent them out promptly at ten,' I reply.

'Good.' He turns away and starts to leave.

'Wesley,' I say. He doesn't respond, he just turns around and waits for me to continue. 'I know it's short notice, but would it be okay if I had tomorrow off?'

'Off?'

'Like annual leave?'

'Whatever,' he shrugs. 'I just need the figures ready for the board meeting by close of play.'

'Of course. Thank you.' He sort of half nods and then walks off, leaving the scent of his over-powering aftershave to clog up the air around me.

I sigh with relief. At least I have the day off. Now all I have to do is sort out my trains and work out where the hell this café is that Suzanne wants to meet me in.

* * *

It's Wednesday morning and I haven't slept at all. I feel a mixture of both excitement and fear about the day ahead. Just to be clear, the two emotions relate to two very distinct parts of my day. The excitement is all about meeting Suzanne. The fear is about what will happen if my husband finds out.

'You're dressed up today,' Lee, my husband, comments, as I join him at the dining table.

I'm wearing a suit and I've actually blow-dried my hair so it looks half decent. 'We have big clients in today. Wesley has insisted on us all looking our best.' I respond with not a flinch to my face. I refuse to feel guilty for deceiving my husband. This is all about me and my dreams, it's nothing to do with him.

'Right,' he says, then he carries on with his cornflakes. That's about all he's said to me since we got out of bed. It's not unusual for us to be so quiet with each other. We've been together for so long now, we're quite comfortable in our mutual silence.

As I start on my own cereal, I look over at Lee. He's engrossed with something on his phone. Probably sports news, knowing him.

There's nothing particularly distinguishing about my husband. He has very short mousy hair and a plain face, and he wears the same boring clothes all the time. He's in his trusty black trousers and shirt with no tie today; his regular work attire. Occasionally, on a really cold day, he'll mix it up with his blue jumper, but that's about as exciting as he gets.

We continue to silently eat our breakfast and then, very consciously, I pop my daily pill in my mouth. I need my heart to be steadied today, more so than any other day I can remember. I'd hate to go through what could be the best day of my life only to find that my weak heart gives out on me.

We finish our morning routine like clockwork, the same as every day, and then we head for the train.

We live just outside of Rugby in Warwickshire and we

both work in Birmingham. We could opt to tackle the M6 motorway each day but instead we get in our car and make the short journey to Rugby train station. We catch the seven fifty-one train, as we do every single day, and we head to Birmingham New Street.

Lee reads *The Metro* and I indulge myself with a book. There was a time a few months ago when I was reading my own book, proofing it before I sent it off to Suzanne Royall. I'd printed it off sneakily at work and had hid it in a file so Lee would assume it was just boring work stuff. He questioned my sudden commitment to my job, but that was about it.

It's been the best year of my life, that's for sure. I've felt moments of excitement this year. That in itself is something to remember. Even on my wedding day I was so sedated on drugs I could barely find it in me to smile. Then we had to make it a small affair so as to not over-stimulate me. Me and my stupid weak heart. This year, though, I've actually felt alive. Even if it ends up killing me, it will be worth it.

At just approaching half past eight, we arrive into Birmingham New Street station. We step off the train, slowly make our way to the ticket barriers, give each other the usual peck on the cheek goodbye, and then head off in our opposite directions, knowing that we'll meet outside WH Smith at half past five this evening ready for our return train to Rugby.

I walk off, as if it's any other day, as if I'm heading to my job just like I normally do. Then I turn around casually and see Lee just going out of sight, storming off to his job in telesales. Looking at him, you'd think he was on his way to the most important job in the world.

Then I realise the time has come. This is it. If my heart wasn't being steadied by drugs I'm sure it would be pounding through my chest right now.

I scuttle back to the board to check the time of my train. The eight fifty is on time and I am about to head to London. I race to the ticket office to purchase my ticket. I need to pay cash. I can't take the risk of Lee finding out. I'm relieved to see that the queue is very short.

Things are going really well. It must be an omen. This is going to be an incredibly good day.

I am about to embark on my first ever trip to London, completely on my own, and I am about to change my life forever.

2. NOTHING'S IMPOSSIBLE

As the train pulls away, leaving Birmingham behind, a few nerves start to kick in. This is a big thing for me. I never do stuff like this.

I can't help but flick back to that night when I couldn't sleep and I first decided to write about David; when I first knew that I had to bring to life literally the man of my dreams. That was in January, it's now December. What a year it's been. The best of my life. I've finally done something for me.

It hadn't been a particularly hard story to write. I suppose that's how I managed it, as I've never thought of myself as having an aptitude for writing. It was as if I just knew everything about David already. The handsome Director of Biomedical Sciences at an enormous research facility in North London. He lives in North London too. Islington to be exact.

That was a tricky bit. I didn't want to change what my dreams had concocted - I love David just the way he is - but I've never been to London. Why my dreams placed him in London, I'll never know.

I did ask Lee a few months ago if we could go there for a day trip so I could secretly do some research, but he said no. It's always the same response: "Too much excitement could be detrimental to your health." If they could see me now!

Although I couldn't do first hand research, the internet helped me loads. I learned just enough about the borough to write about it convincingly. At least I think so. Then the rest of the time I cleverly had him travel up to Birmingham where he occasionally did talks at Birmingham University. That's where the female lead meets him in my romantic story.

She is very loosely based on myself. Just as David is my dream man, she is my dream self. She's an educated woman ready to start a glittering career in marketing; totally independent and passionate to her core. She's got courage and charisma, everything that I'd love to have. But you can't just change your personality.

I look around and it occurs to me that making this journey to London is taking some guts. Maybe I'm not as weak as everyone tells me I am.

Although I don't have the guts to let anyone know what I'm doing. Is it still brave if it's all a secret?

I glance out the window and see the trees whizz by. We'll be there soon. I feel my stomach flutter at the prospect. I decide that as soon as I get to Euston station I must take a few minutes to calm myself. I have no doubt that I'm doing the right thing, but a part of me is still worried that this adventure may affect my health.

About an hour and a half after leaving Birmingham, we arrive into London Euston. I step on the platform and immediately feel a little bounce in my stride. I follow the mass of people, assuming they'll lead me to the exit, when an eerie sensation begins to tickle at my skin.

It increases in intensity as I reach the main concourse. I could swear I've been here before. The wide open space and the vision of hundreds of faces all staring up together at the huge departure screen is freakily familiar.

Logic kicks in. Through my research I've looked at so many pictures on the internet of North London and the surrounding areas, I've probably seen dozens of images of Euston along the way. Of course it's going to seem familiar. It's where David catches his train from when he travels to Birmingham University in my book. When he goes to meet the love of his life.

I try to find a quiet corner, but the station is packed. I eventually find a space at the end of a metal bench and I take a seat. I hunt for my bottle of water that's tucked right at the bottom of my bag and then I sip at it gently before taking a few deep breaths. I need to make sure I'm calm and composed before I even attempt to tackle the Underground.

After a few quiet moments, I feel ready for anything. I stand up and head confidently towards Euston Underground station. I don't know why I was worried. It all seems so easy, like I've done it a thousand times before. My research must have been more thorough than I'd given myself credit for.

I get on the escalator, pulling out my purse on the way down, and then I queue up to get my ticket. I have to pay cash again. I can't take the risk of anything even remotely connected to London appearing on my bank statement. The train was ridiculously expensive buying it on the day, but if Lee ever saw details of London on any bank paperwork, I don't know what he'd do.

Ticket bought, I go through the barriers and head deep underground. It's just two stops on the Northern Line to Angel. It couldn't be easier.

As I take my first ever step on a tube train I feel an anticlimactic disappointment. I thought I'd be wide-eyed with fascination and exhilaration, but again it all feels so easy and normal. It's very strange.

Within a few minutes I'm at my destination. I get off the train and follow the Way Out signs. My research told me that Angel has the longest escalators across the London Underground and as I stare up at them I have my first "wow" moment.

It feels like a long journey rising to ground level and it gives me some time to think through how I'm going to sell myself. I've decided honesty is the best policy. I'm going to be straight and tell her all about my dreams and how they led me to create the amazing David Royall.

I reach the top and head through the barriers into the small but busy station lobby, then within a few steps I'm out on to the main road. This is Islington! In every single way it's exactly as I imagined. But that feels nice. It makes me feel closer to David, like he could almost be real. That's what I wanted to achieve as I wrote the book, and at this moment I feel like I've accomplished a major goal.

With a smile on my face, I head down Upper Street to the small café where Suzanne has asked me to meet her. In my book I imagined David's research facility to be in the opposite direction. A huge building about ten minutes' walk the other way. It's fun to have my fiction brought to life like this.

I soon find the café. I take a deep breath, flick my mind back to the picture I saw of Suzanne Royall on her website, and I make my way inside.

I immediately see her sitting towards the back on a rather large table. She's a glamorous lady wearing a stunning black suit. She has long, thick cherry hair and a beautiful face, and I can't help but find her instantly intimidating.

I take another deep breath. She's here to help me. I give myself a moment to feel proud, telling myself what an amazing moment this is. Then I head on over.

'Suzanne?' I ask.

'Penelope Fox?' I normally love it when people say my actual name, it's so much nicer than stupid Loppy. But on this occasion there is a bitterness in her tone. That's something I wasn't expecting.

'Nice to meet you,' I say extending my hand out, but all I get in return is an icy glare.

I take my coat and scarf off and place them neatly on the

back of the chair.

A waiter appears at our side. 'Are you ready to order?' the young man asks.

'Not yet,' Suzanne remarks. 'We're waiting for one other person to join us.'

'Who's joining us?' I nervously ask, guessing that it must be her business partner or assistant.

'Like you don't know,' she responds, quite to the point.

My pride has now totally been replaced with a deeply uncomfortable sensation. I get the feeling this woman hates me. What have I done? My book wasn't that bad. I really don't know what to say.

'What is it you want?' a male voice suddenly says from behind me and it makes the hairs on my neck stand on end. I shiver as the voice is unnervingly familiar.

The man sits down next to Suzanne. I look across at him and instantly my jaw drops open.

In every single possible way it's the man that I imagined. He's like a real life David Royall. The way he styles his dark brown hair without any particular effort, his crystal blue eyes that are so light yet also have so much depth, his firm mannerisms and serious face that hide how soft he really is inside: it's the man I know so well. It's the man I've been dreaming about and it's the man that I've just written twenty-eight chapters about.

I suddenly realise that he's staring at me with equal levels of surprise.

'I think I have a right to know what's going on here,' Suzanne demands.

I want to reply but I just don't have any words.

'Why have you written a story about my husband?' she spits at me. She now has venom in her eyes.

Royall! It suddenly clicks with me that she's Suzanne Royall. 'Is your name David Royall?' I utter. I find myself glaring in awe at the totally real man opposite me. He doesn't reply, though. He just glares at me in return. There are no words to sum up what the hell is going on.

Suzanne turns her fierce eyes away from me and her next question is aimed very much at David. 'Are you having an affair?'

'Don't be ridiculous,' he snaps. 'I work fifteen hour days and then I come home to you. When do you suppose I have time for an affair?'

'Then why has this pathetic girl written about you? She knows everything about you. Every little detail. Where you work, how you like your coffee, which side of the bed you have to sleep on. How could she know that if you hadn't fucked her?'

This is too much for me. I can feel my heart starting to patter. I have to get out of here. I really don't feel well at all.

'I don't know what's going on, but there's clearly been some sort of mistake,' I say with a shaky voice. 'I'm sorry for any trouble I've caused you. It's just a coincidence. I've never seen this man before in my life and I promise neither of you will ever see me again.'

With that I scramble to get my coat and scarf and I rush out of the café as quickly as I can. I pace back to the tube. It's difficult to run against the drugs that are controlling my body, but I need to get away.

I step in the station and immediately flop against the wall to catch my breath. That was probably the most awkward, embarrassing and awful experience of my entire life. What was it all about?

I suddenly feel a hand on my shoulder. 'Are you okay?' a warm voice asks.

I look up and see the glistening eyes of David. I step away from him, worried what he's going to do next.

'I'm sorry about that,' he says. 'My wife can be a little over-dramatic at times.'

We spend a few moments just staring at each other, breathing each other in. How could he be real?

'How do you know me?' he finally says. Before I get chance to reply though, he adds, 'And how do I know you?'

This second question almost floors me. 'You know me?'

'My wife said your name is Penelope Fox, but that didn't seem right to me. I thought you were Penelope Edwards?'

I glare at him astounded. 'Edwards was my maiden name.' It's a struggle to get the words out, I'm in so much shock.

A serious expression casts itself across his face, like he's trying to work out a very complicated equation. 'People don't normally call you Penelope, do they?' he says. I shake my head and he looks at me with concentration. 'No, people call you Loppy. Is that right?' I nod this time, very slowly. 'But you hate it,' he continues and I feel my mouth dry. I do hate it, but no one in the world knows that. I've been called it for so long, I've just got used to it.

His face starts to soften, like everything is slotting into place, but I feel an eerie prickle across my skin. 'I know you as Penny. Yes, you're Penny Edwards. But I'm the only one that calls you by that name.' No one has ever called me Penny, but just before I go to tell him that, he adds, 'Because Penny was your Grandmother's name, wasn't it?' I shiver against the chill that races up my spine. 'Your family didn't want to get confused so they opted to call you Loppy instead. Why is it I know all that?'

Every word of it is right. It's impossible. 'How can you know me?' I mutter. I'm shaking as I try to find some logic in this inexplicable situation.

'I have no idea.'

This is all so bewildering. 'Is this a joke?' It's all I can think of. It has to be a joke. This must all be a set up; a cruel set up. David doesn't respond, though. 'Are you making fun of me?'

Again, David doesn't respond. I can't tell anything from his unemotional face. Just the way I wrote him. He keeps everything hidden deep down inside. He is exactly the person I imagined him to be, but I know that man can't possibly be standing before me.

Suddenly I want to cry. This is so humiliating. Of course it's all a cruel, senseless joke. Suzanne read my book and decided to get her husband to make fun of me. I don't know why, but it's the only thing that makes any sense.

He still hasn't responded and I can tell I've caught him out. What a nightmare I've found myself in. It's only the fact that I'm half sedated through my heart medication that I'm able to keep control of my senses.

'Shame on you,' is all I say before I turn and make a beeline for the ticket barriers. I don't look back as I make my way to the escalator. Stepping on, I curse the length of it, but I'm worried too much about my heart to start to walk. I need to steady myself. I'm feeling quite overwhelmed.

I take lots of deep breaths and I chastise myself for my foolish behaviour. As if this trip was going to change my life. The whole event has been one massive embarrassment. The only thing I can be grateful for is that no one else in the world knows about it. At least that's something.

As I reach the platform for the tube, I make a pact with myself never to think of David Royall again. What a mess. That was an experience I wish never to repeat.

3. THE UNEXPECTED VISITOR

'I'm getting changed into my dress later,' Siobhan says, sitting on the edge of my desk. She's been wittering on now for quite a while despite the fact that I've barely looked up from my computer. 'You're in the majority wearing Christmas jumpers, though.'

'How unlike me to fit in,' I say with an unexpected bitterness.

'What on earth is going on with you?' Siobhan's harsh tone brings my typing to a halt. I look up at her.

'What do you mean?'

'You've been like it for the last couple of weeks.'

It's been two weeks since that horrendous incident in London, and as much as I've been trying to pretend it hasn't affected me, it really has.

I still dream of David, but now the dreams have dark undertones. He is no longer the saviour of my desperately stale life, he's now a prankster who goes to extreme lengths to make a fool out of me. I feel like I'm in mourning but I'm not sure what I've lost

'Like what?' I ask, as if I have no idea what she can possibly be talking about.

'I don't know. Different. You're normally such a sweet

little thing but recently you've been... gloomy.'

'Gloomy?'

'There's been a definite change in you.'

Despite the fact that I feel sad inside, her words make me smile. She's right, there has been a change in me, and Siobhan is the only person in the whole world who's noticed. I suddenly feel very grateful to have her as a friend. 'Thanks Siobhan, but I'm fine. It's just the pressures of Christmas getting to me. There's so much to do and so little time.'

My phone rings to save me from any further explanation. It's reception. 'Hi Fran,' I answer.

'Is Loppy short for Penelope?' she asks in a hushed voice.

I hesitate, cringing as always at how awful my name is. 'Yes.'

'Right, well you've got a visitor.'

'A visitor asking for Penelope?' I sit up straight. This is most unusual.

'Yes.' Her voice quietens to almost a whisper. 'He won't say where he's from. He said you'd know what it was about when you saw him. It's all a bit cryptic. He looks very dapper.'

'Okay, I'll be down in a sec.'

Siobhan is already heading out of my office. 'I'm here if you need me,' she says, then she disappears.

I stand up feeling quite unprepared for visitors. It's the day of my office Christmas party and I'm dressed in my reindeer jumper, accompanied by my trusty, comfortable black trousers.

I make my way down the stairs to the ground floor. I open the door to reception and immediately place my eyes on David Royall. Or the man who claims to be David Royall. I stop dead still.

He looks right back at me, not a flinch to his face. I step towards him and catch a sniff of his beautiful musk. Just the proximity of him makes me feel weak at the knees. Whoever this man is, he certainly has a startling effect on me.

'Can we talk?' he all but whispers. I hesitate for a moment. Do I really want to be made fun of some more? Then I figure that maybe he's here to apologise, so I nod and gesture for him to follow me.

I lead him to the back of reception where there's a little meeting room that's usually free. He follows me in and I firmly shut the door behind us. There's just a single, small window in the door and apart from that we're blocked off from the world.

We both take a seat opposite one another at the table in the middle of the room. I want to say the tension is unbearable but I actually think it might be sexual chemistry. I'm not quite sure. All I know is that I've never felt anything like it and all of a sudden I feel an utter mess. He makes me wish that I'd actually flicked a bit of make-up on that morning. At least I've washed my hair.

What is he doing to me?

'I can't stop thinking about you,' he utters.

'Please don't,' I reply, looking away from his heavy stare. 'I was so humiliated by what happened in London. Please don't continue to make fun of me.'

'Make fun of you? What are you talking about?'

'Your wife read my book and then she got you to pretend to be David Royall. Why would you do that?'

'I'm not pretending anything. And believe me, my wife is far from a joker. I thought that was pretty obvious.'

'So you're telling me your name really is David Royall?' I ask, sceptically.

Without hesitation, he pulls his wallet out from his coat pocket. I can't stop my mind from thinking how handsome he looks as I watch him search through a wad of cards.

He places his driving licence down on the table before me. I study it carefully. It states, quite clearly, that his name is David Royall. It also tells me that his date of birth is exactly the same as the David of my dreams, and he also lives in Islington.

An eerie chill creeps through me. How can any of this be true?

'I've been dreaming about you for years,' he says calmly. 'I never thought it meant anything until I saw you in that coffee shop.'

I can't think of what to say. He's been dreaming about me too? This all seems so impossible.

There are hundreds of questions swirling around my head, but I can't see how he'd be able to answer any of them. I really don't know what to do.

'I read your book,' he says. 'You know me very well.' I feel my heart start to patter and I try to breathe steadily. 'In fact, I'd go as far as to say you know me better than anyone.'

He leaves his declaration hanging in the air and we spend a few silent minutes just absorbing each other. It's intoxicating. I didn't know you could sit on the other side of the table from someone and feel so much energy from them. It's both amazing and completely bewildering.

'How did you find me?' I finally ask, thinking of a question that I might actually get an answer from.

'I found you online. I never thought I'd be grateful for social media.'

There's another drawn out silence. I am totally lost for words. Is this a miracle? Or maybe just a highly improbable coincidence?

'I don't really know why I'm here,' he says, for the first time taking his eyes off me. 'I have to do a talk at Birmingham University later today and I just had to see you. As I said, I haven't been able to stop thinking about you.'

I feel my jaw drop open a little. 'Do you do a lot of talks at the university?'

'I believe you know the answer to that already,' he replies. The David in my book did many talks at Birmingham University. I thought it was just a convenient reason to place him in a location I'm familiar with, but now it's adding to this bizarre situation and confusing me even more.

We stare at each other again. More needs to be said, I know we're both thinking it, but what can we say? We know each other but live completely different lives. Our paths could never have crossed before, yet I feel like we've spent years together.

I contemplate what this can all mean and for a fleeting second I am almost floating with excitement. Then I quickly grasp a hold of reality. No matter what may seem to be happening, no matter how much I'm desperate for an escape from my sensible, dull life, this encounter with literally the man of my dreams ultimately means nothing. It's certainly a peculiar situation, but it can't mean anything. It's just a big coincidence that is about to end as quickly as it started.

'I'd better go,' he says, as if he's just come to the same conclusion as me. Then he looks deeply within me. He looks at me with more concentration than I think anyone ever has. 'You're about ninety-nine percent the person I imagined you'd be,' he says. I can't reply. He's one hundred percent David Royall to me. Well, except for the fact that he's married.

I open my lips to ask what's missing but I'm suddenly afraid of the answer.

He studies me one more time. 'I can't really know you. I mean, how can I? It's just in every way it seems like the girl of my dreams is sitting opposite me.' He pauses for a few seconds and I try to fight my smile. I'm the girl of his dreams. He just said that. 'Except for one small detail,' he continues. 'The Penny I know is always smiling. If you don't mind me saying, you don't seem very happy.'

My heart sinks. How right he is. And how sad. The only time I ever feel truly happy is in my dreams with him, and now I find out that the only time he knows me to be happy is in his dreams too.

After another short pause, where we once again stare deep into each other's souls, he stands up. 'I'd better go.'

I don't want him to go. I know I'll miss him. But there's

no reason for him to stay. He's not part of my life and I'm not part of his. How could we be?

'I'm glad you dropped by,' I say, leading him to the door. I place my hand on the handle, ready to return him to reception, when suddenly he pushes me back against the wall.

He presses his lips to mine and kisses me. It's the most passionate minute of my life. His warm, soft touch is laced with a desperate urgency and it makes me feel utterly desired.

I realise that I know his lips. I know them very well. It's as if we've kissed a thousand times before. I must have a very vivid imagination.

He steps away and I'm momentarily breathless. I watch as he scans every inch of my face, then I catch him slightly shaking his head. What does that mean?

'I have to go,' he states.

I nod and open the door. I lead him back to reception and we awkwardly say our goodbyes. He quickly leaves the building and I don't take my eyes off him until I lose him in the busy street. He's gone and I can't help but feel sad that I'll probably never see him again.

'Everything all right?' Fran asks.

I have no idea how to respond. All I can muster is a casual nod. I leave the reception area and head back up the stairs. Then suddenly I find myself stop.

I'm still full of that same sense of mourning, but now it's topped with a sprinkle of joy. I replay the kiss again in my mind and a smile grabs my lips.

It might be sad that I'll never see David Royall again, but he's given me a moment of pure happiness that I'll never forget. It's a memory that I'll be treasuring forever, that's for sure.

4. A CHANGE WITHIN ME

For the rest of the day I find that I can't wipe the smile from my face. My sudden change in attitude doesn't go unnoticed by Siobhan but I can easily attribute it to her talk this morning and the excitement of our annual Christmas party. In reality I couldn't care less about the party but I can't exactly tell her that earlier on I kissed a man in the meeting room downstairs. How could I explain that?

At five pm sharp, just like every year, we all head out of our city centre office and make our way up Birmingham's Broad Street. It's Friday night, just a week until Christmas, and Wesley is treating all fifty of his employees to a meal in a private room at a hotel.

After a mediocre feast of tepid vegetable soup, chewy turkey and bland Christmas pudding, those who can face it hit the bars.

My colleagues are already quite tipsy, and if it's anything like every other year, I'm sure it won't be long before they're all slurring their words and falling over each other. I always end up thoroughly bored and glad that I have to leave early.

I can't drink alcohol as it affects my heart medication and I always have to leave around ten thirty as Lee comes to collect me. He worries about me being left on my own late at night, so year after year he goes out with the lads from his office until he summons me to catch the last train back to Rugby. And then that will be another Christmas party done and dusted.

There is a change this year, though. We're all following Wesley to his first bar of choice, when he leads us to one with a karaoke. I swiftly find out that the new girl in the office once auditioned for the X Factor and Wesley is keen to impress her with his mutual love of singing. I can't wait to see his attempts at serenading her. This is worth being sober for.

I've never actually been to a karaoke and I'm quite curious. We walk through to a small side room where the karaoke is being held and I immediately squirm at the appalling noise of the present singer who is attempting to tell us all about his "Summer of '69".

I get my first full view of the stage and I find it surprisingly enchanting. The singer has a mini platform all to himself, with a TV screen in front of him and a microphone in his hand. It's his moment of glory and I can't help but feel jealous. I don't know what it is, but in that flash of a moment I want to sing.

The words of both Siobhan and David echo in my mind. I'm gloomy and unhappy. What sort of life am I leading? I look around at the drunken people surrounding me. Smiles and laughter seem to uplift the room from every angle. I suddenly have my second pang of jealousy.

I never go out. This is the one day of the year that I actually get to enjoy any sort of night life, and I usually hate every second of it. This really is no life at all.

'Lime and soda?' Siobhan bellows in my ear, fighting against the noise.

The memory of David kissing me sparks through my mind. He's only person I've ever met who's actually made me feel alive. Even before I met him, when I was just writing about him, I was more than just useless, boring Loppy Fox. He has given me something to live for, and I

31

know he'd want me to continue to feel that way.

I wanted to write, and I did. Now I want to sing.

'No, sod it,' I say to Siobhan. I have no idea what alcohol tastes like and so I have no idea what I could order. But who gives a crap, it's Christmas! It's time to stop being boring Loppy Fox. 'I'll have whatever you have,' I say.

Siobhan looks at me with confusion. 'I'm going to have a glass to wine.'

'That sounds good to me.'

'It's alcohol, Loppy.'

'I'm fully aware of that.'

'Won't it mess with your medication? What about your heart?'

It's true, I've been warned many times that alcohol will reduce the power of my tablets. But I have to live my life. I'm sick of being so safe. What sort of a life is that? 'What about my heart?' I yell. 'It's bloody Christmas. I want to enjoy myself!'

Siobhan laughs and then kisses me on the cheek. 'You're bloody wonderful!'

As she heads off to the bar I scan my surroundings for somewhere to sit. Then I clock Wesley at the back of the room. He has a book in his hand. I deduce that it's the book of songs and I find myself drawn to it.

'Can I have a look when you've finished?' I ask as I squeeze in next to him.

He turns to me expectantly before his eyes sag with disappointment when he sees who it is. 'Why?'

'I want to sing.'

'You?' He asks with surprise, then I catch the glimmer of a smirk dash across his lips. 'Sure.' He thrusts the large book in my hands. 'I know what I'm singing anyway. It's always best to go with a crowd pleaser.'

I watch him grab a small piece of paper and pen from the centre of the table next to him. He writes his name, his song and a code on it, and then he stands up and walks over to the DJ on the other side of the room. At least now I know exactly what to do.

I open the book. There are hundreds and hundreds of songs to choose from. Where do I even start? I think Wesley might be right that a crowd pleasing melody is a good option, but this may be my only ever chance to sing. There's no one here to stop me and this is rare. I have to sing a song that I really want to do. Something that I know I'll be able to look back on and feel proud of. And from the sounds of the partakers so far, I don't even need to do it well to be appreciated.

'One large red wine,' Siobhan announces, placing the glass on the table next to me. It's massive.

'Thank you so much,' I say.

She clinks her glass against it. 'Merry Christmas!'

I grab it in my hand and take a deep breath. 'Merry Christmas.' Then I privately toast to the new me. The real me. Even if it's just for now, this will be a day I'll remember forever. I take a sip and immediately note how lovely it tastes. My second gulp follows very quickly afterwards.

'You're singing too?' Siobhan asks.

'Yes,' I smile. 'I can't resist. I just saw it and I knew I had to get up there.'

'You go girl! I'm so proud of you.' She clinks my glass again and then starts to dance wildly to the Grease Mega-Mix that's pumping through the speakers.

I look back at my book and flick through the alphabetical list of songs waiting for inspiration. Then I see it. It has to be a show tune. I love musicals. As much as I want to tell myself that this is ridiculously hard, something inside of me is telling me that I can do it. I know I can do it. And if not, what have I got to lose? Everyone is too drunk to care.

I quickly grab a bit of paper and write down my name, my song choice and I find the code next to it in the book. Siobhan snatches the paper out of my hand.

'Ambitious,' she says with a smile. Then she dashes over to the DJ and hands it in for me.

'Next up is Wesley. Can we have Wesley,' the DJ

announces.

I watch Wesley swagger up to the platform like he's a world famous rock star. Not far behind him is Stacey, our new administrative assistant. She's younger than me, I'm sure of it. I'm twenty-eight and she's at least five years younger than me.

That would make her about twenty-three. I quickly flash back to when I was twenty-three and a shiver runs through me. Five years and I still don't remember anything.

I snap out of my moment of seriousness as I see Wesley winking at Stacey who is now standing at the front like a lovesick groupie. She giggles, as if he's made her feel like the most special girl in the world. If only she knew that most of the women in this place had been at the other end of that wink.

The music starts and I roll my eyes. Wesley's sweet but weak voice begins to tell us, '*You're just too good to be true. I can't take my eyes off of you...*'

He's actually pointing at Stacey as he sings. It's so cringeworthy. I gulp some more of my wine down and relax back in my seat.

As the chorus is about to kick in, Siobhan grabs my hand. She yanks me to my feet screaming, 'I love you baby!' I can't help but laugh.

I join in, firstly following the words from the screen, but I soon realise that I actually know all the words to the song. I don't know where from, but I suppose lyrics are easy to pick up. Siobhan wraps her arm around me and we sing together. I'm ever so grateful to have a drink in my hand. I take another gulp.

The show ends and Wesley jumps off the platform and kisses Stacey. Everyone applauds quickly and then ignores the display of romance at the front. How does he get away with it?

Britney Spears blasts through the speakers as the DJ lines up the next song. I feel I should be getting nervous in case it's me, but I'm more hopeful and excited. In fact, I'm very excited. More excited than I think I've ever felt before. More excited than I did sitting on the train going to London.

The room around me seems to have become more vibrant. It's not crammed and annoying anymore, it's bustling and radiant, dazzling with verve and sexual energy. Before I know it, I'm demanding that Siobhan 'hit me baby one more time' and we're dancing together. I'm dancing!

'Next we're looking for... Erm Loppy. Is that right?'

My colleagues around me scream. I think most are shocked as well as supportive, but I can understand that. This is it.

I make what seems like a very long walk, through the crowd and up to the special spot on the platform. I take the microphone from the DJ and I look out at the many faces staring back. A buzz of energy shoots through me and I feel good. I feel really good.

I hear the first notes of *Defying Gravity* from the speaker right next to me and I quickly flash back to seeing *Wicked* at the Birmingham Hippodrome when it toured last year. Siobhan had come with me and it had been a rare girls' day out.

I close my eyes and imagine that I'm up on that stage and the moment is all mine. Then I open my mouth and sing.

'Something has changed within me, something is not the same. I'm through with playing by the rules of someone else's game.'

I can't believe it. This is actually sounding good. I can sing. I mean I knew I didn't have a terrible voice, but this is more. This is totally unexpected.

As the song goes on, my confidence grows. I sweep through the changes effortlessly, like I've sung it a hundred times before. I've listened to the soundtrack a few times, but I've never performed it. I don't know where this is all coming from.

I get to the slower bit mid-way through and I can hear the cheers from my friends. But more, the whole place is now fixated on me, whooping and singing along. That buzz of energy courses through me again and I realise that I don't want the song to end. I don't want this moment to ever end.

I'm alive!

'...*To those who ground me, take a message back from me...*' I feel the words as I sing them. Every syllable resonates within me and I dig deep as I power out, '*Tell them how I am defying gravity...*'

I don't even know how I'm reaching these notes, but it's so easy. No, it's more than that. I feel like it's part of me; like I was born to do this.

The big finale is coming up. This is the money note that I have been waiting for and the adrenaline is now pumping through my body. It's intoxicating.

'*And nobody in all of Oz, no Wizard that there is or was, is ever gonna bring me...*'

The final word for me to sing is 'down'. It's a big one and I take a quick breath before I hit it. As the note comes out of my mouth, I am soaring with elation. I feel incredible.

The note goes on, but it's effortless to hold. I never want it to end. But I know it has to. I'm giving it my all though. At least I'm giving it my all.

As I finish the song, I throw my arms in the air with gusto and I await my applause. Just as I do, a beam of light flashes throughout the room. It's as if there was a huge indoor lightning strike.

There's silence. All eyes stare at each other, wondering where that came from. It was very weird, but I don't let it hamper my enjoyment.

'Loppy, everyone!' The DJ eventually announces. Finally the applause begins and I can't wipe the smile from my face for the second time that day.

5. LIFE AS NORMAL

'Where did that voice come from?' Siobhan asks as I grab my wine and gulp down the last of it. It leaves me a little light headed but it's quite a pleasant experience.

Within seconds, loads of my other colleagues are surrounding me. They're complimenting me on my singing ability, patting me on the back, kissing me on the cheek and generally praising me about the unexpected show I just put on for them. I'm elated.

My phone buzzes in my pocket. It's ten o'clock already and Lee is wanting to know where I am so he can come and collect me. For the first time ever, I feel disappointed. I'm not ready to leave. However, we can't afford to miss the last train back to Rugby, so I don't have much choice. I quickly text him back just as another large glass of red wine is presented in front of me. This time it's from Wesley.

'We've shown them how it's done,' he slurs. Stacey is firmly by his side. She hasn't got a clue how he'll have moved on after Christmas to the next unsuspecting female. Poor girl.

'Thank you. That's very kind of you,' I say, happily taking the glass from him.

'You did good, Loppy. Nice to see you letting your hair

down,' he smiles. 'I demand more of it!'

I can't deny how much fun it has been. This is a version of me I'm definitely liking.

The next twenty-five minutes are some of the most enjoyable minutes of my life. I dance and sing, chat to people in the office I've never spoken to before and I gulp down my wine like it's a precious nectar that I have to drink before it's taken off me.

My Saturday Night Fever routine is in full swing but my laughter is cut short as the dreaded text message buzzes in my pocket. It's Lee and it's time to go.

I say my goodbyes to my friends, I grab my coat from the cloakroom and I step out into the chilly night to greet my drunken husband. He's been out with the lads in the office and, from the smile on his face, I can tell he's had a good time.

He takes my hand and we make our way to New Street Station.

He's talking at me, telling me all about his night, but I'm not really listening. Between the kiss this morning and my moment of glory on the karaoke, I've just about had the best day imaginable. All I want to do is replay it in my mind over and over.

'What are you smiling about?' Lee suddenly asks me, curiously.

'What?'

'You look like you've got a coat hanger jammed in your mouth. Good night?'

'Oh Lee,' I start. I have to tell him. I'm buzzing. In fact I worry that if I don't shout it out I might explode.

'You've been drinking,' he says, stopping to look at me more seriously.

'I had one small glass of wine,' I lie.

'Loppy!'

'Then I sang on the karaoke!' The words burst out of my mouth. I can't stop them.

'You did what?' He's far from impressed. He grabs my

hand more tightly and we start to walk faster towards the station.

'It was amazing, Lee. Did you know I could sing?'

'Yes, you have a beautiful voice. But you could have risked everything.'

'I'm just trying to enjoy myself for a change. It is Christmas. There was no harm done.'

'Not now. But who knows how the alcohol could have affected you. And singing must have raised your heartbeat. You've been really stupid.'

'Hang on, you said I have a beautiful voice. When have you heard me sing?'

Lee stops and looks at me. 'I've known you forever, Loppy. You sing in the shower; you were in the choir at school. I don't know. I don't think it makes me a bad person to know that my wife has an incredible singing voice.'

'Incredible?' I'm touched and totally surprised by his words. 'Why didn't I know?'

'You don't need to know.'

'What does that mean?'

'You're getting excited now. Please calm down.' Lee wraps his arms around me and actually shushes me in the ear. I push him away.

'I've felt more alive tonight than ever before. I've loved it.'

His face becomes angry. 'You stupid, selfish cow,' he says. 'You could have put yourself in danger. Didn't you think about that?'

'I think about it every fucking minute of every fucking day.' I'm suddenly raging with anger in a way that's quite unlike me. I never swear.

'Yeah, well the same here.'

'I just want to live my life. Is that so bad?'

'And what about me?' Lee argues back. 'We've all made sacrifices to keep you safe. You moan about your family being over-protective, but you haven't got a clue what we've been through worrying about you.'

'I wish you all wouldn't bother. You suffocate me!' As my anger increases, my heart starts to race and it makes me light headed. I can actually feel my skin burning with my fury. I storm off in the direction of the train station, fuming with the fact that my husband can't be happy that I've enjoyed myself for a change.

He runs after me, shouting, 'How can you be so ungrateful?'

I am so fuelled with rage that I lose my footing. I stumble and Lee catches me. In a split second I see the anger in his eyes turn to fear. He looks all around to see who's noticed. Somebody has just flashed a torch in our direction. I can't believe how nosey people are illuminating our fight like that.

'I can't lose you, Loppy,' he says. He helps me stand up straight and I see real concern across his face. He wraps his arms around me again, this time holding me really close. 'I can't lose you,' he says softly in my ear. 'You're everything to me.'

'You're not going to lose me,' I say and for the first time I feel a knot of guilt about the passionate kiss I had with another man. Until now it hadn't occurred to me at all that I may have been unfaithful. I guess I have, though.

'Don't leave me, Loppy. Let us protect you. Trust us. All we want is what's best for you so you can stay in our lives and stay safe. We all love you very much.'

'I love you all too. I'm just really bored of my life. It's occurred to me lately that to live so safely is to not live at all. I needed a bit of fun.'

Lee kisses me on the lips. It's wrong, I know, but I instantly compare him to David and I find myself wishing that David were here instead.

My knot of guilt tightens, but I can't be sure if I feel guilty about my unfaithfulness or if I feel guilty about not feeling guilty. It could be either.

'I understand,' Lee says, stroking my hair. 'Maybe we have been holding you back too much. I suppose a little bit of fun every now will be pretty harmless. How about as a

New Year's resolution we look to do something once a month to get you out and about? Like a date night?'

'Really?' I say, very much liking the sound of his proposition.

'Yeah, we could go bowling or to the cinema.'

My moment of enjoying the idea has passed. A night at the cinema does not fill me with joy, especially when we spend most of our evenings in watching films anyway. But I appreciate the gesture. At least he's trying for a change.

'That sounds lovely,' I reply, trying to look enthusiastic. 'We better get a move on,' I say, happily changing the subject. 'We'll miss our train.'

* * *

The memory of that special day has stayed with me but the excitement now all seems like a distant dream. Christmas day has finally come around and life could not be more boring once again.

As with every part of my life, Christmas day has the same old routine. Lee and I wake up, he cooks me breakfast in bed, we swap presents, get showered and dressed, and then we make the ten minute walk to my parents' house.

Lee's bought me a new Christmas jumper and I got him a new bag that he can take to work. None of it is particularly inspiring, but it never is.

I had thought about perhaps getting dressed up for Christmas this year. Maybe even throwing on a dress. I have a couple stored away for special occasions. But Lee has insisted that I wear my new jumper sporting a giant snowman in a bright red scarf and I can't say no.

We get to my parents' house and it's already buzzing with the antics of my noisy family. Tamara, or Tammy as we call her, is there with her dutiful husband and two young sons. She's my older sister, and is a tall, well-built Science teacher. In every way she has an authoritative air about her.

Julian, the older of my two younger brothers, is upstairs.

As usual he'll probably just make an appearance for food and then he'll disappear again. At least he's here, though. Billy, the youngest brother, won't be joining us. I barely see him at all anymore.

I wish I knew why. We used to be such a close family before some inexplicable tensions started to creep in between Billy and my parents. They've always said it's not my business, but it's horrible. He wasn't even allowed to come to my wedding. My dad personally ensured that he was kept away. My desire was apparently totally irrelevant and I was told it was all for my own good anyway.

That's how it's always been with my family. They all dote on me with my weak heart and wrap me up in cotton wool. I know they've all made sacrifices to look after me, so I feel I'm being really ungrateful if I argue with them. But I don't like it.

Since the family feud with Billy, Julian has been very quiet. He's got a job in our local gym and spends most of his time either working out or actually working, and when he is finally at home he'll just disappear on his computer. I have no idea what Billy does for a job, or even if he has a job. All I know is that he lives with his girlfriend, but we're discouraged from speaking with him.

Because I don't know the details, I keep out of it as much as I can. He must have done something really bad, I suppose.

'What are you doing, Loppy?' my dad says entering the living room. I've made myself comfortable in an armchair, trying to ignore my overactive, screaming nephews.

'Merry Christmas!' I reply, looking up at him. He's quite tall with an obvious beer belly, and the first signs of him losing his hair is noticeable through his tinges of grey.

'Get in the kitchen and help your mother. You need steady activity. These little rascals will have you in the grave.'

Every year it's the same. I'm sure Christmas used to be fun.

'Merry Christmas, mate.' My dad shakes Lee's hand. He

then turns to me. 'As you're on the move, Loppy, would you grab that bottle of champagne from the fridge. And the glasses.'

'Who's having some?' I respond.

'Everyone. Except Julian. Leave him out until the food's cooked. We got that fizzy non-alcoholic stuff for you.'

'They do it sugar free now,' Tammy adds as if this is supposed to overwhelm me with joy. 'So we got two bottles.'

I force a smile and then make my way into my parents' spacious, if not a little outdated kitchen. 'Hi mom.'

'Oh good, Loppy. Would you chop the carrots?' she says. She's the shortest member of our family and the only one with blonde hair. My siblings and I definitely look more like my dad.

'Just a sec,' I reply. 'I just need to get the champagne. And something fizzy for me too.'

'Oh yes. Tammy spent ages finding it sugar free. They'd run out in Tesco.'

'Lucky me.'

'Come on, Loppy. We all try our best for you.'

'I know.' I remind myself not to be harsh on my family. It's my affliction that they all try and work around. It's hardly their fault. I should be grateful, and normally I am. At this minute, though, I can't escape the little dark cloud that's hanging over me.

I grab the bottle from the fridge and place it on a tray with six glasses. I take it into the living room for my dad. He's in the middle of what seems like a gripping story so I just leave it on the sideboard for him, before heading back to chop the carrots.

As I stand at the sink scraping away, I hear the pop of the cork and a giggle from Tammy. I peek through the doorway and see their smiles as my dad pours them all a glass. Then he toasts to family.

To family. Even though Billy is in an unknown place and my mother and I are busy preparing the food.

The only time I move from the kitchen is to eat or to go to the toilet. After dinner, Tammy kindly helps me load the dishwasher. I think I'm supposed to appreciate it, like it's actually my responsibility. Why do I feel so bitter all of a sudden?

It's about three o'clock when I finally get to relax. Tammy brings out the Monopoly board and we all play in teams. I get to be in charge of the money while Lee makes the big decisions. I can't help but think how that mirrors our real life, but I daren't say anything. Julian declines the offer and heads back to his online games and we waste a few hours buying property across London.

At seven pm Lee and I head home. We take with us some leftover turkey and we have some sandwiches for supper while watching a Christmas movie. He's quite tipsy but I feel nothing. Just numb. Just like always. There has to be more to life than this.

The next week we spend lots of quality time together, although we do very little, and then on New Year's Eve he takes me out for a meal. We're back home for ten pm though, and we just watch the fireworks on the telly at midnight to mark the beginning of another year.

That's about it. Another Christmas done. This next year has to offer more. Please. Please. All I want is something to look forward to.

6. THE OPPORTUNITY OF A LIFETIME

I've been back at work for a couple of weeks now; it's well into January. Life is pretty much as it always has been but I can't let go of my need for more. Last year gave me a taste of something better. This humdrum life has run its course for me and I have to find a way to improve things.

It's Thursday morning, only just after nine o'clock, and I'm walking through the office with my freshly made cup of decaf coffee, contemplating what I can do to add a little spice into my life, when I notice a kerfuffle brewing in the marketing department. Well, what there is of them. Normally it's a team of six but today there are just two.

'What's going on?' I ask Gemma, the Marketing Executive.

'Everyone's off sick!'

'It's doing the rounds,' I reply.

'We've got that Round Table debate in London today and Rebecca can't make it as she's throwing up, and everyone who could have taken her place is similarly throwing up. I don't know what to do.' Rebecca is our Marketing Manager.

'Why can't you go?' I ask.

'I've got to pick my kids up. If I'd known in advance...

but I won't be able to arrange anything at this late notice. What the hell am I going to do?'

I look at the very young Marketing Assistant standing next to her. He only started in November so I get why he's not an option.

'What's got to be done in London?' I ask.

'Not a lot. It's more just about representing us. We're doing it with a Trade Mag. They're doing all the hard work. All we need is for someone to be there, Tweet about it a bit and then take notes so we can blog about it afterwards.'

'Do you need someone to take part in the debate?' I ask, suddenly backing away from any ideas that may have been forming in my head.

'God no. They'd hate that. We're just the sponsors of it. We're not allowed to influence it in any way.'

'How late does it go on for?' I then ask, the idea now dominating my mind.

'It's only a couple of hours. We just need someone to greet everyone at the hotel at midday, have a bite to eat, then observe the ninety minute debate. It's also right near Euston. They'd easily be back in Birmingham for five.'

'I'll do it,' I say. Another trip to London, another chance for excitement. This is what I need. 'I'll go.'

'What? Are you sure?'

'Becky's just informed me of the situation,' Wesley announces appearing next to me. 'You're going to have to go, Gemma.'

'I can't. My kids.'

'It's fine, I'll go,' I say.

'You?' Wesley actually scoffs at this. 'I don't think so.'

'Why not? I can Tweet and I'm your PA. My job is to take notes.'

'That's not the issue. You'll be representing the company, that's the problem. And you're dressed like that.'

I look down at my brown baggy jumper and black trousers. I have to admit, I don't exactly look like an executive.

'I have a dress she can borrow,' Siobhan shouts from the other side of the office. No matter what's going on, Siobhan always seems to know about it. She's the Sales Manager and has been working for the company for a lot longer than I have. Everyone respects her and we all know not to mess with her. She's a very strong minded lady. But she's also the nicest friend I could ever wish for.

'That's very kind of you, but...' I look at Siobhan's tiny hips and shake my head.

'Give us fifteen minutes and she'll be ready to go,' Siobhan says pulling me away.

'I'll give you fifteen minutes and then I'll decide,' Wesley replies.

'My dry cleaning,' Siobhan explains, nipping into her office across the way from my own. 'It's been here for days. I keep forgetting to take it home. I guess it must be fate.'

'I'll never fit into your clothes.'

'Of course you will. Just because you insist on hiding your fantastic figure behind mounds of wool does not mean I haven't noticed it's there.'

Siobhan shoves a smart black dress into my hands and then she heads into my office and pulls across the blinds. 'You put that on and I'm nipping out to get you some tights,' she says.

'I've shaved my legs,' I say defensively.

'It's the middle of winter, Loppy. You need tights.'

'Oh right, yeah. Thank you,' I say. 'This is really good of you.'

'And this will be really good for you,' she smiles. Then she dashes off.

About fifteen minutes later, as promised, I'm posing for Wesley in Siobhan's smart, figure hugging black dress. It's ever so slightly tight but I'm thrilled that I could get into it at all.

'The girl's got hips,' are Wesley's first words.

'Take my cardy,' Gemma says. She hands me her little black cardigan that normally sits on the back of her chair, just in case she needs it.

'Are you sure?' I ask.

'That dress is stunning but there's not much to it. We can't have more people off sick,' she smiles.

I wrap the cardigan around me and Wesley gives me the nod.

Before I know it, I'm scurrying down to New Street Station to catch the ten past ten train to London Euston.

The train journey was smooth, the map that Gemma gave me led me to the hotel effortlessly and everyone turned up for the debate. Overall the day is a huge success.

It's just before three o'clock when I say goodbye to the attendees, and I'm left with plenty of time to get back to Birmingham without Lee ever knowing I was anywhere else.

Once everyone has gone I pick up my bag and I feel completely satisfied. I can't believe my luck to have another exciting day just one month after my last London adventure. And this one has been far more successful.

I step out onto the street and make my way back to Euston, a smile gripping my face.

I've only been walking for about a minute when a very tall man dressed in dark clothes and a baseball cap approaches me and asks me for the time.

'It's ten past three,' I say, but as the words leave my mouth another man grabs my bag off my shoulder. Before I even have time to react, the one that spoke pushes me to the ground. I land awkwardly on my hip and wince at the impact, left helpless as both assailants run off out of view.

At first the reality of what has happened doesn't hit me. I stand up momentarily more bothered about the bruise I'm likely to get than anything else. Then slowly the realisation that my bag has gone forces itself to the front of my mind. Then it gets worse. My breathing quickens as I contemplate how I've lost my phone, my purse, my train tickets; everything. I'm stuck. I'm in the middle of London and I have nothing. I'm completely alone and have absolutely no way to get home. The bruise is now the furthest thing from my mind.

I look around as if I'll find the answer somewhere nearby but I can't think straight. I don't know what to do. Is this real?

I take a deep breath. This is really real. This really is happening to me. I have to deal with this.

I take another deep breath and decide there has to be a logical resolution. If I take a second to think about it, I'm sure I'll be able to come up with a sensible plan of action.

I could find a phone and call Lee. No, he'd kill me. He'd never let me forget that I'd come to London. He wouldn't let me leave the house again.

I could call the office. But I don't want anyone to know. I feel so ashamed. Stupid, poorly Loppy gets mugged. That'll be the end of my adventures.

I need to get home without anyone knowing.

But that's impossible.

I continue walking towards Euston with a lame idea that Virgin Trains might take pity on me and will let me travel without my ticket.

I focus on my surroundings trying to remember the way back without Gemma's map when suddenly I realise that I know exactly where I am. In fact, I know this very well.

It then dawns on me that I'm only a short walk away from David Royall's workplace. I don't know how I know it. It's that strange situation again. But I know it.

He dropped in on me at work unannounced. He wouldn't judge me. He never judges me.

Before I even have a chance to properly consider it, I find my legs are taking me there. It all feels so familiar and in less than fifteen minutes I'm outside the enormous building of the QAR Research Centre.

It's exactly as I imagined. So much so it gives me a shiver. I look up in awe at the fifteen storey, modern glass building that reflects the dark grey sky. It's a million miles from my little workplace. It's an incredible sight.

I take a deep breath to keep me calm and I head through the large entrance. I can't quite believe I'm doing it, but I don't have many other options.

The light and airy reception is surprisingly quiet. There are a few security guards milling around and, in the middle, behind a huge white desk, sits a receptionist. She's a young woman with straight blonde hair and a perky face, and her smile immediately makes me feel welcome.

'Hello,' I say.

'Can I help?'

'I'm here to see David Royall.'

'Do you have an appointment?'

'No, but he-'

'I'm sorry, I can't help you then,' she replies, shaking her head.

'He'll know what it's about.'

'I'm really sorry, Dr Royall is an incredibly busy man. If you don't have an appointment then you won't be able to see him.'

'You don't understand. I'm a friend of his.'

The girl shrugs. 'There's nothing I can do. He is in the building but if it's not scheduled then I can't disturb him. He doesn't like it.'

'It's really important that I see him.'

'Well, if he's a friend, can't you just give him a call?'

I open my mouth to tell her my unfortunate situation when I realise that even if I get her to sympathise, I don't know his number anyway. Moreover, what if she assumes I'm a family friend and she offers to call his wife? Being honest could get far too messy.

Instead I just nod and shrug my shoulders. I take a step back and scan my surroundings. Anything beyond the reception is blocked by gates. You have to have a pass to get through so there's not even a way I can just go looking for David. This place is serious business.

'Please just give him a call,' I try again. 'If he doesn't want to see me-'

'I really can't,' she replies.

'I promise you, when he knows it's me he won't be mad.' I say the words but I'm not a hundred percent convinced they're true. What if doesn't want to see me?

'I'm sure you're telling the truth, but you're not the first person to try and see Dr Royall and most of them end up being time wasters. If he hasn't let me know you're arriving then there's nothing I can do. My job could be on the line. I hope you understand.'

As much as I'm sure that she's exaggerating about getting the sack for disturbing him, she has the power and I'm stuck. Besides, she's right, if I am the good friend I claim to be, then why don't I just call him? I must seem quite suspicious. 'Thank you anyway,' I say.

I turn around and leave the relative warmth of the reception for the chilly winter air. I don't know what to do with myself. How am I going to get home? And, more importantly, I am now burdened with another worry: am I ever going to see David Royall again?

7. WHAT DO I WANT?

I sit down for a second on a little wall just outside the entrance and I consider my options.

A part of me hasn't forgotten the idea I had of pleading with Virgin Trains to see if they'll still let me travel. I mean I did pay for the journey. I've just had the ticket stolen from me.

I find that I don't move, though. That receptionist clearly told me that David is in the building. He's just metres away from me somewhere. I'm so close to seeing him, I'm not sure I can pull myself away.

I sit and wait on the cold wall, shivering to my core, determined that he'll appear any second. Any concept of time is all forgotten about as I desperately hope that he'll turn up. Before I know it, he's totally consuming my mind.

Then I see him. He's there, right at the back of the reception. He's behind the barriers, chatting to another man.

I scramble to my feet and run into the building, shouting his name like a mad woman. Within seconds the security guards are surrounding me and the receptionist looks horrified.

David glares at me, completely startled. I'm sure not just

from me being there, but also because of the ridiculous entrance I just made. I'll need to explain that.

'It's okay, I know her,' he says, gesturing for the security guards to back off.

I move to the barriers to meet him. As I do, I flash an "I told you so" look in the direction of the receptionist.

'You'll need to sign in,' she says, standing up, still trying to exercise some sort of power over me. 'All visitors have to sign in.'

I turn to David for confirmation and he just nods. I walk around to the reception desk where I'm handed what seems like a very long form for a short visit. Then I'm asked to stand before a tiny little camera and my picture is taken. What is this place?

I'm given my own temporary security pass and I head back to the barrier where David is patiently waiting for me.

'Come with me,' he says as I let myself through. I follow him to the lifts. He presses for the ninth floor and we move up in silence.

The temperature difference is stark and I quickly peel off my scarf and gloves.

We get out and I continue to follow him. We pass a lot of desks and serious faces until we reach a large office at the end. It's deathly quiet, not like my workplace.

I step into his spacious office and the first thing I notice is how immaculately tidy it is. In fact everything is just how I imagined it would be.

David shuts the door behind us and I see him lock it with a key. Without saying a word he closes the blinds across the window so that we're properly alone. I can't help but hope that he's preparing to kiss me again.

I lean myself against his desk, trying to relax in a very strange situation. He fiddles with the blinds for a few moments, even though there doesn't appear to be anything wrong with them, and then he finally turns around and looks at me.

'Why are you here?' he asks. I don't know why but I feel

like I'm in trouble.

'I'm so sorry. I hope you don't mind.' My voice is squeaky, like I'm pleading for forgiveness.

His face softens ever so slightly. 'Of course I don't mind. It's good to see you again.'

He slowly takes a few steps closer to me and I feel that tension that must actually be sexual chemistry appear between us.

'Why are you in London?' he asks.

'For work,' I all but whisper back.

He opens his lips as if to reply but nothing comes out. He takes another step and he's now right in front of me.

For a moment we just stare at each other and then something comes over me. I don't know what it is, but I reach forward and kiss him. I can't help myself.

'What are you doing to me?' he says, taking a step back.

Oh God, I've overstepped the mark. I suddenly feel very uncomfortable. The heat in his office is flustering me and I worry about my heart. I undo my coat and slip it off, taking a deep breath.

'Here,' he says, taking my long black coat off me, but not before quite obviously looking me up and down.

I lean awkwardly against the desk again as he throws my coat on the chair behind me.

He steps back and grabs me around the waist. His warm lips meet mine and he kisses me ardently. He's full of urgency and passion and I don't want him to stop.

He takes a breath. His eyes explore every inch of my face, like he's studying me carefully. 'I want to make love to you,' he utters.

No few words have ever had such an exhilarating effect on me and it takes me a second to catch my breath.

'If that's okay with you?' he says, looking at me square in the eyes. Of course I should say no. Of course I'm not actually going to have sex with him and cheat on my husband. Of course nothing like that is going to happen. Nothing like that ever happens to me.

He takes my silence positively and he moves in to kiss me again. After a peck on the lips, he moves across my cheek and then down my neck and I feel my heartbeat increase.

'You're so cold,' he says.

'I was waiting outside for you for quite a while,' I say. 'The receptionist wouldn't tell you I was here.'

'Oh Penny.' He takes me fully in his arms and I'm helpless. Without thinking about it, I wrap my arms around him in return and we're locked together in a heady embrace.

It's then that I notice how normal this all seems. Just like me walking around London, just like me seeing his workplace: the feel of his arms around me and the sensation of his lips against my skin is so familiar, so safe.

It's as if this is all meant to be. It's like I've been waiting for it all my life. Until this moment there was a huge void and I'm finally filling it with just what I need. And what a very satisfying completion it is.

Then I know I'm not going to say no. I know that I'm going to make love to this man, here, in his office, and I'm never going to want it to end. Nothing in me; not one single pore across my whole entire body wants me to say no. Every tiny little molecule within me is urging me to do this and I am left with no choice.

He slips off my (well, Gemma's) cardigan before kissing me some more. I feel his hands slowly move around me and he starts to unzip my (okay, Siobhan's) dress. 'The second you want to stop, I'll stop,' he whispers in my ear as he carefully pulls the dress open. 'I'll only keep going for as long as you want me to.' I bite my lip to ensure that no words come out. I can think of nothing worse than him stopping right now.

He carefully takes off my dress, then everything becomes a whirlwind of pleasure.

The way he touches my breasts, the way his fingers explore my body, the way he lets me undress him in return. He doesn't even mind when I fumble with the buttons on his shirt and get the zip stuck for a moment on his chinos. It's all so easy and so comfortable. It's like we've done it a thousand times before.

He stops for a second and takes out a condom from his wallet. I'm a little surprised to see that he has one hidden in there but I'm also relieved that we have protection.

He props me on the edge of his desk and grabs my legs. I automatically wrap them around him as he finds his way inside me.

Lust, desire, pure and utter pleasure; every second with him enlightens my body. I'm sure this is how sex is supposed to feel but it most definitely doesn't feel this way with my husband.

With our mouths and our hands, we continue to explore every inch of each other until the final, amazing orgasm takes hold. As our bodies surge with pleasure, I wrap my legs tighter around him and I hold him close.

We stay locked in our embrace for a few moments and only one thought enters my head: this feels a lot like love.

He kisses me gently and steps back. 'Are you okay?'

All I can do is nod.

'I didn't plan for that, you know,' he says.

'You didn't know I was coming.'

'You know what I mean. You're hard to resist.' He leans down and picks up Siobhan's dress from the floor. He takes a moment to look at it before he hands it to me.

'You like the dress?' I ask.

A lascivious smile creeps up on his lips and he nods. 'It's very sexy. It certainly complements your gorgeous body.' I feel my face burn up at his comment. No one has ever said anything like that to me before. 'You do things to me,' he says, stroking my face.

'It's my friend's dress. I just borrowed it for this meeting I had to go to.'

'There's no way it could look better on her. I mean I liked your reindeer jumper, but... this Penny is more like my fantasy Penny.'

Exhilaration flutters in my stomach. I'm his fantasy. He just said that.

'So, you're here for work?' he asks, stepping back and looking around for his own clothes.

'Yes. I had a meeting this afternoon. I have to get back soon. Shit, I have to get back! What's the time? I have to be back in Birmingham for five.'

David looks up at the wall and I follow his gaze to a clock. It's ten to five.

'He's going to kill me! I'm dead. He'll never let me out again.' I suddenly start to throw my clothes on at twice the speed but David stops me. He looks into my eyes.

'Who is going to kill you?'

'My husband. He doesn't know I'm in London. I'm not allowed to go to London. I'm not allowed to do anything.'

'Not allowed?' I can see this angers David and I quite like it. Then his expression changes to confusion. 'Why did you come and see me at four o'clock if you have to be back in Birmingham for five?'

'I was mugged. I didn't know what to do. I'm not even sure how I'm going to get home.'

'Mugged? Oh God, Penny.' David hugs me tightly. 'So you came here for my help?'

'Yes. I didn't know what else to do. And once I was here, I couldn't leave. I had to see you.'

'I'm so sorry. The last thing on your mind must have been sex.'

'I wouldn't say that,' I smirk. I need him to know that I have no regrets. That was incredible.

David smiles in return. He has a gorgeous smile. It lights up his whole face. But it doesn't last for long. Within a few seconds his familiar serious expression returns. But I suppose this is a serious matter. 'We need to get this reported to the police,' he says. 'Then I'd like to take you for dinner.'

'I have to get back to Birmingham.'

'And you will. But please let me take you for dinner first.

It would feel wrong for us to make love like that and then for me to take you straight home. Besides, you must be quite shaken up after your ordeal. You deserve a glass of wine.'

Everything David says is appealing but I haven't got a clue what to do. I find myself just staring at him blankly.

'Tell me, what do you want to do?' he asks.

I definitely know the answer to that question. I never want to leave his side again. 'It would be nice to have dinner, I suppose,' I say with a shrug.

'Then call up... what's-his-name. Tell him you're in London for a meeting and you'll be home late.'

'What?' I say, utterly bewildered as to how David could suggest such an insane idea.

He walks around his desk, picks up his phone and hands me the receiver.

'You need to be in charge of your own life, Penny. It's not right that you're scared to tell your husband you're in London. If you want to go, then I'll take you straight home now. But if you want to come and spend a few more hours with me then you need to stand tall and take charge. All I'm suggesting is that I take you out for dinner, and then I'll drive you home. You'll be home before midnight. But you have to decide what you want. What is it that you really want?'

I look at David. No one has ever asked me that before and I suddenly want to stay with him even more. He's so incredibly lovely. There really is only one possible answer to his question. But what am I supposed to tell my husband?

8. WHO DO YOU LOVE?

'Does your husband hurt you? I mean physically?' David asks with concern, clearly reading something from my terrified face.

'No,' I reassure him. 'He worries about me. All my family do. I've been ill. It's no big deal, but now they all worry insanely about me.' I don't want to tell David about my heart problem. It's nice being normal for a change; not being pitied.

'No one has the right to dictate anything about your life, Penny. You do know that don't you? I'm far from a relationship expert, but I do know it's meant to be fifty fifty. He has to respect your wishes. Just as I am going to. Whatever you want to do, I'll support you.'

The only idea I can contemplate is staying a bit longer with David. Anything else fills me with disappointment. I take a deep breath and decide less thinking and more action. I grab the phone out of David's hand.

I dial Lee's mobile number knowing that he's probably just about leaving his office. It seems to ring for ages and then he answers. 'Hello.'

'Lee? Hi, it's Loppy.'

'What are you doing? Where are you calling me from? Is this a London number?'

'Yes,' I say, as briefly as possible.

'What are you doing in London?' I can tell he's mad.

'I'm here for work. My job expected me to go to London and I had to come.'

'Since when do you need to go to London?'

I have no intention of telling him about the mugging. In fact I may try and never tell him if I can get away with it. For now I just need to make it up as I go along.

'I have to host an event at a hotel this evening,' I explain. 'Then I'm coming home. This is really important to me. Look I'd better go. Don't stay up. Bye.' With that I hang up.

I turn to David for approval, and that's exactly what I get. He looks really proud of me. I take a moment to feel proud of myself.

We finish getting dressed, he deals with a few important emails, and then we head out.

Our first stop is the police station, which isn't too far from David's work. They take a few details from me but they don't think there's a lot they'll be able to do. After that David takes my hand and we walk towards the Underground station.

'Do you mind if we head into central London?' he asks. 'I can't take the risk of my wife seeing us. She works nearby.'

I don't feel guilty but I do suddenly feel a bit terrified. Suzanne Royall is not a woman I want to mess with. 'Of course,' I say before David's other words sink in. A smile grabs my lips as I realise we're heading to a place I've never been to before.

I imagine bright lights, bustling crowds and an electric atmosphere. I can't wait to get on the tube. Abruptly, David stops walking, interrupting my excited thoughts. He pulls me to the right and we enter a mobile phone shop.

Without any delay, he buys a pay-as-you-go phone. It's just a simple one, and I admire how straightforward he is as the store manager tries to upsell loads of extras. He is very to the point with what he wants and I see the strength of character that I always dreamed he'd have being played out in front of me.

He hands me the phone as we leave the shop. 'So you're not without a phone as you sort out your claims. And also, so we can keep in touch,' he says, not a flinch to his face. I take the bag and my stomach tingles. 'We'll get it set up when we sit down for dinner.'

We arrive at Angel Underground station and I'm overwhelmed by the amount of people. It was nowhere near this busy last time I was here.

David very kindly buys me a ticket and then we head towards the Northern Line. I barely let go of his hand. Not just because I feel all loved up, but because I'm also massively intimidated by the crowds.

We make our way to the platform and we stand for the train. It's only a three minute wait but the time seems to drag.

As we wait, the question of his wife starts to niggle at my mind. I have to ask. 'Was she really mad with you?' He looks at me a little puzzled and I realise I need to elaborate. 'After I left the café before Christmas, what happened with Suzanne?'

'Not much,' he replies, gazing down the platform as if nothing more can be said.

'You said you read my book. Did she ask you to?' I add. I need details.

'I told her it was all her imagination and she'd been working too hard. I read your book to highlight the differences between me and your character David Royall; to prove to her that it was all just a strange coincidence.'

'Were there many differences?'

David thinks for a second. 'I'm older than the character in your book. I'm thirty-four, you had him at twenty-eight.'

I shrug. 'I suppose I made him the same age as me.' As

I say it though, I realise that I've always thought of David as older than me. I wonder why I wrote him as twenty-eight?

'And he's single. But I think that was about it. The rest was pretty much the David Royall standing before you. It was rather unsettling to read, if I'm honest. Let's just be grateful that Suzanne doesn't know me as well as you.'

As much as his words send tingles of delight through me, they also confuse me a little. 'But she's your wife. She must be closer to you than anyone.'

David very slightly shakes his head. 'Suzanne and I have an understanding. Let's just say, it's more a marriage of convenience. We were both lonely, we came together. We're there for each other when we need it, we satisfy each other's matrimonial needs, then we give each other space to get on with our lives.'

'What?' I say. I've never heard of such a relationship.

'I'm not one for love and romance,' he says. I can't hide the look of disappointment on my face and he catches it straight away. 'But I've also never had sex in my office,' he quickly follows up with. 'You do things to me, Penny.' I know he wants to say more but he doesn't. He just pretends to see if the train is arriving. Lucky for him, it does just seconds later.

As we make our way to Kings Cross and then change to the Piccadilly line, we don't say a word. I desperately want to know what's going on in his head, but he doesn't look like he wants to talk.

We get off at Covent Garden and I follow him down the platform towards the lifts. We silently wait and the urge to know more starts eating away at me. Within a couple of minutes we're stepping into a lift and by the time we've reached the cold night air I'm ready to burst.

'Do you have an open relationship?' I ask as I stop in the middle of what feels like a thousand people.

'What?' David responds, quite shocked.

'Do you sleep with other women? Does she sleep with

other men?'

'No. Never. It's a marriage of convenience but it's still a marriage. We're faithful to one another.'

'You were,' I whisper, but any guilt I felt before Christmas is long gone. I don't feel guilty at all.

David stares into my eyes as if I'm the only one present and the swarm of people around us seem to slowly fade away. 'There's something between us, Penny. Something neither of us can explain. But it certainly runs deep. I am not one to cheat on my wife, that's not me at all, but I also know that we need to explore what's happening here. I have never felt this way. I feel more for you than I've ever done for my wife.' He stops himself.

I stare back at him. I want to say it. This might be my only chance. I have nothing to lose. I can't see myself ever coming to London again. Lee will lock me up after this. 'I love you,' I say. 'I don't know how, but I know I do.'

David's face softens. 'I love you too, Penny. I'm sure of it. I know it because you're the only woman I've ever loved.'

I want to return the compliment but I know I love Lee. I admit I have much stronger feelings for David, but I've been with Lee since I was fourteen years old; I know I love him. I think so anyway. But why does it feel so much better and far more intense with David? Why can I not stop thinking about David?

'Is this the start of an affair?' I ask as I look at the phone he's given me. In reality, no one else in the world needs to know I have this phone. It's now my secret way of contacting the man I'm having an affair with. Yet still I don't feel an ounce of guilt. Just pleasure. So much so I have to work hard to stop myself from smiling.

David contemplates my question. 'I suppose, technically, that's the word for it. But I would like to see it more as an exploration of an impossible situation that has brought us together. We've spent no more than about three hours together since we first met, yet we both know, categorically, that we're in love. That needs exploring.'

I grab his hands. 'I don't want to let you go,' I say.

'Then don't,' he says back. He smiles and kisses me gently. We spend a moment just smiling gleefully at each other before he quickly glances at his watch. I take a quick peek too and I see it's already just after seven. 'Do you like Mexican food?' he asks.

'I like fajitas when I cook them at home,' I reply, trying not to feel sad that the time is ticking by. 'But I don't eat out very often.'

'Then you're in for a treat. This is one of my favourite restaurants.'

David leads me on and within a few minutes we arrive at a rustic, buzzing Mexican restaurant, and true to form it all feels eerily familiar.

We eat delicious food, I drink two beers not once telling David about how it may affect my medication (and I realise I very much like Mexican beer) and we talk about everything and anything that comes to mind. We already seem to know so much about each other, but we still find there isn't a moment of silence. I can't believe how well we get on. I don't think I've ever enjoyed anyone's company more.

At nine o'clock, we head back to the Underground. We walk to Leicester Square this time. At my request we take a quick detour around the square so that I can see it for real, and then we head back on the Piccadilly Line and make our way towards Islington.

David leads me most of the way to his apartment. I just wait around the corner at the very last moment in case his wife is lurking about. Within a few minutes he pulls up beside me in his sophisticated looking car and I hop into the cream passenger seat, instantly relaxing against the plush leather comfort. It's a million miles away from Lee's little rust bucket.

We drive out of London and up the M1, back to Rugby. It only takes us a couple of hours, and, just as David promised, minutes before midnight he pulls in at the end of my road.

I'm dreading what Lee will say to me but I feel worse about saying goodbye to David.

'Call me tomorrow? Let me know you're okay?' he says, kissing me on the lips.

'Yes, definitely. You have my number too. Don't be a stranger.'

'One way or another, I'll be seeing you very soon. I have to,' he says.

We kiss again and then I know I have to let him leave. He still has another two hour drive home. 'I can't thank you enough for tonight. For everything,' I say.

'I'm always here for you,' he says. Then he kisses me again.

9. THE REAL PENELOPE FOX

It's Friday and it hasn't even occurred to me to look forward to the weekend. Life is just too good as it is. How can a day when I was mugged turn out to be so perfect? It's really made me start to believe in fate.

I'm typing away at my desk but all I can think about is David. Wonderful, gorgeous, in love with me David.

It's been non-stop all morning with Wesley demanding that I catch up on all the stuff I couldn't do for him yesterday, but around lunchtime I'm finally given a minute of peace and quiet.

I stand up quickly and shut the door to my office. I promised David that I'd speak with him today and I can only do it in work time.

I slyly grab the mobile phone that David bought for me out of my bag and I bring up his number. Then I dial it on the office phone. That way anyone who's passing by won't be suspicious and should leave me alone.

The phone seems to ring for an age and I can feel myself getting nervous. I hope all this excitement isn't having a detrimental effect on my health. That would be typical: I finally meet the love of my life and I die of heart failure.

Did I just think of David as the love of my life? Surely

that should be my husband. This is all so very confusing.

'David Royall,' a stern voice answers relieving me of my taunting thoughts.

'Hi, it's Lop... Penelope,' I say.

'Hello.' He sounds very pleased to hear from me so that's good.

'I hope it's not a bad time but I did promise to call and let you know I'm all right.'

'I'm very glad you called. I've been worrying about you.' I think that's the first time in my life that I've heard those words and it hasn't irritated me. I love the fact that he's worrying about me.

'I'm fine. You must be exhausted, though. What time did you get home?'

'Around two. But I'm working from home this morning so it's been a nice easy start to the day. It's good you called now though, I have a meeting in an hour.'

'You must do very worthwhile work,' I say. The David in my dreams was in charge of a facility that did all sorts of medical research. He oversaw groundbreaking work. I suppose the real David Royall must be exactly the same.

'I like to think so. Anyway, I'm eager to hear how things went with your husband. I hope you stood your ground.'

'I certainly did,' I say, unable to stop my beaming smile. 'It was quite unlike me. I was a new woman. Thanks to you. I got home and he was waiting up for me. He was fuming. He said he'd been trying to ring me for hours and I'd been deliberately ignoring him. I had to tell him that I'd been mugged. I hadn't really got a choice.'

'Of course.'

'He wasn't happy. He screamed at me, telling me I couldn't be trusted to go off on my own and he wouldn't allow it again. He said he was going to phone my boss up demanding that I'm no longer sent on business trips and all that rubbish.' There's a fierce lack of response on the other end of the line and I can tell David's getting angry. I just know it.

'But then I had a moment of clarity,' I continue. 'It just seemed so obvious. I turned it all around on him. I told him that if he insisted on wrapping me up in cotton wool and he wouldn't let me experience the real world, then I was never going to be prepared for it. I said it was just inevitable that something bad was going to happen and his overprotective, suffocating, molly-coddling ways were ultimately to blame.'

'You said that?'

'It was amazing. I then added that I'd gone to the police all on my own and had arranged for them to see me home safely, finishing with just how competent I really am if I'm allowed to be.'

'I'm so proud of you. What did he say?'

'We argued for a while but he eventually backed down. What could he do? He's always had such a meek wife but suddenly I was taking none of it. It felt great.'

'So, you're really all right?'

'Yes. Apart from missing you.'

'Tell me about it. I'm working on coming up for a weekend to see you. We could spend a Saturday together or something.'

This makes me sit up straight. I want to see him so badly, but I can't see how I can justify going off for a whole day mysteriously. As exciting as an affair is, in reality I'm still very much a married woman and I have a very large family that demands my time.

'Is everything okay?' David asks after I don't reply.

'It's just... I'm not like you. My husband always likes to know where I am. We do everything together.'

'Don't you want to see me?'

'More than anything.'

'If you don't want to-'

'I do. Believe me, I do. Look, leave it with me. I'll figure something out. You give me a date and I'll somehow make myself available.'

'Okay.'

There's an awkward silence for a moment.

'I have to go,' he finally says. 'I'll text you tonight. I love you.'

'I love you, too.'

I hang up and rest my head in my hands. This affair malarkey is going to be much harder than I thought. But how can I not have David in my life?

That Friday night, Lee and I order our usual takeaway and, just like every Friday, we watch a film. It's all extremely boring. We have nothing to talk about. We're just stuck in these walls night after night leading the dullest lives imaginable. I can't even remember what we have in common anymore.

I sit in my baggy jumper feeling unattractive and uncomfortable. I don't want this life anymore. I want some enjoyment.

It's not really conceivable for me to just get up, leave Lee and walk into the arms of another man. That's just far too complicated and messy, and it's so far from realistic that I can't even entertain the idea. But what I can do is make myself feel better about me. So I hatch a plan.

As always, in our ever-predictable cycle, the next morning Lee's alarm goes off at eight. His Saturday routine is to get up and make himself a fried breakfast, which he enjoys while watching some mindless television. On the other hand, I usually stay in bed for as long as humanly possible, too bored to even be bothered to get up. It hasn't occurred to me before, but that's why I lie in. What is the incentive to get up when the most interesting thing that awaits me is going to Sainsbury's?

This morning is different, though. This morning I am going to find the real Penelope Fox.

I wait for Lee to go downstairs and I sneak my mobile out from my bag. I text David good morning with an insane amount of kisses and then I call for a taxi.

Next I jump in the shower, throw on some jeans and a

jumper and head downstairs.

'What are you doing up?' Lee says munching into his scrambled egg. He looks totally thrown.

'I'm going shopping,' I announce.

'Since when? I need to bleed the radiators today, I don't have time to take you shopping.'

'Don't worry,' I say as I see the taxi pull up outside. 'I'm having some Penelope time.'

With that I grab my door keys and I leave, not looking back once.

'To Rugby train station, please,' I say as I get in the back of the car. There's a huge satisfied smile on my face.

I have an active driver's licence but I haven't driven in five years now. I don't like to think about it, but I had a heart attack behind the wheel. It was bad. Really bad. But it could have been so much worse and I always try to find peace with that thought.

Not that I can remember any of it.

I shudder. I really do hate thinking about it. Instead I reflect on how I've never considered a taxi before and I suddenly feel strangely independent. It's a new sensation and I'm liking it.

I arrive into Birmingham City Centre about an hour later and I head straight to a department store. I know exactly what my plans are.

First stop is to get a make-over. I ask the sweet but incredibly made-up lady on the counter to give me lots of tips and I buy tons of make-up from her.

Next stop is the hairdressers. I usually go to a family friend in Rugby, but today I'm going to a fancy salon. I don't have an appointment but they're able to squeeze me in thanks to a last minute cancellation. Luck is definitely on my side!

Then it's time for the outfits. I felt incredible in that dress the other day, so I search for lots of other similarly flattering dresses. I can't wait to show off my new look to

David next time I see him. I hope it's soon.

I get home at about quarter to three and I can tell Lee is peeved by the sharp tone he greets me with from the kitchen.

I decide it's best to give him a wide berth and I dash straight upstairs to dump my many bags. I grab one of the more casual dresses that I bought - a blue jersey dress - and I quickly slip it on.

I admire myself in the full length mirror that hangs on the back of our bedroom door. I look so different. I look good. Really good!

Feeling the need to show myself off, I hop down the stairs to face Lee. He is loading the dishwasher and he doesn't see me at first.

'Where the hell have you been?' he asks.

'Birmingham,' I simply respond.

'What on earth were you...' He stops when he catches his first glimpse of me.

'What do you think?' I say, posing for him.

I have more make-up on than I've ever worn before, but it's somehow created a very subtle effect. My new shorter hair bounces playfully off my shoulders thanks to my new layers, and the dress clings elegantly to my proud size ten.

'You look gorgeous,' he utters. I don't know whether to feel flattered by the clear surprise in his tone or not. 'What's brought this on?'

'I thought it was time for a fresh start. I'm sick of being poorly old Loppy. I want to start enjoying my life.'

He walks towards me and kisses me on the lips. 'You look... really different.'

'I feel really different.'

'Maybe we have been letting things get a bit stagnant. I suppose it wouldn't hurt if your husband took you out for dinner tonight. I'll be the proudest man in the room with you looking like that.'

It's nice what Lee is saying, but his words seem to have no effect on me at all.

He kisses me again and this time it's a proper, deep kiss. I know he's getting excited.

'Sod the dishwasher,' he says and he grabs my hand. 'What else did you buy?'

He leads me up to our bedroom where my bags are all laid out on the bed. I pick one up to show him but he knocks them all on the floor.

'Did you get any new underwear?' he says, pushing me down on the duvet.

I shake my head but he's already working his way into my bra. It feels all wrong.

He kisses me again and I know exactly what the kiss means. I suddenly feel sick with guilt.

'I can't,' I say sitting up, almost banging my head against his, so urgent is my need to halt the action. We haven't had sex in weeks and I know I should be enjoying this moment with my husband, but I just can't. It wasn't my intention to get him all excited. My plan was to look more attractive, but I did it for me.

I did it for David.

'What is it?' Lee asks. 'Come on.' He tries to kiss me again but I push him away.

I can't deny it. The truth is I don't want my husband. No, it's more than that. I actually feel like I'm cheating on David. How can that possibly be?

'It's my heart,' I lie. 'My chest is hurting me. It's really hurting suddenly.'

I expect him to throw his arms around me with concern but he just stares at me blankly.

'It must be all the excitement,' I say. 'I think I need to rest.'

'You never have chest pains,' he argues.

It's true. In all the years I can remember having this heart condition, I've never once had an issue with it. The drugs have been tremendous.

'It's probably just indigestion,' he states. I can tell he's really annoyed and it totally throws me. I could be on the verge of having a heart attack and all he's concerned about is getting his leg over. After all the molly-coddling he does, I can't believe my health is suddenly of such little importance.

'I'll just have a short lie down,' I say, getting into bed. 'Maybe then we could go out for that dinner?'

'All right,' he mumbles with irritation. 'But after dinner we're coming straight to bed. And we won't be sleeping.' There's a glint in his eye and it fills me with guilt. All I can do in return is nod with feigned enthusiasm.

He heads off back downstairs and I sigh. What am I going to do? I don't want to have sex with my husband. I feel sick just at the idea of being unfaithful to David. What is that about?

Then it occurs to me that David could still be having sex with his wife. I have no right to interfere in his marriage, but the very thought of it hurts me. I lie on my back and stare up at the ceiling, as if it will somehow give me answers.

What if David's having sex with his wife at this very minute? I can't even call him, not with Lee hanging around. What am I going to do?

I take a deep breath and decide the best course of action is to talk to David at the first moment available. Honesty is the best policy. Although I don't have a right to interfere in his marriage, I at least have the right to know where I stand.

I struggle with these thoughts as I lie there for what seems like hours. This is all getting deeply complicated. Rather than a cheeky affair on the side, I'm now totally in love with a man I'm not married to. I can't see how any of this is going to end happily.

10. BURNING QUESTIONS

Monday morning finally arrives and I'm so relieved. I've somehow managed to avoid Lee's over-excited libido all weekend but it hasn't been easy. It's also been torturous not being able to speak to David. I haven't even texted him with so many negative thoughts spinning around my mind.

I get into work and I head straight for my office. I throw my coat off, turn my computer on - so I look like I'm doing some work - and then I grab my secret phone out of my bag. Lee has kindly sorted me out a replacement mobile from the one that had been stolen so I now have to be careful I'm using the right one.

I start to dial David's number on the landline when I realise I haven't shut my office door. I stand up to close it when Siobhan appears.

'Morning! Bloody hell Loppy, you look amazing.'

I'm wearing one of my new dresses, I've used some of the new make-up techniques I've been taught and I have made quite a lot of effort with my hair. This is the new me and I'm determined to stick with it. Even though it did take me ages this morning.

'I got so many compliments when I wore your dress last week. I liked it, so I've updated my wardrobe a bit,' I respond.

'It suits you.'

'Look, I've got a really important call to make. Shall I drop by for coffee when I'm done?'

'Yes! We need our Monday morning catch up.'

Siobhan has barely stepped away and I've shut the door. I scuttle back to my desk and quickly dial David's number. I have a burning question to ask him and I keep my fingers crossed that he answers.

'David Royall,' he says after just a couple of rings. I note an inquisitive tone to his voice.

'Hi, it's Lop... Penelope.'

'I was hoping it would be you when I saw the Birmingham number. How are you?'

'Stressed,' I say honestly. I don't have time for small talk. I need to get to the point.

'Why? What's the matter?'

'On Saturday night Lee tried to have sex with me.' As I utter the words I realise how ridiculous they are. It's hardly shocking news that my husband wants to have sex with me. But this is an extraordinary situation all round.

There's a stony silence on the other end of the line. Maybe I need to make it sound better. 'I didn't want it, though,' I add. 'I felt awful. I felt like I was cheating on you.' However, again there is no response.

I shuffle nervously in my seat. 'It's like I'm married to you and I'm being unfaithful with my husband. How can that be?' Still David doesn't say a word and I think I might throw up. 'I haven't slept with him,' I clarify. 'Not in weeks now.'

To my incredible frustration, David continues his silence. I decide that his lack of response is obviously because he thinks I'm moronic. But I have to know where I stand. I have to ask. The jealousy is driving me mad. 'Are you still sleeping with your wife?' I blurt it out with such urgency, I half expect him just to hang up.

Thankfully, I finally hear him sigh. 'Hang on,' he says.

'Let me get back to my office.'

I hear shuffling and I assume that he's walking past all of those desks. As I wait, I find I can't control the anxious tapping of my foot on the floor. This is no good. I have to stay calm. This relationship will be the death of me.

'Are you still there?' he asks after a few moments.

'Yes.'

'The answer is no, Penny. I too am suffering with the same dilemma. I have no desire to sleep with my wife. In fact, I'd go as far as to say I have no desire to sleep with anyone else for the rest of my life, except for you.'

This time it's me who's speechless. A little smile grabs my lips.

'This has all got very complicated, very quickly,' he continues, quite seriously. 'I need to see you.'

The smile leaves my lips as quickly as it came. 'See me, like to break up with me?' I shakily ask. Bloody hell, that sounds like I'm his girlfriend. What am I? His mistress?

'Of course not,' he replies, very firmly. 'It's just a lot seems to be happening. It will be much easier to speak in person.'

I nod. Not that he can see me, but I don't quite know what to say.

'I have to work this weekend,' he says with a touch of frustration in his voice. 'We're in the middle of a major project and I need to be here. Hang on.' Everything goes quiet for a few moments. Then he comes back to me. 'I can probably do Sunday. Just for a few hours. Can you get away?'

I look out my window and see Siobhan returning with her mug of coffee and an idea forms in my head. 'Yes, but it will have to be in Birmingham. Can you get to Birmingham?'

'Of course. I'll get the train. It will probably be easier anyway. I can do some work then.'

A warmth glows inside of me as I consider the effort he's willing to go through to see me. 'Great. Text me what train you're getting and I'll meet you at New Street. But I'll need a couple of days' notice to prepare. Will that be okay?'

'Of course,' he says, and I can hear the love in his voice.

'I can't wait to see you.'

'I can't wait either. Love you.'

'Love you.'

I place the phone down and a huge weight lifts off me. This is one crazy situation but at least we're totally in it together.

Before I've even had chance to gather my thoughts, my phone makes a funny ring. It's a call back. Wesley's been trying to get hold of me. I press the button to return the call.

'Loppy, I need you in my office. And grab a coffee for me on your way.'

I do as requested and head to the kitchen. I hate it when he says he needs me.

He's the owner of the business and when he's not sleeping with the staff, it's pretty much all there is to his life. As a company, we develop Business Intelligence software. Everything else aside, Wesley is incredibly clever and incredibly well respected across the industry. He started the company from scratch seven years ago and now we're fifty staff strong and we sell the product all over Europe.

I grab the two mugs, having made myself a coffee as well, and make my way to Wesley's office. I have my notepad under my arm, a pen behind my ear and an uncharacteristic bounce in my step. My call with David obviously had a positive effect on me.

I enter his office, place the mugs on his desk and then automatically shut the door. Whenever I'm summoned with "Loppy I need you", I know it's a door-closed meeting.

I go to sit on the chair on the other side of his desk when his wolf whistle halts me.

'You look hot,' he announces.

I am literally stunned. I don't know what to say.

'Where has this Loppy been hiding?'

I shrug. 'I felt like a change.' I sit down and grab my

notepad and pen, ready for action. I cross my legs only to become very aware of how much of them is on display. I've opted for flesh tights and I'm starting to regret it.

I look across at Wesley and he's grinning with a glint in his eye that I have never seen directed at me before.

'New dress?' he asks.

'Yes. I went shopping at the weekend.'

'I may need to give you a pay rise. I think lots more shopping trips will be needed if this is the result.'

I don't know what to do with myself. It's completely inappropriate but I can't deny I'm flattered by the attention. I feel the need to somehow justify my change. 'I think going to London last week woke something up inside of me.'

'Right, you and me, get us booked on a train to London.'

'Oh, okay.' I assume he's joking and I snigger.

'I'm serious. The Biz-Show Exhibition is next week. Get us booked up and sort out the trains. Becky's going one day to recce it, we'll go the other day. Liaise with her.'

'What?' He never asks me to go anywhere with him. I've been sort of less PA more typist really.

'You heard. Book it in my diary and cancel anything else I have.'

I stare at him blankly.

'Is there a problem?' he asks, quite seriously.

'No. I'll get it sorted.'

He nods and then leans back in his chair as if he's considering something very important. 'You're married aren't you?' he finally asks.

'Yes,' I reply with caution.

'What has your husband made of your new look?'

I flash back to the weekend and my efforts to avoid Lee's excitability. I wish I'd been with David instead. I can't wait for David to see my new look. I'd repeat those office antics with him any day of the week.

As I recall my visit to London, a little smile escapes on my lips.

'That good, eh?' Wesley chuckles, reading my silence in

his own way.

I just shrug. What am I supposed to say?

The black dress I'm wearing shows more cleavage than I've ever dared to reveal before and I'm very aware that Wesley is now glaring at my chest.

'You like my new look then?' I ask, desperate for something to say.

'Oh, very much so, Loppy. Very much so. You seem so different. So much brighter. I'm very happy for you. And your husband.'

This comment makes my skin crawl, but I feel the need to be polite. 'Thank you.'

'In fact, Loppy, I insist that you ditch the jumpers for good.' He chuckles afterwards but I sense he's not joking.

'You said you needed me?' I prod.

'Hmm,' he nods, still very much staring at my chest. 'I have to go to Europe. There are problems in Spain and Germany with those shitty sales reps. Do you want to come?'

I'm gobsmacked by this request. As much as I'd love to travel and see somewhere different, I'm painfully conscious of the timing of this offer.

'I couldn't,' I say, shaking my head for extra clarification.

'Sure you could. I need you.'

'It's not good for me to travel, what with my heart and everything.' Lee is always telling me that travelling is risky for my health. Although it's funny when he wants to go to Lanzarote for two weeks, I can fly then. Still, it's the perfect excuse now.

'Oh right, yeah. Shame. Maybe next time. I need you to arrange all the details, book hotels, the usual stuff.' He fills me in quickly on his itinerary and I make the relevant notes.

'I'll get on to it now,' I say standing up.

'I meant it about that pay rise, by the way. How long have you been here now? Must be a while.'

'Five years,' I say.

'Has it been that long? Consider it sorted then. I'll speak

to Finance and I'll get back to you.'

I'm taken aback by the power of a dress and make-up, but I don't intend to turn down extra money. 'That's very good of you.'

'It's a fresh start all round,' he says as he watches me leave.

11. A SHORT-TERM SOLUTION

By Sunday I feel like a new woman in so many ways. Not only have I been getting more attention than I've ever had before – including from my husband – but I also feel more in control. David has given me the confidence to take a stand and it's paying off really well.

Lee is very kindly dropping me off at Rugby train station. I've told him I'm going for an afternoon of girly time with Siobhan where she's going to teach me some new make-up techniques. In reality, my husband is dropping me off at the train station so I can meet the man I'm having an affair with.

Why is this not making me feel guilty? This really isn't acceptable behaviour for a decent person, yet nothing in the world has ever felt so right.

He waves me goodbye from the car and I agree to call him on the return journey to come and collect me. It can't be late. I don't want to invite lots of questions. But I know it's going to be really hard to tear myself away from David.

I get on the busy train and I will it to move quickly. I send a quick text to David to tell him that I'm on my way and he texts me back immediately saying how he can't wait to see me. I text him back to return the sentiment and then we spend the next thirty minutes exchanging soppy messages like we're over-excited teenagers experiencing love for the first time.

My train finally arrives and I can't wipe the smile from my face. I know David's already here and he's been waiting for me for a few minutes. I scramble through the ticket barriers and head towards Starbucks where he told me he's standing, and then I see him.

With no thought at all, I throw my arms around him and we kiss, like we've not seen each other in months. It's only been about ten days, but it's felt like forever.

'Hi,' I say, glowing after our long embrace.

'Hello,' he smiles. 'You look beautiful.'

'Thank you,' I reply as my body tingles with joy. Of all the compliments I've had this week, none have meant more to me than those few words.

'Shall we grab that coffee then that I promised you?' he asks, referring to one of our text exchanges.

I nod and grab his hand. It should be more prominent in my mind that Lee and I both know people that live in Birmingham, but I find I just don't care.

We walk out the station and up New Street to a coffee shop. It's fairly busy and we join the queue.

'Let me see if I know how you take it,' he says, studying me. 'White, no sugar?'

'Yes,' I smile. 'But can you make it decaf?' I quickly try and find a way to change the subject as I don't want him to probe as to why it has to be decaf. The whole "I can't have stimulants because of my weak heart" conversation needs to come soon, I know. I have to tell him. But not just yet. I don't want those pity eyes just yet. 'I'll go and find a seat,' I say, moving away as quickly as I can.

Within a few minutes he finds me by the window upstairs looking out onto the busy street. He places down our coffees and we sit for a minute in silence, breathing each other in. He's so handsome.

Before I know it, my right hand is holding my coffee mug and my left hand is intertwined with his across the table.

'What are we going to do?' I ask. He regards me but says nothing. 'No, I mean it. What are we going to do? Here we are, and it's amazing, but in a few hours...' I drop my voice and look around, but no one is interested in us. 'In a few hours I'm going home to my husband. I can't bear the thought of it.' I shake my head as the awful question once more floods my thoughts. 'You haven't slept with your wife, have you? I know I have no right to ask, but it sickens me to think of you with anyone else. Even if it is your wife.'

'Penny,' David soothes, squeezing my hand. 'Of course not. I was honest the other day when I said you're the only woman I want to be with. But that does leave us with quite a quandary. Which is why I wanted us to meet. To discuss it properly.'

'Discuss what exactly?' It has to be bad news. I can feel it.

'Our future.' I hold my breath. Do we have a future? 'We've found ourselves in the most peculiar of situations,' he continues. 'I can't stop thinking about you. As much as I despise the idea of messing my wife around, we have to find out what this is all about. There's a deep connection between us, and I have to admit that I've never felt this way before about anyone. So I think we owe it to ourselves to explore this. But we also can't live like this long-term.'

'I agree,' I say, but I'm not sure where he's going.

'My wife is a sexual woman,' he says, and I instantly feel nauseous. Why did he have to tell me that? 'And in our mutually convenient marriage, sex has always been a core part of how we've worked together.'

Part of me really doesn't want to hear any more, but I also have far too many questions. 'Do you love her?' I ask.

David shakes his head. 'It's a marriage built on respect. I care for her, yes, but I don't love her.'

'But how can you have sex with someone you don't love?'

David gives me a look that says "are you serious?" and I

feel very silly.

'Do you think she loves you?' I ask, remembering how angry she was when I met her.

David remains quiet for a minute. Finally he says, skirting my question completely, 'I'm lucky in that Suzanne and I lead very separate lives. I can be working late with a great number of demands on me that ultimately mean I'm able to avoid her in bed. But what about you?'

'Don't worry about me,' I say, still with half a mind on my question. Suzanne's anger definitely ran deep. I'd put money on the fact that it's more than a mutually convenient marriage for her. But I suppose I don't know anything about them. And I can see David is not going to tell me. Not that he should. It's really none of my business.

'Do you have a plan?' he asks, nudging me from my moment of contemplation.

'Yes. It's no issue at my end. There's nothing for you to worry about.' I absolutely cannot say more than that and luckily David seems to respect my lack of elaboration. He just nods.

The reason I don't want to say any more is that my plan all revolves around my weak heart. It's been a hindrance in my life for far too long, it's about time it starting working to my advantage. I'm going to make a doctor's appointment this week for a check-up and then tell Lee that they've found my heart is having spasms or some crap like that. I'm going to tell him that I've been warned not to have sex for the foreseeable future as it could cause extra strain on my already weak organ. He can't really argue with that.

'While we both have short-term plans, we can't sustain this life for long,' David says, quite wisely. 'It's not only going to be hugely difficult, it's also not fair on anyone involved. Whether they're aware of it or not.'

'So, what are you saying?' I become worried about the answer.

'I think we need to give ourselves a deadline. I propose three months. In the next three months we'll promise to stay faithful to just each other and we'll make every effort to spend as much time together as possible. We'll call as often as we can and, at the very least, we'll text every day. Then, at the end of three months, we make a decision. We either decide to commit to one another completely and we find a way to make this work for good, or we go our separate ways and admit that we just can't be together.' He squeezes my hand tightly. 'This plan allows us time to explore these sudden feelings for each other but we also minimise the hurt that we cause to ourselves or anyone else.'

He's really thought this through. I can't believe it. It sounds like a very sensible suggestion, except for the huge leap at the end. Could I leave Lee? Would I have to move to London, change my job, leave all my family? The thought terrifies me. Then I contemplate a life without David and I stop breathing. I can't even begin to imagine that.

That's a startling thought on its own. How can I feel so strongly about someone I've only just met? Although I suppose he has been in my life for over a year, albeit not physically. This is all most peculiar. Taking some time to properly evaluate this strange situation we've found ourselves in is definitely the best course of action.

'Okay,' I say. 'Three months to explore us and find out the best way to move forward is a good plan.' I break into smile. 'And to kick start it, I already have our next get together sorted. If you can make it? I really hope you can make it.'

David says nothing, he just waits for me to give him details.

'On Thursday I'm coming to London with my boss. I can't believe it, he's actually taking me on a business trip with him. It's funny, he's barely noticed me before, but I show a bit of cleavage and I'm off to London.'

'What?' David doesn't seem pleased.

'I told him I had a friend that I wanted to catch up with. He said it was no problem for me to get a later train back. I've booked the last train of the night so we get the whole evening together. How great is that!'

David has a very stern look on his face. 'Are you busy?' I ask as I become worried. Why isn't he more excited? 'Do you have plans already?'

'Penny, that wouldn't matter. If you're going to be in London then I'd move heaven and earth to be with you. What concerns me is that you've connected this trip to London with an inappropriate reaction to your appearance.'

'I guess,' I say, hesitantly, although my mind is more focussed on how lovely his comment was. 'He wouldn't stop staring at my chest.' As soon as I say this, David instantly lets go of my hand. His whole body tenses. It's rare for his emotions to be on display like this and my elated sensation vanishes. I appear to have upset him. 'I'm not going to Spain or Germany with him,' I add in a desperate attempt to make the situation better.

'Why does he want you to go to Spain and Germany?'

'For work. He's got to sort out a few problems over there. I am his PA. It's not that strange that he asked me to go with him. Not that he's ever invited me before. Mind you, he's never wolf whistled at me before either.'

'He did what?' This is the first time I've heard David raise his voice and I'm a little stunned. 'Penny, I need you to tell me what happened.'

I watch him cautiously. He seems really mad. I thought he might see the funny side. I take a few moments to think of what to say. I suppose all I can do is be honest. 'On Monday I went into his office and he told me I looked hot. I know it's completely inappropriate, but it's just what he's like. He's like it with all the women in the office. Well, all the attractive ones.' I pause as the reality of the situation occurs to me. 'I guess this means he finds me attractive.'

'Did he make any advances towards you?'

'No.'

'Are you sure?'

'Yes. The most he did was make a quick reference to my sex life. It was a bit awkward but it didn't mean anything.'

'Penny! Did you report him?'

'What? No. Who would I report him to? Besides, why would I want to? He gave me a pay rise. And not a little one. Four thousand pounds.'

'You do realise that this is sexual harassment?'

'No it's not.'

'Yes it is. Right, what are you going to London for? Do you need me to join you?'

'No. It's an exhibition. It's at Olympia. There will be hundreds of people there.'

'Send me the details. Any problems, I won't be far away.'

'Okay. But he's not going to do anything.'

'I'll be the judge of that.'

'And I'm not going to let him. What do you take me for? I have a husband and a... a you. I don't need any more complications, thank you. He's a slime ball, yes, but he's my boss and he's just noticed me for the first time. Getting a four thousand pound pay rise is a small price to pay for being leched at a little.'

'Penny-'

'And him seeing me completely differently also means that I get to go to London where I can spend time with you.'

'That's not-'

'So it's win win as far as I can see.'

'Penny-'

'I don't want to hear any more about it!' I'm not really mad with David but I give him a look that says enough is enough. It's very nice that he cares, but the new me is all about taking a stand and Wesley Parker is one man I can deal with.

For a moment we just stare at each other. David can clearly see that I'm not willing to discuss it anymore but I can tell the whole subject is prickling him quite badly.

I decide a change of topic is needed. 'You said you had a big project on at work. What's that all about?'

David sighs. 'It's complicated.'

'Were you working all day yesterday?'

'About five or six hours. That's all.'

'I suppose at least you have a genuine reason to be working late. It must help with avoiding your wife.'

'Yes, that's true. This project is running for the next five weeks, so I'll be legitimately busy for a while.'

'You will be free on Thursday, though?'

'I will be there, Penny. Don't worry about that.'

As we start to make plans as to what we can do on Thursday night, the tension soon dissipates and the next couple of hours fly by.

Before we know it, I'm kissing David goodbye. The only small relief is that I'll be seeing him again very soon.

12. THREE MONTHS

The following Thursday I meet David outside Covent Garden Underground station and we have an amazing evening together. And that kick starts the most incredible three months.

I did as planned and paid my doctor a visit. Of course he didn't find any change in me. He just gave me a new prescription and sent me on my way. But I've told Lee a very different story. I put on the dramatics and explained that the doctor has warned me off any sexual activity for three months. Lee was annoyed and upset, but my health has to come first.

He's calmed down a lot since, and we're back to our boring old relationship.

But life is not quite as boring as before.

I've started yoga classes. Or at least that's what Lee believes. I told him I wanted to do yoga as it's good for my condition, adding that the doctor says it will strengthen my heart so I can have sex again. I know it's incredibly mean and manipulative, but I don't have much choice. And I find I don't really care.

Full of encouragement, Lee drops me off two days a week at a nearby high school where he thinks my yoga classes are taking place.

It isn't a total lie. I am going there to join some other ladies in a mutually fun activity. But it isn't yoga.

After realising a new passion just before Christmas, I've joined a choir that's run by the music teacher. There are a few school kids, but mainly ladies of all ages.

I couldn't tell Lee the truth. He wouldn't like all this fun I'm having. He'd only worry about me unnecessarily. But I knew he'd be fine with yoga. Yoga is good for a steady heartbeat. Yoga is good for sex.

After just a few weeks of practising, we have our first performance and I'm honoured with a solo. We're doing songs from the musicals and I am blessed with singing *I Dreamed a Dream* from *Les Misérables*. And just to top off this fantastic moment, David comes to see me. He's so supportive and really seems to enjoy it. Everyone believes he's my husband and we don't correct them. We just look at each other and we both know it's a huge step forward in this exploration period.

After that, the yoga apparently goes up to three classes a week, with one being on a Saturday night for three hours. That becomes precious time between David and myself. It costs him so much in effort and travel expenses to come and see me, but we relish every second.

I'm a little surprised that Lee just goes along with it all. But then again, he's granted free time to go out with his mates rather than looking after his ailing wife, so I guess it's win win for both of us.

On a couple of occasions I tell him that a friend is going to drop me off home (the friend being David) so Lee can have a few drinks and not pick me up. There's a close call one night when as soon as David stops at the end of my road, Lee's taxi appears next to us. I have to hide in the footwell until he goes into the house.

Other than that, though, our scheming seems to go very smoothly.

To add to our good fortune, my boss also, inadvertently,

aids our affair as I became his new PA that he's never without. I'm in London at least once a fortnight and Wesley is more than happy to support my so-called London social life. If he's ever tied up with difficult clients he doesn't mind me having lunch with my "friends" and he has no issue with me getting later trains back.

Lee becomes frustrated with the longer hours I'm suddenly appearing to work, but it's all gone hand in hand with my massive pay rise. When I tell him that I've been promoted and this is now part of my job, he has little choice but to believe me.

Yes, okay, I'm shoulder deep in a web of lies and the slightest twitch could send it all crashing down around me, hurting so many people that I love. But I find that I just don't give a crap as I have literally never been happier. I feel like me. I feel complete. I feel like the girl in the book I wrote and it's all like a dream come true.

* * *

I put the phone down and a few butterflies flutter in my stomach. That was David. Our three months are soon up and we've planned in the final piece of our exploration so that we can make a decision once and for all about our future.

Over the past couple of months, all we've really had are scraps of time together. A few hours here, a few hours there. We've repeated our exploits in his office a few times, and there have been a few occasions in his car, but it's never felt like we've been properly together. We've never had uninterrupted time together, and we haven't experienced simple things like falling asleep next to one another. So that, we decide, is the final thing we need to do to know how we feel.

He's just told me that he's booked a hotel room for a week on Saturday in London. We're going to have a whole weekend together undisturbed. All I have to do is tell Lee that I'm going away.

It's only Tuesday though, I have ages to think about that. There's no question in my mind, I want this weekend. I need this weekend. And as it stands at the minute, I can't imagine a life without David.

My phone rings. It's Wesley. 'Hello.'

'Loppy, can you pop down to my office please?'

I'm unnerved by the polite and chirpy nature of his tone. 'On my way.'

I grab my notebook and pen and make the thirty second walk to his office.

He's sitting behind his desk with a big smile on his face.

'You might want to shut the door,' he says and I do as requested. Then I take a seat and poise myself ready to take notes.

He does nothing but regard me with a cheeky grin for a few moments. Finally he says, 'I got you all wrong. I'm normally very good at judging people, but you're a sly old fox.'

'Pardon?' I'm not sure whether to feel proud or offended.

'Tell me. Your husband, does he work in London?'

This totally confuses me. 'No. He works just down the road.'

Wesley's smile broadens. 'I thought as much. Well then, Mrs Fox, I would like to know who it was that you were kissing so enthusiastically last week in London?'

My jaw drops open. I have no idea what to say. I'm really not prepared for this.

'I had my suspicions when you were taking every opportunity to go and meet this mystery friend. I've been with a few married women; I recognised the signs. Then I finally got the chance to follow you last week. I knew it! Who is he?'

I'm completely thrown. I suddenly feel quite sick. 'It's none of your business.'

Wesley shrugs. He walks around his desk and sits on the

edge of it, just in front of me. 'We could make it my business.'

I am completely lost for words. Is that a threat?

'I'm not judging you, Loppy. Far from it. We were never meant to be a monogamous race. It's unnatural.'

'It's not what you think,' I say. 'It's a complicated situation.'

'It's not a problem. You don't have to justify it to me.'

As I'm scanning my brain for what I can say alongside worrying about what he might do with this information, he puts his hand on my leg. 'Is there room for a third man in your life?'

I stand up, alarmed, almost falling over my chair as it bangs to the floor.

I feel embarrassed and stupid. I glare at him awkwardly before I turn on my heels and scuttle out of his office as quickly as I can.

I shut myself in the safety of my own office and I feel numb. I don't know what to make of any of it. Is he going to tell people my secret, or use it against me? Will he try and force me to be his play thing?

David has warned me several times, and I knew Wesley was a flirt, but I never expected that. I feel violated.

I plonk down on my chair and bang my head against the desk. I just don't know what else to do.

'Loppy?' Siobhan says, knocking on my door as she opens it. 'Loppy!' She runs to my side and hugs me. 'What's happened? Gemma just said you'd run out of Wesley's office looking a bit shook up.'

I hug her back. I feel so stupid. 'It's nothing.'

'Loppy.'

'Wesley just tried it on with me.'

'What?' She's fuming. 'What did he do?'

'Oh God, Siobhan.' I need to talk about this. I need the release. I need a friend. I stand up and shut my office door again. 'It's nothing I don't deserve.'

'How can you say that? Tell me what he did!'

'Nothing much.'

'It seems like quite a lot. The bastard.'

'He felt it was justified.'

'It's never justified.'

'No, you don't understand.'

'I don't think you understand.'

'No.' I look her square in the eyes and I take a deep breath. 'I'm having an affair.'

'With Wesley?' The look of shock on her face almost makes me laugh.

'No! Definitely not. But he's found out about it and he just saw it as a green light to proposition me.'

'What?' Siobhan shakes her head. This was clearly the last thing she expected me to confess. 'You need to tell me everything. In fact, no, sod this. You never get mad, you never get emotional, you never take action. So this time I'm doing it for you.'

She marches towards the door. 'Where are you going?' I ask.

'Just turn your computer off and get your coat on.'

13. AN AFTERNOON OFF

'What are you going to do? I need this job,' I plead with Siobhan.

'Don't be daft, just get your coat on.'

She leaves and I look at the time. It's just after midday and I tell myself she's taking me out for lunch. She's just taking me out for lunch.

About five minutes later she reappears in her coat with her bag. 'Come on then.'

'Where are we going?'

'Wesley thinks we've both been working too hard of late and he's said we can use the company credit card to reward ourselves with a champagne lunch. Oh, and he added that he doesn't expect us back this afternoon.' Her face is full of smug satisfaction but all I can concentrate on is the word champagne.

'I can't have champagne. My heart. With everything going on at the minute, I need my medication to work.'

Siobhan looks at me sternly. 'Loppy, you were fine at Christmas. Besides, sometimes in your life you just need to give in and go with the flow. This is one of those times. Now follow me.'

Siobhan takes me to a really fancy restaurant. It's

stylishly decorated with mainly a business clientele, all suited and serious.

She swoops in and so many eyes are cast her way. She has a way of making people stare, like they're totally in awe of her.

A waiter shows us to a table and she orders two steaks and a bottle of Moet.

'A bottle?' I ask in disbelief.

'We have been granted carte blanche with our sleazy boss's credit card. We'd be fools not to make the most of it.'

'But my heart.'

'From what I saw before Christmas, having a glass or two of wine does your heart the world of good. We might have to go and find a karaoke again later.'

'Later? I really shouldn't drink. What's Lee going to say?'

'I was wondering when we were going to get on the subject of your husband.'

I sit silently. Should I have told her? It felt good to tell someone. And I trust Siobhan more than anyone. Well, except for David.

The waiter brings over our champagne. He pours us a glass each before leaving the bottle in a little cooler to the side of our table.

'I'd like to make a toast,' Siobhan says raising her glass. I mirror her. 'To one good thing coming from that slimy bastard.'

We clink glasses and I hesitate. I have to meet Lee in a few hours. What will he say?

Then I think about the fact that I'm planning a weekend away in about ten days' time with another man. A man that I'm considering spending the rest of my life with. Sod it, I need a drink.

I take a sip and it's divine. It's such a refreshing experience, and within seconds I'm taking a gulp.

'One more sip and then I want to know everything,' Siobhan says. 'An affair? Who is he? It is someone in the office?' She seems enthralled.

I take another gulp before placing my glass down and shaking my head. 'No. You definitely don't know him. He lives in London.'

'In London? So, you met him recently?'

'That's the weirdest part. I mean really weird. Not the Christmas just gone, the one before, I started to dream about this man. The dreams were so vivid, and so sexual.' I can't believe I just said that. I must be getting drunk.

'Anyway,' I continue, 'I couldn't stop thinking about this man so I wrote a book about him.'

'A book?'

'A novel. He was the main character. His name is David Royall and when I came across Royall Literary Agency I thought it was fate. Well, I suppose it was.'

'He's the agent? You're published?'

'No. The agent was his wife. I sent her my book and she requested a meeting with me. But it turned out she'd invited her husband along too. Her husband being David Royall, the exact same man in my book.'

Quite rightly, Siobhan looks confused. 'You based it on him? I don't know what you mean.'

'No, I'd never met him before. But it was him. The man that I'd been dreaming about for like a year was suddenly sitting opposite me in the flesh. In every way it was him. But then it got weirder still because he said he'd also been dreaming about me. We'd never met before, but he knew all this stuff about me. Stuff he couldn't possibly have known.'

'Are you sure you haven't met? Like a drunken shag or something? You know, perhaps he was lingering somewhere at the back of your subconscious?'

'Look at my life, Siobhan. I've done nothing with it. I've been with my husband for half of it. I'd never even kissed another man until David showed up at our office.'

'You kissed him at our office?'

'Yes.' I can't help but smile. 'He tracked me down and we had a very unexpected but very wonderful kiss in the downstairs meeting room.'

'What?!'

'Then when I went to London in your dress, I got mugged.'

'He mugged you?'

'Not him! Some horrible blokes on the street. They stole my bag.'

'Why am I just hearing about this?'

I shrug. 'I didn't want to talk about it. Besides, I've been on cloud nine ever since.'

'You enjoyed getting mugged?' Siobhan looks utterly perplexed.

'No! But after I got mugged, I didn't know what else to do so I went to see David. He looked after me. He took me out for dinner then drove me home, and we've spoken practically every day since. More than that, barely a week has gone by where we haven't seen each other.'

'Wow!'

I take another gulp of champagne and I find I'm bursting to tell her more. This is quite unlike me but it's a liberating experience. I drop my voice. 'We had sex in his office.'

'What? Really? Was it good?'

'Amazing. Mind-blowing.'

'So, is this just a sex thing?'

I gulp down more champagne and shake my head. 'I love him.' I quickly knock back the rest of the glass. 'Siobhan, I love him more than Lee. I love him more than my husband.'

'Bloody hell, Loppy.' Siobhan looks at me with a mix of pity and surprise. She grabs the bottle of champagne and fills up my glass again. 'What are you going to do?'

'We've set ourselves a deadline. That's next weekend. Either we decide to stay together and leave our spouses, or we say goodbye and go our separate ways.'

'Oh my God. What are you going to do? Are you going to leave Lee?'

'Is it bad that I'm considering it?'

Siobhan glares at me firmly. 'Who makes you happier?'

I pretend to consider her question, but the answer is obvious. 'David. Any day of the week. But it's not that easy, is it.'

'Oh Loppy, I want to tell you what to do. I really do. But it's not my business and it's not my place. All I can do is give you my honest advice. Ask yourself this: if you look back in fifty years' time, what will you regret more? Will you regret it more if you leave your husband and take a chance on a new, exciting relationship, or will you regret it more if you let, in your own words, the love of your life get away?'

'It's not just about me though, is it?'

'When you're eighty-five and sitting in an old people's home are you going to feel satisfied that you made choices to please other people?'

I gulp down more champagne as her questions sink in. Again, the answers are all simple. I know what I want to do, but is that what I really should do? I could gain a lot but also lose so much.

Steaks eaten, second bottle of champagne drunk and we stagger in the direction of New Street station for a final tipple before I have to meet Lee.

I've finally managed to change the subject from Siobhan's extensive probing regarding the logistics of a sex life with a man who lives a hundred miles away, and we're now laughing heartily about the antics in our office. I don't think I've ever laughed so much.

At about twenty past five we head into the train station together and Siobhan gets straight on her train. I, however, have to wait for Lee. I stand in our usual meeting point and I can't wipe the smile from my face.

'What's up with you?' he says as he approaches me. At first he looks curious, then he looks mad. 'Are you drunk?'

'No,' I giggle.

'You're off your head!' He's so angry it sobers me a little.

'If you knew the day I've had.'

'Did you get the sack? Who drinks in the afternoon like

that?'

'I didn't get the sack. I was given the afternoon off.'

'Bullshit.'

'How dare you!' I know I'm slurring and I try to compensate for it by standing up tall, as if that's going to make a difference. I glare at him with the aim of showing him how I'm not in the mood to be messed with, but I just end up stumbling and he has to steady me.

'You're an embarrassment,' he says, trying to lead me to the platform. He holds me on the escalator and I start to giggle again. The escalators are an exciting place when you can't stand up straight.

'Did you know that the highest escalator in the UK is at Angel Underground station?'

'Where?' Lee asks, clearly irritated.

'In London!'

'Really interesting.'

'I like Angel.' Images of David flicker through my mind. 'But I can't tell you why.'

'That's good, because I don't care. What I want to know is why you've not been to work this afternoon and why you're steaming drunk?'

We arrive on the platform and Lee leans me against the wall.

'You know Wesley, my boss?' I say. He just nods. 'He tried it on with me.'

Lee looks at me with disbelief. 'What?'

'Siobhan got mad and told him that we either go out on his credit card or she'll sue him.'

Lee shakes his head. 'So this is some bullshit story the two of you have concocted to get an afternoon out on the piss?'

'No, it's true. He was touching me.'

'I touch people at work all the time, they don't turn around and threaten to sue me. You're lucky you've still got a job.'

'But Siobhan said he was harrassmenting me!' I slur.

'You need to sort it out with him tomorrow. Don't get the sack, Loppy. With your heart condition, you won't get a job anywhere else. That's if you make it through the night. Look at the state of you.'

The train pulls up and I suddenly feel sad. Lee manhandles me on to the packed train and I think I might be sick.

It's going to be a long journey home.

14. A DOWNHILL MARCH

After my two hour nap when I get home, I wake up dizzy with a very dry mouth. I grab a glass of water and I feel the urge to cry. I never cry. This is all getting far too much for me now.

I sit down next to Lee on the settee. He's watching some quiz programme on the telly and his face is venomous. It's very uncomfortable.

I wish I was with David. I find myself yearning for him.

'Have you had dinner?' I ask in a soft voice.

'Yes. You'll have to sort yourself out. I couldn't wake you. What an embarrassment.'

I take a deep breath. I want a hug so badly but not from Lee. I need to speak to David.

'I might pop out and get some chips then,' I say.

'I'm not going for you,' he responds.

'I didn't ask you to.'

'Good.'

'Can I get you anything?'

'A mask for when we get on that train tomorrow so no one will recognise us after your display.'

'Display? What display?'

'That couple had to give up their seats because you were

falling all over the place.'

I sigh. I have never, ever been drunk before; let alone in that state. It was fun and then utterly horrible, and now I feel dreadful.

'I'll be back in a few minutes,' I say standing up.

I grab my bag, checking that my secret mobile is in there, and I head out the door.

Just two houses down, I pull out my phone and call David.

'Penny? Are you okay? What's the matter?' he asks, answering after just one ring.

I realise that we never speak at this time of day. It's nice he sounds so worried. 'I've had a terrible day.'

'Where are you?'

'I'm just walking up the road to get some chips.'

'On your own? Where's what's-his-face?'

'At home.'

'What's going on?'

'I got drunk. He's in a bad mood with me.'

'Oh no, how terrible of you.' I appreciate his sarcasm, but if he knew the truth about my condition he'd probably be just as worried as Lee.

'Oh, David. It's all gone to shit.'

'Tell me what's happened.' He has such a caring tone, it instantly makes me feel better.

I sigh as I look around to check that no one is listening. 'My boss has found out about us. He saw us in London. He took it as an open invitation to come on to me.'

'He did what?' I have to hold the phone away, David is so angry.

'He asked me if I had room for another man in my life.'

'I knew it. I'm going to kill him.'

'I told Siobhan and she confronted him. He gave us his credit card and the afternoon off. She took me for steak and champagne at his expense.'

'She sounds like a very good friend. Do you need me to come up?'

'I'd be lying if I said I didn't want you right now, but it's not practical. Aren't you at home?'

'Not yet.'

'You're working late?'

'Yes. Well no. I am at work but I don't need to be here. I'm just catching up on a bit of paperwork. Okay, I'm also playing Spider Solitaire.'

'What? Go home.'

There's a small pause before he speaks. 'It's a bit tricky at home right now. Suzanne is nagging me that we need some matrimonial time. Just two more weeks.'

'Oh.'

'Are you sure you don't need me to come up? Or I could just head straight to Birmingham and knock out your boss?'

This makes me smile. 'I'd love you to. But...'

'Have you reported him?'

'Reported Wesley?' I ask.

'Yes.'

'To whom?'

'Penny, he's sexually harassed you at work. You need to report him. It's not right.'

'Is it sexual harassment, though?'

'Yes.'

'But all he did really was ask me-'

'You can't hit on your staff members, Penny.'

'He does it to everyone, though.'

'If I acted like he did I'd find myself before a tribunal before you could even say wrong.'

'So you think I need to report it?'

'You have to.'

'Okay. I'll see what I can do tomorrow.'

'You must. You said he's like it with everyone. One day he's going to go too far and we're in a position to stop that happening.'

'Okay,' I nod. Reporting it had never occurred to me. He's so slimy I just considered it to be typical Wesley as opposed to an offence. Although, thinking about it, I am dreading going into work tomorrow. I hope I don't have to see him.

'I'd better go,' I say, reaching the chip shop. 'Don't stay at work too late. Although it does make me happy to hear you're keeping your distance from her.'

'And you keep your distance from that son of a bitch.'

'Lee?' I ask, shocked. I know David isn't Lee's greatest fan but...

'No, your boss.'

'Oh! How am I meant to keep my distance from him?'

'I mean it, Penny. I'm worried about you.'

'Okay,' I nod, not seeing at all how I'm supposed to avoid the man I assist on a daily basis.

'I love you. Call me tomorrow.'

'I will. Love you too.'

The next day at work I feel wretched. This must be a hangover. Siobhan has gone to get me a cup of coffee and I'm just staring gormlessly at my computer. I'm going all out caffeine today. Sod my heart, things are too bad for me to care right now.

I'm back in my jumper and trusty trousers as I had no desire to make any effort this morning. This does not feel good.

'Here you go,' Siobhan says placing two mugs down on my desk. She takes the chair opposite me. 'So how did Lee react? We were off our faces.'

I pick up my mug and sip at the boiling liquid. 'He was fuming. He hasn't stopped ranting on about what an embarrassment I am.'

'You did explain it though, didn't you?'

'Explain what?'

'Why I took you out.'

'You mean about Wesley?'

'Yeah.'

'I told him all about it. Both in a slur last night and in more detail this morning.'

'Why do I get the feeling it didn't go well?'

'He told me that we were clearly just pushing our luck; angling for an afternoon off. He has informed me, in no uncertain terms, that I'm not to see you anymore and I need to apologise to Wesley.'

'What?!' Siobhan slams her mug down she's so mad. It makes me feel better. 'What a fucking bastard! Sorry, I know he's your husband, but where does he get off being so insensitive. No wonder you're having an affair.'

I can't help but smile at her comment. 'David is at the other extreme.'

'You told him?'

'He said you're a great friend and I have to report Wesley for sexual harassment.'

'Bloody hell, Loppy, you have got two different men there. I know who gets my vote.'

'I know we were joking about it yesterday, but is it sexual harassment? David was quite adamant.'

'Of course it is, Loppy. He's a vile sleaze. There's no way he should be allowed to go around hitting on all of his staff. It's disgusting.'

'Shall I report him then?'

'In an ideal world I'd tell you to go for it and never look back. But, sadly, I think the reality is far more complicated.'

'What do you mean?'

'Firstly, Loppy, who are you going to report it to?'

I shrug. 'HR?'

'And who's Head of HR? Patricia. The woman who Wesley had a fling with a couple of years ago. The only reason she got that promotion is because she gives great blow jobs.'

'Siobhan!'

'Well it's true. We all know it. The problem you've got is that everyone around here seems to adore Wesley. It's like he's untouchable. All is always forgiven. He must have one hell of a big wallet.'

'Couldn't I go to the police or something?'

'But then what? You'd have to leave your job. He owns the company. And ultimately it's just your word against his. It's not like anyone is going to back you up. Well except for me, of course. But Wesley's adored. It's like he has some sort of hypnotic effect on every other woman but you and me. It's crazy.'

'So, what should I do?'

'I hate to say this, I really do, but absolutely nothing. I seriously can't see any way you can win if you pursue this. It's shit but that's the way it is.'

I know Siobhan is right. And if I'm honest I much prefer the idea of letting it go. I don't know how I'm going to tell David, but I just don't want to create a load of problems for myself.

My phone rings and I jump. 'It's Wesley!' I take a deep breath and I pick up the receiver. 'Hello.'

'I need you in my office.' Then he hangs up. All the pleasantries are long gone.

'I've been summoned,' I say standing up.

'Good luck. Don't take any crap!'

I slowly make my way to his office. I go in and he immediately demands that I shut the door. Reluctantly I comply and I take a seat. He does not look happy.

'I've just been taking a look at the online banking. You took the piss a bit yesterday didn't you.'

'What? I don't know.'

The truth is that I really don't know. Siobhan took charge of everything.

'I can't believe you told Siobhan that I'd come on to you. I merely asked if you were open to multiple relationships as you clearly aren't the monogamous type. I hardly think that can be justified as a come on. Do you?'

I don't know what to think. It's all a bit vague and all I really want to do is forget about it. I just shrug.

'Have you gone around telling anyone else?'

'No,' I say.

'Good. And I think we need to keep it that way. I'm a

fun time guy, that's for sure, but I never cross the line. I'm sickened that you could suggest such a thing. And now Siobhan will never look at me in the same way again. Your silly lies have been costly, Loppy. Do you understand?'

I really don't know how to react. David would probably be punching him by now, but there does seem to be a logic in what he's saying. Maybe I did just get it all wrong.

'I'm not going to say anything,' I mutter.

'Then I won't tell anyone that you're having an affair,' he says to my great surprise. 'You look after my interests and I'll look after yours. Do we have an agreement?'

I just nod, completely lost for words.

'Go on then. I don't need anything else.'

I head back to my office full of confusion. I want to be mad with him but I can't be bothered with the hassle. All I can think about is that in just over a week's time I'm seeing David and, all being well, my life might just change forever.

15. DECISION TIME

The next week and a half drags by. Wesley has reverted to treating me like I barely exist and Stacey is once again flavour of the month. I've just gone in to work, kept myself to myself, and then headed home and thought of David. He's all that's got me through it.

Everything that was good seems to have vanished. I haven't seen David in over two weeks, my choir has split up as the music teacher has been pulled into other commitments, and Lee has started trying to control me again. He's even been turning up so we have to have lunch together to ensure I'm kept away from Siobhan. It's all gone downhill and I couldn't be more relieved to be getting away. Thank goodness the day has finally arrived.

I wait for Lee to get up and start his usual Saturday morning routine and then I quickly get ready, making as little noise as possible. With his controlling ways returning, I haven't been able to find a way to tell him that I'm going away for the weekend. Instead I've decided just to announce it on the spot and then run as fast as I can. What is he going to do?

At nine o'clock on the dot I look out the window and see David's fancy car. It seems to sparkle in the mid-April sun and I feel the dread that I've been carrying around for the last two weeks drift away.

I go downstairs with my overnight bag and get ready to make the speech I've been practising all week.

'Where are you going?' Lee asks from the settee. He's just finished his cooked breakfast, apparently oblivious to my movements upstairs.

'I'm going away for the weekend. You've been suffocating me too much of late. I need some time to figure out what I want.'

'What?' He looks like the world has just knocked him down and for the first time I feel sorry for him. 'You're leaving me?' As he utters these words his shock quickly morphs into anger.

'I'm just going away for the weekend. On my own.'

'Where? You can't just leave. I won't allow it.' His demanding tone wipes away any sorrow I momentarily felt.

'I'll see you tomorrow night.'

I open the door and scuttle out as quickly as I can towards David's car. I get in the back, pretending it's a taxi as planned. It's one hell of a flashy taxi, but I doubt Lee will notice.

'Get back here now!' Lee shouts from the doorway in his pyjamas.

'Is that him?' David asks as he turns the engine on.

'Please, just drive on.'

'No problem.'

I can't look back. I imagine Lee standing in the middle of the road waving his fist in the air with indignation and it's too awful to witness.

As we turn out of my road, I sigh with relief. David continues for a couple of minutes before pulling over so I can join him in the front.

'This is it,' I say, squeezing his leg. He cups my face with his hand and kisses me. It's such a long, deep kiss and I can tell he's missed me.

'How are you?' he says, swiping my hair out of my eyes.

'Happy now.'

'What a rough couple of weeks you've had.'

'You're not mad with me, are you?'

'Mad?'

'I know you wanted me to report Wesley, but I just needed it to go away. He'd make my life a misery.'

'I'm not happy that the bastard is going to get away with hurting you, but I do understand. He's the owner of the business. That can't make it easy.'

'Working at that place is never easy. But I don't have to worry about it now for another two days. So let's focus on happy stuff. How are you?'

'Relieved that this day has come and I finally get you all to myself. Properly.'

He kisses me again and I can't help but smile. With everything else going on I'd almost forgotten that we are now going to be totally alone together until tomorrow night. No disturbances, no clock-watching, no torturous end of night goodbyes. This is going to be heaven.

He starts the engine again and we head towards London, where David's booked a city centre hotel. He can't afford to be far from work and he's warned me that he may need to drop in tomorrow morning.

When he first told me this, the reality of our situation hit home. Should we both agree to leave our spouses and start a life together, I know that I'll have to relocate.

That's fine, though. That's what I want. It's daunting, but if that's the only way I can be with David, then so be it. It's the only choice I could ever be happy with. Besides, my reasons to stay in the Midlands have been getting smaller by the day.

I look at his face, concentrating on the traffic. He'd be a fantastic poker player. I can never read him at all. I'm pretty sure he's thinking on the same lines as me and he will want to leave his wife, but we've been very careful not to talk about it yet. We've deliberately decided to make our own minds up without any influence from the other person. That way we'll know we're both happy with the decision.

It's a pleasant journey and we share small talk and play car games and pass the time with lots of laughter. I can't believe two hours have gone by when David is leaving his car with the hotel valet.

We follow a porter who carries our bags for us and we enter the plush hotel somewhere near Hyde Park. It's like nowhere I've ever been to before and David whispers in my ear about how he wants it to be a weekend we remember forever.

That does sound promising.

We check in to our luxurious room. It's not overly spacious but it's pristine and the bed is like sitting on clouds. After a little bit of unpacking, we decide to head out for a walk.

We take the tube to Embankment and then walk hand in hand by the Thames. David points out a few of the key sights that I could never have seen before, but as with so much in this city, they all seem weirdly familiar. I remind myself that London is on the telly a lot. I bet it's a place that no one is ever surprised by.

We find a pub not far from Westminster and we indulge in a leisurely lunch. David insists on treating me and I feel like the most special girl in the world. I'm having such a wonderful time. It's already mid-afternoon when we make our way back to the hotel.

Within seconds of entering our room we're all over each other; hands exploring skin and clothes flying everywhere. The energy levels are polar opposite to our relaxing lunch. I don't know how we managed to wait so long.

I feel my heart start to patter with excitement and I suddenly grab a hold of my senses. What am I thinking? I've been so stupid.

'Oh God!' I say, pushing David back and looking for my bag.

'What is it?'

I haven't had my tablet today. I normally take it every

morning. I've never forgotten, not in years, but today I haven't taken it. With all of the emotions that I'm no doubt going to be experiencing this weekend, I need it more than ever.

The fear that my heart will give out on me just when I've found true happiness drives me into a panic.

'Where's my bag?' I ask, spinning around, not able to see it for looking.

'It's here, by the door,' David replies, clear concern across his face. 'What's the matter? I have protection, if that's what you're worried about?'

'No. It's...' Now I have to tell him. I have to. If he's going to commit to a life with me then he needs to know that it may be cut short. It's only fair. I really should have told him earlier.

'Sit on the bed with me,' I say, taking my bag from him.

We sit down together and he looks very worried.

'There's something I haven't told you. I know I should have done. I know it's huge, but you're the first person who's close to me that hasn't taken pity on me, that hasn't wrapped me up and suffocated me. I wanted it to last a bit longer.'

'What is it?' He actually looks terrified now.

I take his hand. 'I have a heart condition.'

His face grows very serious. 'What sort of condition?'

'I have a weak heart. I'm not allowed to get too excited or do anything even remotely stimulating or it could kill me.'

'What?' He looks confused. 'What's your diagnosis?'

Now I'm confused. 'That's it. What I just told you. I have a weak heart.'

'Well, what's caused it? What are they doing about it? You need to tell me everything.'

'It's just a weak heart. I'm just unlucky. I have to take these pills.'

I get the little tub out of my bag and David takes it from me. He reads the label.

'Penny, these have nothing to do with your heart. What

are you taking these for?' He's becoming angry.

'What are you talking about? They've been prescribed for me. They're for my heart. They keep me calm; keep my heartbeat steady.'

'Yeah, they'll keep you calm all right. You realise what the active ingredient is, don't you?'

I shake my head. I haven't got a clue what he's talking about.

'This isn't heart medication. They're inhibitors. They're like anti-depressants. They control your mood. Yes, they'll steady your heart, but not because you have a defect. They affect your brain.'

'What?' I can't believe what I'm hearing. He's obviously mistaken. 'No. No.'

'How long have you been taking them for?'

'I don't know. I tried a couple of other things first but they said I wasn't reacting well enough.'

'How long?'

'These particular tablets? About four years.'

'Four years?' Now he's really mad. He stands up and paces the room, still grasping the tub in his hand. 'I need to know everything, Penny. I need to know exactly what's been happening with you. For starters, who the hell told you to take these?'

I hesitate for a moment, before meekly replying, 'My GP.'

'Your GP?' He stops in his tracks and glares at me. I feel like I've done something really wrong. This is awful.

'I was told to take one a day or I could die,' I say, feeling the desperate need to defend myself.

Still with his ferocious face, he shoves the tablets in his jeans pocket. 'I would never normally advise anyone to just stop taking drugs like these. They're so strong, you really should be weaned off them. But you are not letting another one of these drugs pass your lips until we get you checked out. Properly. By someone I trust.'

'What are you going to do?'

'Penny, these tablets have been controlling your mood not your heart. So the first thing we need to do is find out if there really is something wrong with your heart. Either you've been given totally incorrect medicine, which is highly dangerous...'

He looks gloomy and I feel my heartbeat quicken as if it's trying to tell me something. 'Or?' I nudge.

'Or someone is trying to keep you sedated.'

16. MATTERS OF THE HEART

David scans the floor and finds his jumper. He picks it up and throws it on before reaching into his pocket and pulling out his mobile phone. Without saying a word, he dials a number.

I watch him, not knowing what to do with myself. What he just said was quite shocking, but I can't believe it's true. He's got to be mistaken.

'Hello, this is Dr David Royall. Could you tell me if Dr Reeves is working today, please?' There's a pause. I have no idea who he's talking to nor what they're saying in response. 'Thank you. No, no, that's all I need to know.'

David ends the call and pops his phone back in his pocket. He looks deadly serious.

'Get dressed, we're going to get you checked out,' he says.

I do as he requests and we head down to the concierge. David's car is brought around for us and we drive out of London.

I've no idea where we're going and David is very quiet. I just don't know what to make of it all. How could my doctor be wrong? I mean he's not just my doctor, he's my second cousin; he's family. Surely he'd have my best interests at heart? No, David is the one who's mistaken. He's not a medical doctor. He's clearly misunderstood the situation.

We pull into the car park of North Middlesex University Hospital. Once we're all parked up, David takes my hand and leads me into the main entrance. He seems to know where he's going and I don't need to ask as we follow a trail of signs to the cardiology department.

When we get there, he stops at a reception desk. A nurse smiles at him. 'Can I help?'

'Can you let Dr Reeves know that I'm here to see him, please?' David asks.

'Do you have an appointment?'

'No, but my name is Dr David Royall and I work for QAR Research. I've been helping Dr Reeves out with some samples. I think he'd appreciate my visit.'

'No problem, just bear with me.' She picks up the phone and dials a number. She turns away from us and I can't make out what she's saying.

After a few minutes she turns back and places down the receiver. 'He's with patients at the minute, but he said if you can wait then he'll be with you as soon as he can.'

'Thank you,' David says. He takes my hand again and leads me to some chairs in the waiting area.

And there we wait indefinitely.

Time seems to drag and David is not up for much conversation. He's so deep in thought.

I really don't know what he's going to say to Dr Reeves nor really how Dr Reeves is going to help us. I want to ask, but I'm a bit too nervous about what the answer might be.

I'm positive that David has got this all wrong and those tablets really are helping my heart. I think I am anyway. Okay, there's a small part of me that's contemplating the notion that I've actually been given sedatives and not heart medication. It sounds too ludicrous to be true but I can't swipe the thought from my mind.

'David,' a male voice finally says from next to us. It's

been over an hour and I'm hoping this is Dr Reeves.

He's a tall and skinny man who stands very upright. There's something quite formal about him. 'Thanks for seeing me, Sam,' David says as he shakes his hand.

'What is it I can help you with?' the man replies. He doesn't come across as very friendly.

'Is there somewhere we can talk?' David asks.

Dr Reeves just nods and we follow him through a door into a little examination room. We all take a seat and Dr Reeves looks at David expectantly.

'This is Penny, a good friend of mine. She's just told me that she's got a weak heart and she's been taking tablets to help with her condition. This is what she was prescribed.'

David takes the tub out of his pocket and shares it with Dr Reeves. He looks immediately puzzled. 'For a heart condition?'

'Apparently so. I need to know if there is in fact something wrong with her heart and I was hoping you could help.'

Dr Reeves looks at his watch and a flash of stress appears in his eyes. He stares at David thoughtfully. 'Yes, all right. I suppose I owe you this. Come this way.'

Dr Reeves leads us to another examination room. This one has a bed in it next to a machine. He mumbles something to a nurse who shuts the door behind us, and then he asks me to sit on the bed. David stands at the back of the room out of the way.

'Penny was it?' Dr Reeves asks as he takes a seat next to me. I just nod. 'Could you detail your symptoms for me.'

I take a second before I answer as I'm not totally sure what he's asking me. 'I have a weak heart,' I eventually say.

'Yes, but what are your symptoms?'

'I don't understand what you mean.'

'Pains in your chest? Fatigue? Shortness of breath?'

'No,' I say shaking my head.

'You have no symptoms?' He stares at me, waiting for me to elaborate, but I really don't know what to add. 'Okay then, when were you first diagnosed?'

'Erm... when I was seventeen. So about eleven years ago.'

'Seventeen? And what brought about this diagnosis? Something must have happened?'

I shake my head again. 'I don't really remember. Sorry.'

I can tell he's getting annoyed with me, as if I'm being deliberately difficult. But I'm just being as honest as I can.

I look across at David and he forces a supportive smile, but I know he's far from happy. I hope he's not mad with me. I should have told him sooner.

'Right Penny, let's take a look,' Dr Reeves says. 'Can you take your top off please and lie down?'

I turn to David again and he nods. Slowly I take my T-Shirt off and lie back.

'I assume you'll be familiar with an ECG,' Dr Reeves says quite passively.

'No,' I reply. 'I've never heard of an ECG. What is it?'

At this I see him turn to David. They share a look I can't decipher. 'What tests were run to determine your diagnosis?' Dr Reeves asks me.

'I don't remember initially,' I reply. 'But I do have regular check-ups with my doctor.'

'When you say doctor, do you mean your GP?' Dr Reeves asks.

'Yes,' I say. 'He checks my blood pressure and a few other things. He always checks on me before he gives me my prescription.'

'Have you ever seen a specialist?'

I shrug. 'My GP is my second cousin so he knows me quite well. I guess he's never needed to refer me to anyone else.'

Again, Dr Reeves turns to David. I wish I knew what that look meant.

'Okay,' Dr Reeves says. 'Just relax. You'll need to stay very still.' I take a deep breath and watch as Dr Reeves carefully places some sticky pads attached to some wires onto my arms, legs and chest. They all appear to be connected to the machine next to me.

When I'm fully patched up, he spends some time operating the machine and then a piece of paper prints off. He studies the data and shakes his head. Oh God, it's bad. I hold my breath as I prepare for the worst.

He addresses David. 'There's nothing wrong. In fact, this is looking good. Extremely good.'

'How conclusive is it?' David asks, coming forward for the first time.

'There are limitations, but I have to say I'm quite confident this is an extremely healthy heart.'

'That can't be right,' I say.

'Why is she on those pills?' David directs his question at Dr Reeves but he just stares back at David with no answer at all.

Dr Reeves turns to me. 'You say you've been taking these pills since you were seventeen?'

'No, just for four years.'

'Well, what did you have before that, when you were younger?' he asks.

I shake my head. 'I don't remember.' I take a deep breath and turn to address David. 'I'm sorry but there's something else I haven't told you. I know I should have done, but I didn't want the pity eyes. I'm so sick of everyone pitying me all the time. It was so nice to be treated like a normal, healthy person for a change.'

David is looking at me like he's about to punch a hole in the wall and I'm worried how he's going to react. I really should have been more honest with him but I didn't see how it mattered. 'I was in a car accident,' I state. 'I had a heart attack behind the wheel. See! How do you explain that? I have a bad heart. Twenty-three year olds do not have heart attacks. There must be something really wrong.'

'You were in a car accident?' David asks, as if he's somehow challenging me.

'Yes. It was just over five years ago. It was awful. When

I woke up in hospital I couldn't remember anything. Nothing from the five years before. Nothing from when I was about seventeen. Can't you see, that's why my family worries so much about me. You can't imagine how frightening it is to wake up and not be able to remember anything.'

David turns very pale. He looks quite ill suddenly. This is clearly all too much for him to absorb. I really hope this won't push him away.

'Thank you, Sam,' he says. 'I think I've got all the answers I need.' He turns to me. 'It's time we have a talk with your family. We're leaving right now.'

I have never seen David more serious, and that's saying something. Dr Reeves removes all the sticky things from me and I grab my top. I barely have time to throw on my jacket before David's out the door.

We get back to his car and he doesn't hesitate in revving the engine and driving us back up towards Rugby.

'What's going on?' I ask as David joins the M25.

He doesn't respond, he just shakes his head. I'm reluctant to push it as I'm not really sure I want to know anyway.

I sit quietly instead and obsess over the idea that my diagnosis could be incorrect. It can't be true. I've visited my doctor so many times and it's always been conclusive. I have a weak heart. Although it does raise a mini alarm bell to me that I've never had one of those ECG things before. Or maybe I have and I just can't remember. That's the hardest part of all, having so many blanks.

David is being very sensible. When faced with a conundrum such as this, asking those involved will always help. I'm sure my mom and dad will shed some light on it all and there will be a very simple answer. Maybe my heart issue is so small or niche that it's not detectable on that ECG thing?

I want to refuse to believe that I don't, after all, have a heart problem. The very notion that I've been taking medication for years for something that's not wrong with me is unnerving to say the least. More so, the idea that my family has suffocated me with worry for so long... I don't know what I'd do if it suddenly turned out I had a healthy heart.

No, it can't possibly be true. It's unthinkable really.

Like a flash, the reality that I'm going to visit my parents with my lover hits my brain and I start to panic. 'How are we going to explain you to my family?' I ask David.

'You're going to let me do the talking, okay?' David replies, quite firmly.

I nod and I have to admit that I'm happy with that. I trust he will do the right thing, and I know I'd just get flummoxed. He could pretend he's a doctor or something. Well he is, really, so that's what he will probably do.

I sit back but I can't stop chewing over the idea that I have a healthy heart. 'Can we have the radio on?' I ask, in the hope that it will stop me overthinking everything.

'Of course,' David says, flicking the knob.

I scan for some music that I like and then I sing along, trying very hard to only focus on the song and nothing else.

For the best part of two hours I try and block out my questioning mind and concentrate on the radio. David has hardly uttered a word and I'm stiff with tension when we finally arrive outside my parents' house.

I go to grab my key from my bag, which I always have with me, when I hesitate. This is a completely spontaneous visit, it's now about nine o'clock at night, and I'm with a man whom they have never met. I decide to ring the bell.

We wait for a few seconds before my dad answers the door.

'You forgot your key?' he asks, only seeing me at first. Then he clocks David and all the colour drains from his face.

'You know me, don't you?' David says.

Panic sets in. Lee must have told them that I'd gone away. He must have said I'd left him and then I turn up with another man. They've put two and two together and got exactly four. They know I'm having an affair and they're clearly not impressed. Well, of course they're not going to be impressed.

'Oh my God,' my mom says as she approaches the door. What am I going to do? David and I haven't even had our chat yet. What if he doesn't want me and then Lee leaves me anyway for being a cheater?

My mom darts off into the living room, and I see through the gap in the door that she's picked up the phone. She's probably calling Lee so he can attempt to punch David's lights out.

My family loves Lee. He's their third son and he gets treated better than I do. This is not going to be an easy evening.

My dad and David are just glaring at each other. The tension is unbearable. My dad is doing his stand up straight thing to try and intimidate David, but David's standing firm. He's composed as always; not flinching at all.

This is ridiculous. I take a step inside and head into the living room. But I'm grounded to a halt when I catch the words of my mom's conversation.

That's not right. That doesn't add up. What the hell is going on?

'Yes, he's back,' she says. 'David Royall's back.'

17. LIES, LIES, LIES

'How do you know his name?' I ask, confronting my mother. She just stares at me palely. Her eyes slowly turn to my dad for support but neither of them say anything. All four of us are standing in the living room glaring at each other but no one dares to speak.

I catch Julian's head peeking around the doorway from upstairs. He takes one glimpse of what's going on and legs it back to the safety of his bedroom. Probably a wise decision.

'Well?' I push after I see no one is willing to speak. 'How do you know who David is?'

There's still nothing but silence and it's starting to become quite frustrating. 'Okay, I have another question,' I try. 'David has just taken me for a heart test. An ECG thing. The doctor said he can't find anything wrong with my heart. Why is that?'

Again, my parents just stare at each other. It's clear neither of them have any intention of answering my questions.

'I think you need to tell us everything,' David says. 'Including what happened to us both five years ago.'

I turn to David with confusion. Did I mishear that? 'I

was in a car accident five years ago, too,' he tells me as my jaw drops open. 'And I also can't remember a thing from the few years before it happened. Something very odd is going on here and it's about time we were told the truth.'

'Bloody hell, it really is him.' Tammy's sour tone suddenly hisses from the front door. 'Where the hell have you come from?' It's becoming quite apparent that not only does my whole family know who David Royall is, but he is also very unwelcome in this house. I look around and I am completely lost for words. What on earth is going on?

'Shall we sit down?' my mom says.

'I'd rather stand,' I say. I'm far too edgy to sit.

My dad focusses his attention fully on Tammy. 'They know they were in a car accident,' he explains, 'and David's told her that there's nothing wrong with her heart.'

'Is it true?' I ask, hoping for an answer on something.

'How did you two find each other?' Tammy asks instead and I feel my body tense.

'We bumped into each other in London and we couldn't work out how we knew each other,' David quickly replies. I'm grateful that he doesn't mention my book, or our affair. This is complicated enough.

'Bloody London!' my dad hollers. 'Lee should never have let you go there.'

The tension in my body flares into anger. 'Let me? He doesn't own me! Besides, why? Because it's bad for my heart? Is there anything wrong with my heart? Will someone just tell me!'

'Okay, okay, calm down,' Tammy says, shushing me. 'We'll tell you. We'll tell you everything.' She glances at David quickly. 'David was your doctor.'

'What?' I ask.

'In the years you can't remember, David was your doctor.' I just gawp at her with confusion. 'What I'm about to tell you is probably going to freak you out,' Tammy continues. 'We thought it would give you a better life if you didn't know when you woke up from your car accident. We

125

just wanted what was best for you.'

'What are you talking about?'

'There's never been anything wrong with your heart.'

The words strike me hard. There it is. Confirmed. It's so hurtful. I actually feel physical pain from all the lies and manipulation. 'Then why have I been taking those pills?' I ask.

'You've been sedating her,' David states.

'Yes, but for your own good,' Tammy responds, all of her focus still very much on me.

I feel hurt, upset and confused. I don't know how to react.

'Loppy, you're not normal.' Talk about kicking a girl while she's down. Lies and manipulation aren't enough, let's throw in a few insults. 'You're special. Very special,' Tammy adds.

I just shake my head. Is that meant to make me feel better?

'You have an ability,' Tammy continues.

I'm completely lost. Rather than wanting answers, I'm now terrified of what's coming next.

'When you were seventeen you became able to... You can... This is going to sound very strange...' Tammy takes a deep breath. 'When you were seventeen you suddenly developed the ability to control light. As in, like, sunlight.' I question to myself whether I'm actually still conscious. This has to be some bizarre nightmare. 'We don't know why, and it was as freaky as hell at first, but that's what you can do,' Tammy finishes.

There is a moment's silence. Everyone watches me, waiting for me to react to this crazy revelation. But I just feel numb. I don't know what to make of any of it.

Tammy continues, 'After a few months we realised that we had to find you help to figure this all out. We needed answers. David was recommended to us as he's a really clever scientist.'

'But he did bad things!' my mother shrieks. It's so loud

and unexpected it makes me jump.

'What do you mean bad things?' I ask. How can this get much worse?

'He took you away and used you,' she replies.

'He did all these horrible experiments on you, Loppy,' Tammy says. 'When you were allowed to come home you were so broken; all prodded and poked and experimented on. You were his lab rat and it was killing us all to see. You pleaded with us to help you get away from him, but he had all these powers of authority and stuff. It was horrendous.'

'Then one day we got the phone call,' my dad chips in with.

'Phone call?' I ask.

'He was driving recklessly and he almost killed you,' Tammy says.

I shake my head. This doesn't make sense. 'David?'

'He can't be trusted,' Tammy continues. 'It was a blessing when you woke up with amnesia. We could finally give you the freedom you desperately desired. We did it for you.'

I turn to David, utterly baffled. None of it feels true, but why would they lie? I mean lie any more. I need him to say something but he is glaring at Tammy with venom in his eyes. 'Why sedate her?' he asks, quite to the point.

'To hide her ability,' Tammy replies, not at all intimidated by David's glower. She addresses me directly again. 'We knew that if you no longer had this ability then you'd properly be able to get away from him, so we made sure you were able to control it.' I just stare at her, still totally lost for words. 'You need adrenaline to be able to do your light thing. The tablets kept you calm and steady, stopping you from building up the power. Relating it to your heart just tied up all the loose ends.'

This is all so massively overwhelming. I don't even know how to start processing it. I need to get away. I don't think I can trust a single person around me. I shake my head and move towards the door, when suddenly Billy races in.

'Loppy!' he says, hugging me. It's the most contact I've had with him in years.

'Billy, get out of here now,' my dad orders.

'No!' Billy shouts back. He's so firm and strong. Gone is the little boy I knew years ago. 'He's here now. This has to end. You can't stop me telling her now. Not now he's back.'

My dad grabs Billy and actually manhandles him out the front door. 'They're lying to you!' he screams. It's so desperate, it shakes me to my core.

David follows them and yanks my dad, trying to get him to let go of Billy. My dad takes a swing at David, but David's quick and flinches out the way. 'You bastard!' my dad says, trying for another punch but again missing. David's very agile.

Billy takes advantage of my dad's focus on David and runs back into the living room. He grabs me. 'Don't listen to them!' he pleads.

'Back off,' Tammy says, pushing Billy back towards the door. 'He's just trying to get attention.'

'That's enough!' Julian roars from the doorway. 'Enough! This has ruined our family too much. We have to stop the lying. Loppy has the right to know the truth. I called Billy as this has to end now.' I stare at my brothers, bewildered. What are they talking about?

Everyone stops and the atmosphere calms.

'We've kept our mouths shut for too long,' Billy says, looking at the faces around him. 'Everything's changed now. David's back and they need to know the truth.'

'If you don't tell us the truth, I'll find it another way,' David states. 'I won't rest until I get to the bottom of all this.' Everyone in the room is silent. We all just stare at each other like a stand-off. 'She's your daughter, your sister,' David pleads. 'How can you treat her like this? She absolutely has the right to know the truth.'

My family continues to pass glances between one another until Billy finally squeezes my shoulder gently. 'I have no clue what you were just told, but I bet it's a load of crap. The truth is, Loppy, when you were seventeen you developed an ability.'

'Tammy told me that. That I can control light and I do it with adrenaline.'

Billy relaxes a little. 'I'm glad to hear it wasn't all a load of bollocks.'

'Billy!' my mom says. 'Language.'

He shakes his head and exhales sharply. 'We were all really scared for you,' he continues, 'but you just took it in your stride. You were amazing. Then a few months later you left for university.'

'University?' I can't believe it. 'I've been to university?'

'You have a degree in Business & Marketing.'

'What?' My head starts to spin. This is getting harder to take by the second.

'While you were there you did some digging and found that David, a hugely respected scientist, was visiting the university to do a talk.'

'Birmingham University?'

'You remember?'

I take a second to search my brain, as if now it's all been confirmed the memories should just pop back in there. But I can't recall a thing. 'It's somewhere in my head,' is all I can say.

'You went to his talk and then asked if you could spare a few minutes of his time.'

'So he was my doctor?' I start to feel relief that at least Tammy hadn't lied too much, when Billy shakes his head.

'He was far more, Loppy. The way you told it, it was love at first sight. He couldn't do enough to help you. No matter how weird it was that you had this ability, he listened to you and accepted everything. He loved you and you most certainly loved him.'

'He experimented on her!' my mother exclaims.

'Yes he did,' Billy says, piercing his eyes at my mother, 'but with your consent, Loppy. You were vague with the details. You said you didn't want to put us in danger by knowing too much, but you were letting him experiment on you. He was helping you learn about your power. You seemed happy.'

'Who's happy being poked and prodded at every day?' my dad says.

'Was I living here?' I ask, trying to piece everything together.

'You lived with David,' Billy says. A shiver runs through me. 'You were engaged.'

My jaw drops open for what feels like the hundredth time in the last ten minutes. I turn to David and he looks as shocked as I am. 'What about Lee?' I ask.

Billy shakes his head again. 'You left Lee just days after you met David. You barely saw each other anyway after you started university. You outgrew him and you fell in love with David.'

'Why did you never tell her?' David asks as I feel myself becoming quite lightheaded. This string of revelations is really starting to take its toll on me.

Billy turns to David. 'I wanted to. I hated the lies. But after the car accident, this lot were all so happy. It meant they could get their Loppy back.' Billy looks at me but he's getting a bit blurry. 'You lived in London and you had a highflying job as a copywriter for a major marketing agency.'

'A writer?' I whisper.

'You have a real flair for it. You were soaring ahead in your life and they hated it. They blamed David for taking away their little girl.'

'That's not true!' my mom says. 'We were worried sick about you. You were so pale and thin. He was using you.'

'I wanted to tell you everything when you woke up,' Billy says, 'but they wouldn't let me. For years they would never let me near you. One of them was always with you. They wanted to keep you in their safety bubble. They wanted to stop you being their freaky daughter that made something of herself.'

'Don't simplify it, you stupid boy,' my dad spits.

I hear them arguing again but I can't make out the words anymore.

I take a deep breath. This is all far too much information. It's so confusing yet I know in my heart it's all absolutely true. I haven't been having an affair with David, I've reconnected with my fiancé. I haven't got a heart problem, I've been tricked into taking drugs to hinder my special powers.

As the truth swirls round and round, the room becomes distant. It gets hazier and hazier and then, finally, it all goes black.

18. LIGHTNING STRIKES TWICE

'Penny. Penny.' David's soft voice slowly brings me back to reality.

I'm lying on the carpet and my hip is a little sore. I look up and all I can see is David's face. He's kneeling down next to me and he seems very worried. 'Penny, are you okay?' There is such concern in his voice, it fills me with warmth.

'Her name is Loppy!' The moment is ruined by my dad's anger. I quickly glance around. A room full of people who are supposed to love me yet only one is checking that I'm okay.

I turn back to David. He is very handsome. His blue eyes are like oceans and all I can think about is swimming away with him to a deserted island and never coming back. It suddenly feels so very dark here and his eyes are the only light.

'How are you feeling?' Again, his caring tone soothes me. I can physically see and hear how much he loves me and it makes my heart flutter. If we never broke up, can I still think of him as my fiancé?

'Get up you stupid girl,' my dad orders with his ever-predictable lack of sympathy. David scowls at him but it doesn't seem to have any affect. 'There's nothing wrong with her. This is just typical Loppy, wanting attention. She got herself into this mess, showing off with her special powers and then running away to London with some self-centred scientist. Now she wants sympathy from us.'

'All of this is her fault, is it?' David hisses.

'If she'd just stayed at home with her family then none of this would have happened. I warned her. She's careless and stupid and she's put us all through hell trying to pick up the pieces of her reckless behaviour.'

David looks back at me and sighs. I can tell he's trying to let my dad's words wash over him, as hard as it is. He strokes my face. 'I'm sorry, I should never have taken you off those pills so suddenly. I should have weaned you off gently. It was an emotional decision. I should have known better.'

'Get up now. Stop embarrassing yourself,' my dad says.

'She's not faking,' David argues. 'You had her on incredibly strong tablets.'

'They were the only bloody things that would work.'

'She's very strong,' Billy explains. 'She heals.'

'What do mean, heals?' David asks.

'She's never been sick, not once in her whole life. She said it was something to do with her blood. You knew why.' Billy looks at David with sorrow.

'Can we leave now?' I whisper to David. He looks down at me, as if he's not heard me correctly. 'I'd like to leave now.' A small smile flashes across his lips and he nods.

He helps me to my feet and I look away from all my family.

'Where are you taking her?' my dad asks. David just glares at him in return, saying nothing. I can't look at my dad. I can't look at any of them. I just keep my focus on David.

He puts his arm around me and we make our way to the door. I don't know what happens behind me. As we shut the front door I hear the arguments start up again but we quickly head to David's car.

He drives on for a minute or two and then he pulls in at the side of the road. He turns off the engine and faces me.

'Are you okay?' he asks.

I don't know what to say. What am I supposed to say?

He squeezes my hand. 'We have a lot of figuring out to do. I don't know how much more help your family is going to be, though.'

'Have they been helpful at all?' I ask, then I can't help but smile. It's all been far too stressful. The smile is the only thing keeping the tears away.

David thinks for a moment. 'Do you believe we were engaged?'

I look into his eyes. Of all the things that I've just been told, it's the one thing that never occurred to me to be a lie. Does David think it's a lie?

I feel so full of emotion, I don't really know what to do with myself. I just stare down at my lap, lost for words, too afraid to ask any more questions.

'I want you to come back to London with me,' David says. This grabs my attention. 'We'll have to check in to a slightly cheaper hotel, but we'll stay together. Call in sick for the week. Let me look after you. If nothing else, I want to keep an eye on you as you withdraw from those awful drugs. I shouldn't have been so careless. You need to keep me posted on your symptoms. Any fatigue, muscle aches, headaches?'

I think carefully. 'I have a sore hip, but that's from where I landed when I fainted. Lightheaded-ness, I suppose.'

'We need to give you something-'

'No. No more drugs.'

'But-'

'No. This is much better.'

'We'll see. I'll be keeping a close eye on you.'

'I've never called in sick. Ever. Billy was right about me never being ill.'

'Well, that's going to be step two. I apparently knew something about your ability once, so I can find it out again.

We'll get to the bottom of everything, don't worry.'

'What's step three?' All I can think about is David. I want to talk about us. After all that's just been revealed, where do we stand? But David just regards me. He doesn't say anything for what feels like an age.

'There's so much,' is all he finally mutters.

'One day at a time,' I nod. I don't want to push it. Now I'm worried I have. 'Let's take it one day at a time,' I say.

'I think we have to.' I know he's right but I hate it.

I look ahead and I'm about to tell David to pull away when logistics hit me. 'I better grab some clothes and things. I'm going to be in London for a week?'

'For starters,' David smiles. This gives me a glimmer of hope that he's thinking of the future. With so many blanks in the past, I have my sights very much set on the future.

'Would you drop me off home quickly?' I ask.

'Are you sure?'

I just nod in reply and David drives us the short journey to my house. He pulls up at the end of the driveway.

'Do you want me to come in with you?' he asks.

I don't know what I want. Will Lee be there? Most probably.

I consider Lee. My husband. But we broke up. I was engaged to another man yet I ended up marrying Lee.

I try to remember whether, at any point, I actually wanted to marry Lee. When I woke up from the crash I was so confused. Everyone told me I was engaged to him. I never questioned it. Why would I? The last thing I remembered was being with him.

The bastard.

'I'll be fine. I won't be long.'

I walk to the door and I feel a fire burning inside of me. It's like nothing I've ever experienced before. I turn my key in the lock and head straight upstairs. I'm not sure if I want to see Lee or not.

The choice is taken out of my hands, though. As I reach for my suitcase under the bed, I hear Lee enter the bedroom.

He is completely silent and I decide to ignore him. Just the thought of him makes me angry. I know my family lied too, but I'd like to believe that somewhere along the line they wanted to protect me. With Lee, I can't help but think he did it all for his own gain.

I open the wardrobe, not turning around once, and I start to pack my clothes.

'He hurt you, you know,' Lee finally says.

'I see my family have called you.'

'They're worried about you.'

'I'm sure they are.'

'You really are selfish.'

This makes me stop what I'm doing. With a bolt of anger shooting through me, I turn around. 'You tricked me into marrying you even though I'd left you for another man. I didn't want to be with you, but you got me to marry you anyway. I think that makes you the selfish one.'

'We did it for you.'

'I didn't want it!'

'Have you any idea of the sacrifices we've all made? You've become such a boring bitch. Every day all you do is mope about and moan.'

'Maybe that's because you've been sedating me.'

'For your own good. To keep you safe. It's nice to know you're grateful. All I've done for years is look out for you and your weak heart-'

'I don't have a weak heart!'

'No, you have freaky powers that scared the crap out of me when you first used them. But I didn't walk away. I've always stood by you, Loppy.'

With a frustrated sigh, I continue with my packing. He'll be wanting an award for bravery next.

I zip up my suitcase and push Lee out of the way. I struggle a bit as I start to carry it down the stairs and Lee tries to grab it from me.

'Get off me!' I snap.

Lee wins the battle and yanks the bag from my hands,

almost knocking me off my feet. He places it behind him on the landing, as if to hold it hostage. 'You were going to spend the whole weekend with him behind my back, weren't you?'

I feel a great urge to slap Lee, but I resist. I refuse to answer. All I can think about is how I'm going to get my bag back.

'Did you know about your ability?' he asks.

I sigh. 'Why did I leave you last time?'

'What?' This seems to throw him.

'You heard me.'

'You're not leaving me again.'

'I was never yours for you to marry.'

'But we are married. It's all legal.'

'Not for much longer.'

'You're not leaving me again.'

I smile. 'It's not many men who get left for the same man twice. But you've only got yourself to blame, Lee. You stole my life from me. You've taken some of the best years of my life, I refuse to give you one second more.'

'It's not happening.'

'I'm not being controlled by you anymore.'

'I love you, Loppy.'

With this I feel the strike of anger in my belly. I take a few deep breaths before telling him, in no uncertain terms, 'My name is Penelope.' Then I summon up all my strength and I push him aside.

I think it's the surprise more than anything that knocks him over, but I don't care. I grab my bag and struggle down the stairs as quickly as I can.

'Loppy!' he screams, but I'm already at the door. 'Loppy, you bitch!'

I slam the door shut and drag my suitcase towards the car. David gets out to help just as the front door swings open.

'Loppy!'

Everything stops. David and Lee remain motionless,

glaring at one another.

'Is there a problem?' David calmly asks me after a few moments.

I shake my head and he takes the suitcase from my hands. Being sure to keep my back to Lee, I quickly jump in the passenger seat.

I focus my attention on the driver's seat so I'm completely facing away from Lee and the house. I can't bear to look. After a few seconds of silence, I hear David move. He places my suitcase in the boot, slams it shut and then walks back around to the driver's side.

'It has to be true that we were engaged,' I say to him as he straps himself in.

'I know,' he replies, quite seriously.

'What were you going to tell me today? When we had our chat. Were you going to end things with me or leave your wife?'

David looks past me and I know that Lee is still there, staring at us. 'So many forces have tried to keep us apart,' he says, turning his attention back to me. 'It's quite remarkable. Yet despite all the odds, we've found our way back to each other. I loved you before enough to propose and I know in my heart that I love you just as much now. You're the only woman I've ever loved. For me there was never a choice. I want to spend the rest of my life with you, Penny. You're the only thing that matters. In fact, I'm starting to believe that you may be the only thing that's ever mattered.'

I swallow back an urge to cry. That might be the most wonderful thing than anyone has ever said to me. It's also such a relief to hear. 'Good. I'm so glad,' I tell him. 'Because I've just left my husband.'

David looks past me again and I know that Lee must still be there, like an idiot. An unwanted, cruel idiot. David squeezes my hand. 'Don't worry about him anymore. It's all going to get better from now on. Things are on the up. This moment marks the start of the rest of our lives.'

19. AN EXTRA LAYER OF CONFUSION

It's nearly one o'clock in the morning when we arrive back at our fancy hotel room. It seems such a shame that we haven't been able to enjoy it.

David is refusing to acknowledge how tired he is, but his whole face is deceiving him. He flicks the lights on, rests my suitcase on the floor and then hugs me tightly.

'You should try to get some sleep,' he says, kissing me gently on the head.

'I think right about now I could sleep for a week.'

'We get to wake up together tomorrow.' I can't see his face as I'm nestled into his chest, but I can tell he's smiling.

'We must have done that hundreds of times before. That's so weird.'

'Come on.' David heads towards the bed and I grab my pyjamas from my suitcase. I can't sleep without my cosy pyjamas.

He pulls back the duvet and plumps my pillow before heading into the bathroom. I change into my pyjamas and snuggle up under the Egyptian cotton. The bed is so ridiculously soft, I know I'll have no problems sleeping; no matter how many thoughts are spinning around my head.

As I pull the duvet up around me, I spot my wedding

ring still wrapped around my finger. I don't want that anymore. I'm not with Lee anymore. This is a fresh start and I want that part of my life to be well and truly over with.

I nip out of bed and throw the ring in my case. Then I tuck myself back under the duvet.

David returns just as I'm curling up. He strips down to his boxers and then slides in next to me. It feels so familiar and safe, and I forget about Lee as quickly as I whipped off my ring. At least now I know why. No wonder I never felt guilty.

David puts his arm out and I nuzzle in against his chest. We wrap ourselves around each other and a huge sigh leaves my body. This is the most wonderful, comfortable moment that I can ever remember having.

His warm skin is so silky and I find I quickly start to relax curled up in his arms. Although I don't recall ever feeling like this before, I'm woefully aware of how much I've missed it.

As that notion sinks in, a mixture of both anger and sadness torments my soul. My family has stolen so many moments like this away from us.

I start to process all of the times we could have had together and all of the things we've missed out on. All of the holidays and home cooked meals. Just going to the supermarket together; living our everyday lives. Our wedding day. I begin to wonder what our wedding day would have been like. Had we made plans? Had I tried on dresses? What about a venue? I think about the smile I would have had on my face all day. It certainly wasn't present on the wedding day I ended up having.

I'm so lost in thought, I don't notice myself drifting off, and before I know it I'm fast asleep.

I wake up with a start. I instantly turn to check on David, but he's not there. Panic sets in. Those awful dreams.

I take a deep breath as the sound of the shower trickles through. He's in the bathroom.

I spot his laptop on the desk at the other end of the room and I feel as if I've missed half the day. I scan the bottom of the TV in front of me where I remember there's a clock and I see it's approaching half past nine.

I hear the shower turn off and within a couple of minutes David appears.

'Morning,' he smiles, seeing I'm awake. He walks over, wrapped up in a fluffy white dressing gown, and sits down next to me on the bed.

'Morning. Have you been working?'

'Yes. Just for a couple of hours. I couldn't sleep.'

'I had horrible nightmares.'

'Are you okay?' he asks with concern. I just nod and smile in reply. For so long David has been the centre of my dreams, but last night all I dreamt about was my family kidnapping me. They all really hated me.

He kisses me gently and holds my hand. 'I've booked us into a slightly cheaper hotel for the week. I hope you understand. It's near Waterloo. I thought it best to steer clear of anywhere my wife may be.'

I forgot about her. A pang of sickness punches me in the stomach as I think about it. How can he be married? I try and swipe it from my mind. 'I can draw out some money,' I say.

'No.'

'But you can't-'

'We're in this together, Penny. You have enough going on, the least I can do is sort out somewhere for us to stay.'

I squeeze his hand. He makes me feel so loved. I can't remember ever feeling this way before. Some husband Lee turned out to be. I close my eyes for a second and thank the universe that David is back in my life. I'm so grateful that I've been rescued from that prison I was in.

'I thought we could check out of here, go straight to the new hotel, and then I want you to come to work with me.'

'Won't I just be in the way?' I ask.

'If you'll let me, I want to take a sample of your blood.

Your brother told us there was something in your blood that stopped you getting ill. I think that's a really good place for us to start. So, if it's okay with you, I'd like to take a look.'

'You can do that?'

'Yes. I assume that's why you came to me in the first place.'

'You're very clever,' I say. 'I'd really appreciate it if you could take a look at my blood. You're about the only person in the world I trust right now, so you're the only one that's going anywhere near me.'

'Good. Get ready then, we have another big day ahead of us.'

Within the hour, we're driving away from the fancy hotel. We make the decision to drop off David's car at home first. I wait in a nearby coffee shop with my bags in case the dreaded Suzanne is around. David is going to tell her that he'll be on the road for work for a few days and then he can easily pack and disappear with no questions asked.

I did broach the subject of whether he was going to tell her about me, but he said that would only open up a messy can of worms and he didn't want to waste any time at the minute. He suggested that it would be better for us to have our week together undisturbed and then he'd tackle the issue of Suzanne after that. I agreed with him. I know it's not going to be a five minute conversation. I don't like it, though.

In fact, I hate it. At least Lee knows I'm not coming back. Suzanne thinks all is wonderful and that David is all hers. It makes my blood boil.

Just as I'm chewing over how my boyfriend/fiancé/love of my life – whatever he is – is not telling his wife that he's now with me, David arrives at the coffee shop. He's far quicker than I expected.

'Are you okay?' he asks. My body is clearly stiff with tension.

'Of course,' I reply, forcing myself to relax. I must let go of my frustrations. I remind myself that he wants to be with me, not her, and any delay is just logistics. Wouldn't I rather he be with me now than having a long, meaningful conversation with his wife about how he's leaving her? That could take all day. I must keep telling myself that.

We head towards the nearest tube station and by midday we're settling in to our new hotel room. My earlier frustrations soon drift to the back of my mind as David and I explore our new home for the week.

We both unpack our clothes and try to make the small but comfortable room feel as homely as possible, before we make our way back up the Northern Line towards David's office.

We alight at Tottenham Court Road station for a quick lunch break. We head down Oxford Street and find a sandwich shop.

As we sit in the window and watch the world go by, I get that eerie sensation again that I've been here before, and for the first time it dawns on me that I probably have. I used to live in London. I worked here. No wonder everything feels so familiar.

After we've gulped down our lunch, David grabs my hand. He's heading somewhere with purpose.

He doesn't say a word and I follow him willingly. He stops outside a computer shop. 'I want you to write again,' he says.

'What?'

'We're getting you a laptop and I want you to spend your week writing. I'm going to have to work lots, so when we're not together I want you to write. Unless you want to go out exploring?'

I love everything about what he just said. I feel a warmth travel through me, radiating my soul. He wants me to explore. He wants me to write. He wants me to do what I want to do. 'What do you want me to write?' I ask.

'I really enjoyed your story about me, but if you don't mind I'd rather you didn't share my life with the world. It was a bit too close to home. So I think you should write a new novel. One that we really can get published.'

A sickening sensation rumbles in my stomach as I recall that meeting with Suzanne. I thought I was getting published once. Still, when I think about what I've gained from that moment, it was actually the best thing that could ever have happened.

I start to smile until reality hits. 'I can't afford a laptop. I need to save. I don't know-'

'Penny, stop it. This is a gift.'

'You can't!'

'I can. I can do whatever I like. Will you accept my gift?'

I really want to say yes. Everything in my life has changed. Being able to write - to do what I've clearly always loved doing - would be a great way to kick off this new start.

'I could pay you back?' I offer.

'For a gift?' David shakes his head at me.

He enters the shop. Just like when he bought me the phone, he handles the shop staff brilliantly. He keeps them to the task in hand, not standing for the endless extras they try to sell him. He's so patient and firm. He's incredible.

He hands me the bag and I proudly leave with my brand new laptop. It's not a big one, it's one that I can easily carry around with me. I'm a writer on the move and it's very exciting.

Our final stop is David's workplace. I have to sign in as always before I'm given my visitor pass and then we head up to his office.

He fires up his laptop and helps me set up my own. In between doing work, he keeps checking on me. We're sitting opposite one another at his desk and I feel so close to him.

When it's all set up, I flick open Word and I'm ready for action. I've decided not to overthink my creativity and, to begin with, just write about what I've been going through. If not a novel, I'm sure it would make an interesting memoir.

As I start to type, David excuses himself. I assume he's going to the toilet but he comes back a few minutes later with a test tube thing and some purple gloves.

'Is it still okay if I take a sample of your blood?' he asks, very politely.

I suddenly feel incredibly nervous. 'Can you do that?'

'Yes,' he nods. 'I'm not qualified to see patients, but I know what I'm doing. I won't hurt you.'

He rolls his chair around so he's sitting next to me and I take off my cardigan. My short sleeved dress leaves my arms free for him to access.

He pops the gloves on, wraps a Velcro thing around the top of my arm and wipes around the inside of my elbow with a cleanser. As he feels for a vein, I turn my head away. I trust him completely, but I'd rather not witness it.

My arm stings sharply as the needle breaks through and my skin prickles with a sense of déjà vu. I know I've definitely experienced that sting before.

Not a few moments later and David is sticking a plaster on me. 'All done,' he says, kissing my arm.

I study the tube in his hand. It doesn't look like he's taken much blood. 'Is that enough?' I ask.

'Yes. I don't need a lot. Will you be okay if I pop to the lab?'

'Can I come?'

'Sorry, Penny. This is a very secure building. You need clearance to get in the lab. But I won't be long. Besides, it looks like you're well into another masterpiece.'

I look back at my laptop and grin. 'It's a start.'

David disappears and I bite my lip. I read over my notes about the last few months.

What a strange turn of events. If I hadn't written that novel then I never would have found David. More than that though, if David hadn't married a literary agent then we never would have met again. I suppose I should be grateful that he met Suzanne.

I don't know what I thought before, but I now definitely believe in fate. The universe wanted us to find each other. Or maybe that's what they call serendipity?

An idea sparks in my head. David may not want me to write about him, but I can write a novel about our story. And what a story it is to tell. I could change the characters but the idea of a love so strong that it defies all the odds is definitely worth writing about. It all began with that life changing email from Suzanne Royall. Who knew my life would never be the same again?

I start typing and the pages just fly away beneath my fingers. It feels amazing. I feel free.

I don't know how long I've been in my story world for but I'm brought hurtling back to reality when David slowly re-enters his office. He looks pale and worried.

He places before me a little test tube that's sitting on its own in a yellow plastic rack. I don't know what I'm supposed to be looking at. 'What's that?' I ask.

'That's your blood.'

'The bottom bit?' I ask. That's the only bit in the tube that looks red. The top bit looks like really pale urine.

'All of it. I've spun it in the centrifuge to study its composition. The top bit, the clear stuff, that's your plasma.'

'Ugh.' It looks a bit gross.

'The bottom bit, that's your red blood cells.'

'And what about the green bit?' Right under the large layer of plasma there is a layer of bright green goo.

David doesn't answer me. I turn to him and his face looks even more serious than it normally does. 'What is it?' I push, nervous about what he's about to say.

'I have absolutely no idea, Penny. I've never seen anything like it.'

20. A BRIGHT REVELATION

'What do you mean you've never seen anything like it?' I ask, totally confused.

'Just that,' David replies. 'I've worked with hundreds, if not thousands of blood samples in my career, but they have never looked like this. There are four main components to blood, Penny. That's a scientific fact. It doesn't change. Well, not normally. This fifth element makes absolutely no sense.'

I don't know how to feel. 'Is this bad?'

David sits back in his chair and stares at the tube. 'I can't say.' He shakes his head and sighs. 'I don't get this. I don't get any of it. If I was studying your blood, I would have made notes. There has to be documented notes on what I did. I've been working here for ten years, you'd think I'd have notes somewhere. But I've never come across anything that I haven't known about and I've just had a thorough search through some old project files and there's nothing. Where would I have kept my notes?'

I don't know what to say. We remain silent for what seems like an age. I'm trying very hard to think of something intelligent to say, but the truth is I don't really understand any of what's happening. I'm utterly lost.

'I'm not going to let you down, Penny,' David finally says. 'There are a lot of unknowns here but I want to give you answers. I'm going to give you answers. If you'll let me.'

'Please. I need answers. We need answers.'

'The only problem is that in order to do that... I'm going to need another sample of your blood.'

'Take it,' I say, holding out my arm. I'm more than happy for him to take my freaky blood. Maybe if we got some answers then we could start to piece together why the last five years have been taken from us. And, just as importantly, maybe we can figure out what happened in all those years we can't remember.

'Not now,' he says. He kisses my arm where the plaster still is and takes my cardigan off the back of my chair. 'Let's give your arm a rest. Besides, it's been a big couple of days and I want to be on form when I start to analyse your blood.' He opens his mouth as if to say something else, but he stops.

He holds out my cardigan and I slip my arms in. Then he starts to pack up his laptop. I copy him and put my own laptop away, tucking it back in its box and then into the carrier bag.

'I think I need a laptop bag,' I smile.

David looks at the clock on the wall. It's nearly five pm. 'It's a bit late for shopping now, but why don't you look tomorrow morning?'

'When do you want to take my blood again?' I ask, hoping that he will say soon.

'We've got another major project starting tomorrow,' he says. He pauses and I can tell he's mentally scanning through his schedule. 'I should be done with all my meetings by three. How do you feel about getting here for four? I can take a few samples and you can make sure I get away on time. We could have a full evening together.'

'Would you not look at the samples straight away?'

David takes me in his arms. 'I hate to say this, but it could be a very slow process, Penny. All I know at the minute is that you have an unknown fifth part to your blood. I'm going to have to run a variety of tests on it. It could take weeks, maybe even months before I have any sort of answer for us. And I'm going to have to do it all around my other work. But I promise, I will give it as much attention as humanly possible, and the minute I find out anything I will let you know.'

I shrug with disappointment. 'I always thought science was fast paced. They solve murders overnight on CSI.'

David smirks. 'Sadly that is not reflective of real life. In the real world science takes time. But we get answers; we always get answers. Trust me, Penny, I will get you answers.'

I kiss David warmly on the lips. 'I know you will.' I don't tell him that science suddenly seems really boring.

We head back to Waterloo, hand in hand. We ditch our laptops at the hotel and then David takes me out to a flashy bar for a cocktail. It's the first time I ever remember having a cocktail and it's quite exciting.

Not knowing what I may or may not like, I close my eyes and point at the menu. I end up with something intoxicated with rum. It tastes divine. It has quite a kick to it, but it's also thrilling to the taste buds.

We grab a bite to eat afterwards and I feel liberated. I can order whatever I like. I have the most stimulating food and drink I can think of, followed by an espresso. Sod it, I don't have work tomorrow and I've been deprived for no good reason for far too long.

For the first time in my new memory, David and I are spending time together without disturbances and without watching the clock. No matter what the last twenty-four hours has thrown my way and despite the many stimulants I've just consumed, I can never remember being this relaxed. My life finally feels just as it should be; against all the odds.

David insists on paying for the bill and then we slowly walk back to our hotel. We're now arm in arm and I feel incredibly loved up.

Each step we take under the romantic moonlight seems to morph our love into pure and yearning lust. The closer we get to the hotel, the more we're touching each other, the deeper our kisses get, and by the time we reach our room, I'm ready to burst.

The door has only just clicked shut and David and I are engulfed in a sexy, passionate kiss.

Breathlessly, he leads me to the bed. I kick my ballet pumps off while he yanks at his jumper, and within seconds we're kissing again. His hands reach back to unzip my dress and I scramble to free myself from my clothing with as little time away from his mouth as possible.

He throws his jeans to the floor and we press ourselves next to each other.

I just love the feel of his skin against mine. I have literally never felt so excited. Every inch of me is screaming with pleasure and I think I might explode.

Interlocked with such a desperate desire, before I know it he's inside of me and our bodies are thrusting in time to an ecstatic rhythm.

Nothing in my life has ever felt so intense. I get lost in the rapture and my body starts to shake. As much as I want to watch David and be with him completely in this mind-blowing moment, the overwhelming joy is almost too much and I have to close my eyes.

I feel the climax coming and I want to scream. I'm tingling all over with delight.

Then it starts to burn. But it's a good sort of burn; it's amazing.

Just as the pleasure is peaking, David suddenly stops. He urgently backs away from me.

I open my eyes and try to catch my breath. I know something is wrong. 'What is it?' I say. Have I upset him?

'Did you not see that?' he asks.

'See what?'

'The room. It just lit up. Like a sheet of lightning had crashed through it.'

'Is it the lamp? What is it?' I start to look around but everything seems normal. Except for David's face. He's appears utterly shocked.

'I think it came from you,' he says.

'Me?'

'You just created a flash of light, Penny. I think I've just witnessed your ability.'

21. LIGHT RESEARCH, HARD WORK

I sit up straight and try to absorb what David is telling me. 'It's true then? You think it was me.'

I can see David searching his mind for logic.

'Do you think this light thing has anything to do with the green blood you found?' I ask.

'Green cells,' David corrects. 'At this point I would definitely assume they're related. For you to have two anomalies that are completely distinct from one another seems highly unlikely. It's far more plausible that they're linked. But that's what I'm going to find out.'

'Should I be worried?'

David puts his arm around me. He holds me close. 'No. And I know that for a fact.'

'How?'

'Because we've been here before; we just don't remember. Your brother made it quite clear that you were happy, though. Of all the things that your family told us, it was blatant that the issues were with them and not you. So, if you were happy before, when we knew a lot more, we can safely say that you don't have anything to worry about now.'

I smile and kiss him. 'You're very wise.' We hold each other for a few moments and I start to feel better about everything. 'Do you think this light thing is just going to go off randomly? Do you think I can control it?'

'I don't know,' David replies. 'Let's find out.'

David stands up and puts on his pyjamas. I follow his lead and slip myself into my pink matching set. I stand opposite him, waiting for inspiration. 'What do I do?' I ask.

'Okay, let's break this down.' I can see his brilliant mind at work. 'Your family told us that your ability was connected to adrenaline, hence the fact that they were sedating you to control it.'

A flash of anger stabs through me as I remember how they'd been manipulating me for years, but I don't say anything. He's deep in thought and I don't want to distract him.

'But let's also think about your green blood cells,' he continues. 'If we run with the assumption that these blood cells are linked to your light ability then it has to be connected to your blood flow, surely.'

'Take it slow,' I request. Science was never my strong point.

'Do you understand the effect that adrenaline has on your heart?'

'Makes it beat faster?' I ask cautiously, worried that it seems too easy to be right.

'Yes, that's right. At its most basic level, adrenaline causes the contraction rate of the heart to increase. And the faster your heart beats, the quicker your blood flows around your body.'

'I get that.'

'So, if we factor in all we know, we could hypothesise that the movement of these green cells around your body is, somehow, conducting light. But they have to be moving quickly. It's only when your blood flow is increased that the light takes effect.'

'So I need to get my blood moving quickly for it to work?' I think I'm following it.

'If we take what your sister said to be true, then if you

increase your heart rate to a significant level you should be able to create this light. Then, to stop it, you need to slow down your heart rate again. It seems most peculiar, but let's give it a go.'

'Okay,' I say, trying to work through the logic in my head. I consider the flash of light that David just witnessed. 'I suppose my heart rate was going a bit off-the-chart crazy when it happened a few minutes ago.' I can't resist a cheeky smile.

'Yeah?' he smiles back, raising his eyebrows.

'Oh yes,' I nod and smirk. I run over to give him a quick cuddle.

'Right, sorry,' I say, backing away again. 'If I'm understanding this correctly, basically the excitement spiked my heart rate and then that charged these green blood cell things and that made me able to create light.'

'Charged? Yes, I like that. You're charging them somehow. I have no clue how that could be possible, but it seems like a great working theory. Let's go with that.'

'So I need to raise my heartbeat.'

'Yes.'

'How? Shall I go for a run?'

David considers my question for a moment. 'Tell me how you feel about everything.'

'About what?'

'We've not talked in any depth about what happened to us. For some unknown reason we were split up against our will. Tell me how you feel about it.'

'I don't know if I want to-'

'Tell me, Penny. Let it out. Get in touch with those emotions. Let the anger take hold of your body and see how it affects you.'

I see what he's doing. I've spent years not being angry about anything. I've been stuck maintaining a temperate level, no matter how badly everyone was treating me. Without thinking any more, I say the first thing that comes to mind. 'I'm furious.' That felt good. 'They stole five years of our lives. We were going to get married.'

'We were planning our wedding day.'

'They forced me to marry Lee. Oh my God!' As I think about the truth my heart starts to pound. 'I'd barely got out of hospital when they whisked me down the aisle. They told me Lee and I had been planning our wedding for two years. It was all such bullshit. They did it to control me; to trap me in a marriage so they could stop me getting back with you.'

'And I bet also to change your name so I couldn't find you. I knew you as Penelope Edwards.'

'Loppy fucking Fox! Everyone knows me as Loppy Fox. My family tried to eradicate Penelope from my life. I hate Loppy!'

'They hid you away in every way they could.'

'They imprisoned me in my own life!' I want to cry now as I start to process the reality of what happened. My thoughts turn to David. 'And you're married now.' As I say the words, I feel a tingle across my fingers.

'Yes I am. I'm stuck in a marriage. I didn't want to say anything before but it's not going to be easy for me to leave Suzanne. And to be honest, I don't know if I want to.'

Fear, anger, sadness, regret, in fact every negative emotion that I'm capable of feeling rages through my body and my fingers burn.

Without any warning at all, a ball of light suddenly flashes from my hands. It's incredible. And it feels like such a release.

'You did it!' David exclaims. He rushes over and hugs me. 'I'm sorry. That was a lie. I wanted to push you to the edge so we could get this to work, but it was nothing but a lie.'

'What?' I say, hugging him back.

'The minute I can get away from Suzanne, I'm leaving her. You're the one I love. I just wanted to give you a push to get the light to flare.'

I'm tearful as I hug David tightly. 'That was so mean.'

'I'll never do it again. I promise. But you have to

remember it, Penny. Use your emotional memory as you practise. I'm sorry.'

'It's okay,' I say, kissing his cheek. 'As long as you didn't mean it.'

'I don't want her. I never did.'

'It's always been me?' I ask. I need this reassurance now, more than ever.

'Even when I didn't know you were real, you were still all I could think about. I still wanted you more than my wife.'

A smile warms my lips. That's true for the both of us. I shrug my shoulders, trying to calm the emotion. 'I suppose you got me to light up.'

He kisses me softly. 'Just remember how you felt. And remember how you calmed yourself.'

I do feel calm again. It's amazing. I close my eyes to remember what I did. But I'm only given a second before David is kissing me again. And this time it's a little bit more passionate.

I kiss him back and within seconds we're wrapped up in a fervent embrace.

He pushes me towards the bed and those memories are long gone.

Our desire for each other is taking charge and I feel my fingers start to tingle with that wonderful burn.

David's alarm goes off at six thirty the following morning and by seven o'clock he's left for work. It seems crazy early to me. I'm starting to think I'm in love with a workaholic. I can't help but wonder if he was always like this. That's something for me to ask him.

I try to go back to sleep, but I can't. I'm going to call Wesley at nine o'clock to phone in sick and it's playing on my mind. I've never called in sick before; ever. This is strange new territory for me. Even more so in that I'm not actually sick.

David has justified it by telling me that I'm not in a fit

state to work; not with everything that I've been through. I suppose I have to agree. Work is the last thing I need to deal with right now. We also joked about how I could say I'd seen a doctor. It's not a lie!

I have one hundred and fourteen minutes to go until I need to call Wesley. I feel sick. What if he knows I'm lying? What if he knows I'm in London?

It did occur to me that I could just tell Wesley the truth. Well, a version of it. I could say I've left my husband and I'm going through a rough time. But he's not the sort of man you can say that to. He'd hear me somehow tell him that I fancy him or something.

Claiming to have the flu is a much better excuse. Not that I know what having the flu is like, but David's briefed me on the particulars.

One hundred and twelve minutes.

As I get more and more nervous, it dawns on me how alive I feel. I couldn't remember the difference, I'd been on those drugs for so long, but now I'm actually feeling like me again. Although at times like this, being sedated did have its advantages. This countdown is torturous.

I try to sleep again, but I just keep playing out Wesley sacking me down the phone and I can't switch off.

As eight o'clock hits, my nerves increase, and that's when the tingling on my fingers begins. This then unnerves me even more, and within minutes the tingling starts to burn. I get lost in a cycle of nerves and fear and before I know it I'm shooting flashes of light around the room.

I take a deep breath and decide that if I can't sleep and I'm doomed to clock watching for the next fifty-two minutes, then I might as well spend the time learning about my ability.

I do as David suggested and I recall emotions from over the past couple of days. It works. As I get angry or sad and I work myself up, the tingling starts, then as I calm myself it goes away.

I practise over and over, working myself up and calming

myself down. In fact, I'm getting good at it.

Just as I'm getting into a rhythm, the alarm on my phone chimes. My heart practically leaps out of my chest, both from the suddenness of the alarm and also that the time has come, and I shoot a bolt of light across the room. It's quite impressive. I think I might enjoy this ability when I can control it.

I grab my phone and switch off the alarm. The dreaded nine o'clock has arrived. I quickly practise my poorly voice before dialling Wesley's mobile. He's never far from his mobile.

'Loppy,' he answers after just a couple of rings.

'Morning Wesley,' I croak. It's an Oscar-worthy performance but he doesn't respond. 'I'm really sorry but I've got the flu. I'm so poorly.'

'You're sick?' he says with surprise.

'My turn I guess.' I follow this with a weak cough.

'So you're not coming in?'

'I don't think that would be wise. But fingers crossed I get better very soon.' *I'm sure I'll be better by next Monday*, I think to myself with a naughty smile.

'Right.' He actually sounds lost and for a moment I feel useful. 'Well, take care and keep me posted.'

'Will do. Speak to you soon.' I hang up with my fake cough, just for effect, and a wave of relief washes over me. I think I may have even enjoyed that. It's a rare treat to get one over that creep.

With a self-satisfied smile, I jump in the shower. I'm now eager to start my day.

I begin by scoffing down a Full English breakfast at a local café before returning to our hotel room to do some writing. At half past one I break for lunch and then I take in a few sights on my way over to David's office.

He's all ready for me and by half past four he's taken a few samples of my blood and I'm playing scrabble on my phone as he finishes off some work.

He treats me to dinner on the way back to the hotel, but

we don't have a late night as he has to be at work again for just after seven in the morning. And then my day virtually repeats itself.

I text Wesley on Tuesday morning, being far too ill to speak, and then I crack on with some more writing followed by a little bit of further sight-seeing. I also make sure I do lots of practising with my light ability whenever I get the chance.

By the time Thursday comes around, I'm ten chapters into my novel, I've become quite adept at throwing light around, and I've enjoyed lots of London's tourist hot-spots. I'm having the best week ever!

David has been getting home – well back to the hotel – for about six o'clock each night, but it's now half seven and there's no sign of him. Finally he calls.

'I'm so sorry Penny,' he says. 'I've been in the lab. I've had a breakthrough. It's only little, but I've found out something about your blood.'

'What? What is it?'

'Meet me in Covent Garden. Let's go for dinner and I'll tell you everything.'

22. IN THE BLOOD

David won't tell me a thing until we're sitting in the restaurant. It's the lovely Mexican one, the restaurant we visited the first time we had dinner together. Well, the first time that I can remember.

We order our fajitas and I stare at David eagerly.

'It's not a lot, like I said,' David says with a smile. He gulps down some of his beer and takes a deep breath.

'Go on.'

'I've been focussing on your green blood cells, as you know. Firstly, I can't see that they interact with your red blood cells, but it's not conclusive yet whether they react with your white cells.'

This means nothing to me. 'Is that bad?'

'No, not at all. It's very early days but it could possibly account for why you're never ill.'

'Except for my terrible flu at the minute,' I smirk and then I pretend to cough. I feel very excited, and David too is beaming. It's amazing to have... What is he? My boyfriend? My fiancé still, as we were once engaged and never actually broke it off? I suppose he's just my David for now. It's amazing that my David is studying me and finding out so much about me. I'd love to have that ability. He's so clever.

'I'm predicting a miraculous recovery from that flu,' David smirks back, then he leans in closer to me and drops his voice. 'Seriously, though, I've found something more definite out. When your blood flow increases - so when your heart is beating faster - the green blood cells expand. It's like they get a boost from your accelerated heart rate.'

'Wow. Why do they expand?'

'I have no idea.' He reads my expression and I find I can't hide my disappointment. 'No, don't you see? This is really exciting. I've proven today that there's a significant change to the anomalous cells when your heartbeat increases.'

I shake my head. I haven't got a clue why that's meant to be exciting.

'We already know that your adrenaline levels impact your ability to control light,' he explains. 'And now I've found the same trait in the green blood cells. There is a physical change to the anomalous cells during the same conditions that cause you to expel light. It can't be a coincidence.'

'So these green blood things, they're definitely connected to why I can shoot light out of my fingers?'

'They have to be. We haven't proven it yet, but we have a very strong connection now.'

'So, what is it then?'

'What's what?'

'The cause of the light?'

'I don't know yet.'

'But you're nearly there?'

'It's a step in the right direction.'

'Well, when will you know?'

David just looks at me blankly and I feel my face screw up. 'You have to have patience for science, don't you?' I say.

David chuckles. 'Yes, you do. But it pays off.'

Our fajitas arrive and we lighten the conversation as we munch. I admire David's enthusiasm and I love that he's on the case trying to find out why I'm different, but I can't say that I'm as excited about this revelation as he is. I was hoping for actual answers. This doesn't really tell us anything.

We head to a bar after dinner and David promises me a later night. He says he won't go into work until eight tomorrow. I think this is my moment to challenge him.

'Have you always been a workaholic?' I ask as we take a seat on a small table near the window.

He looks thrown by my question and I smile to indicate that it's not an issue just a query.

'My work has always been an important part of my life,' he states.

'You work such long hours, though.'

'It's my job. We're doing research that could change the human race.'

'I suppose when you say it like that,' I shrug.

He sighs. 'The truth is, at my level, I shouldn't really be involved in the day to day lab work, but I can't help it. I got the promotion to director because of my knowledge and experience, but it hit me hard not being involved on the science front-line anymore. So now I try to do both. I have all the red tape of being a director and I also get in the lab and work with my team as much as I can. I can't let it go.'

'And that's why you have so little time for anything else?'

'I get to lead the team and make all the important decisions, but the lab work is where it really happens.'

I smile. I love his passion for it. As much as I wish we had more time together, I know I wouldn't have him any other way. 'Will you tell me about it? What sort of research is it?'

'It's complicated and boring.' This is always the sort of answer I get from him when I ask about his work.

'How can it be boring if it's going to change the human race?'

'It won't interest you.'

'Why can't I be the judge of that?'

He sighs and shrugs his shoulders 'Okay, if you're sure.

But I warn you, most people glaze over after about a minute.'

'I think we both know I'm not most people.'

'That's true,' he says with a cheeky grin. I stick my tongue out at him and giggle. 'The projects I've been working on are heavily focussed on trying to understand the immune system better,' he tells me. 'We need to find alternative medicines to antibiotics. That's why I was so enthused about that finding earlier. The fact that you don't get ill, I can't get it out of my head. It has to relate to those blood cells.'

'Oh my God,' I say.

'What is it?'

'This can't all be a coincidence. Could my blood have somehow influenced your work before?'

David smiles. 'I thought something very similar. Except for the fact that I can't find anything, anywhere, that even remotely suggests that you were in my life before. We have such stringent paperwork trails. I can't see how I could do all of this work - even off the radar - and not leave a single trace of it anywhere.'

'Are you sure?'

'Believe me, if there was anything I'd left from before, I would have found it by now. But let's not get deflated. We'll get there again. And with the added bonus this time that I have a hell of a lot more experience.'

I hold my glass of wine in the air. 'To solving the mystery of Penelope Fox,' I say.

David shakes his head. 'Can we toast to solving the mystery of Penelope Edwards?' he asks.

I clink his beer bottle. 'To the mysterious Penelope Edwards.'

'Now I'll drink to that!' David chuckles, then he clinks my glass in return and we both sip our drinks.

We sit for a minute, both individually mulling over everything that has happened to us in the last few days. It's been massive, but I don't feel overwhelmed. I suppose somewhere deep inside of me I already knew all of this.

I'm actually more interested in the future. 'What do we do next?' I ask.

'Next?' David asks.

'What's going to happen after this weekend? Am I just moving back to Birmingham?'

'Oh Penny,' David grabs my hand and squeezes it gently. 'I'm so sorry. With everything that's been happening and the fact that all the time we've spent together has just felt so normal and easy, I forgot all about next week. I forgot that this wasn't our life.'

'Do you want it to be our life?'

'I don't want to live in a hotel, but I want to live with you.'

'I want to live with you too.' I squeeze his hand in return as delight flutters through me. 'Do we have to live in London?'

David hesitates. 'Would that be a problem? I need to be near my work. And not just because it's my job, but because I'm in the perfect position to help you. We need me to have this job.'

I shake my head. 'It's fine.' It really is fine. It's exactly how I want my life to be. 'I lived here before. It's where our life is. I still have to go back to work, though. Even if it's just to hand in my notice. I have to give a month's notice.'

'Okay. But that doesn't stop us finding a place together, does it?'

'I guess not.' I'm now bursting with tingles of elation.

'Perhaps you could contact some estate agents tomorrow, get some viewings booked in for Saturday? I promise I won't work this weekend. Or as little as I can get away with.'

'Do you think we'll be able to get appointments, just like that?'

'Of course. Especially when we have money to spend.'

'I don't have any money to spend.'

'I do.'

'But-'

'The only thing you need to worry about for now is settling in to a new life.'

'I want to pay my way.'

'I know you do and you'll get a job in no time. You could find out where you worked before and pay them a visit. Or, more likely, you'll be selling that fantastic book of yours. But before all that, your life is about to be turned upside down. Take a few weeks to settle. I said it before, Penny, we're in this together. You're moving across the country to relocate, leaving everything you know behind. The least I can do is make it as easy as possible for you.'

I squeeze his hand again and thank my lucky stars that I've met such a wonderful man. 'Okay, I'll hand my notice in on Monday and then we're on the countdown to living together.'

'No, I want us to be living together straight away. How do you feel about commuting long distance for a few weeks?'

'You mean commute from London every day? That's going to be really difficult.'

'All right, we'll get you a hotel for the week and you can come home at the weekend.'

'Home to London?'

'Your new home.'

A huge smile overtakes my face. I live in London! It's thrilling.

I think about our future life together when one last question suddenly taunts my mind. My smile fades as I ask, 'What are you going to do about Suzanne?'

David sighs. 'I've been thinking about that. I need to get it sorted. If it's okay with you, perhaps I could drop you off back in Birmingham on Sunday afternoon? Then I'll go straight home and tell Suzanne the truth. She needs the truth. It's only fair.'

'It's one hell of a truth to digest.'

'Maybe I'll leave out the light and the green blood cell bits,' David says with a small smirk.

'Yes, that might be wise.'

'We'll get you that hotel room booked tonight.'

'No,' I say as an idea forms in my head. 'Perhaps I could ask Billy if I could stay with him. It won't be for long and I think I'd like some time to get to know him again. With everything that's happened, I've barely spoken to him in years. It'd be nice if we could reconnect.'

'What a lovely idea.'

'It's also really close to my house. Well, where Lee lives. I could pack up my stuff slowly then too. Nip in and out quickly. That might make the transition easier.'

'However you want to do it. Just let me know how I can help.'

I lean over and kiss David. 'I love you.'

'I love you too.'

I'm on a mission on Friday and within an hour I've made four appointments with estate agents.

By the time we've viewed the second place on Saturday, we know we've found the perfect apartment. It's very luxurious with three massive bedrooms. We sign the paperwork and it's all settled. I'm going to be living in Islington!

We're able to move in on Wednesday, so David plans to spend another few nights at the hotel and by next weekend we'll be in our own home.

It's a rare day that David doesn't actually work and we indulge in twenty-four hours of quality us time before the sadness that Sunday brings. I can't believe I have to say goodbye to him.

He drops me off at Billy's house mid-afternoon on Sunday, after treating me to a Sunday roast in a country pub nearby. I try so hard not to cry as he drives away. I know I'll see him again in a few days' time. It's just been the best week I've ever had. To my recollection.

Billy is great, though. He was more than happy for me to stay. He's riddled with guilt, but I don't really blame him for anything that's happened. It's thanks to him that I know the truth.

He and his girlfriend cook me my first home meal for over a week - although I'm a bit full from lunch - and by ten o'clock I'm curled up on their sofa dreading Monday. I've never handed in my notice before. That I can remember. But it's all for the best and it represents the start of the end of my current life. A life I've not really enjoyed.

My phone chirps and I look at it. It's a text from David.

All sorted with Suzanne. Went as well as can be expected. I am now officially all yours. Back at the hotel, missing you. Goodnight xxx

I text back how pleased I am and wish him sweet dreams. I feel happier now, and totally relieved.

I lie back and think of the wonderful week we've had. Within seconds sleep has grabbed me, but I'm pretty sure the smile doesn't leave my lips.

23. A SPOTLIGHT ON THE PROBLEM

I arrive into work extra early on Monday to make sure I can print off my letter without anyone noticing. David helped me put it together. I didn't even know what a resignation letter should say.

I seal it in an envelope and write *Wesley Parker* in my neatest handwriting on the front. I then underline his name just for effect.

Now that's out of the way, I turn my attention to my emails. Having been off for a week I'm expecting hundreds, but when my inbox opens I see I have just forty-seven. That seems low. I normally get more than that just in one day.

'How are you feeling?' Siobhan asks, swinging into my office, still with her jacket on. She's the only person I don't want to lie to. I have to tell her some semblance of the truth. 'The flu is awful,' she continues.

I close my office door and drop my voice. 'I didn't have the flu.'

'Oh sorry, that's what Wesley told me.' She seems very confused.

'I've left Lee.'

Her jaw drops open and her eyes light up with intrigue.

'It's very complicated,' I explain. 'I found out that I don't have a heart problem. It's too long a story for now, but I couldn't stay with a man who'd lied to me. So I'm perfectly healthy and perfectly in love with a man who is not my husband.'

Siobhan grabs her head as if it will somehow help her to compute everything that I've just told her. 'You don't have a weak heart?'

I shake my head.

'And Lee knew that?'

I nod my head.

'You've left Lee for David?'

'Yes. Last weekend.'

'Wow! How could he lie to you like that? That's absurd.'

'Trust me, it's very complicated.'

'Well, I can't say I'm upset. I was never overly impressed with Lee. But what are you going to do? Isn't David in London?'

I grab the letter from my desk. 'I'm handing in my notice today. We already have a flat in London.'

'Bloody hell, Loppy. I can't believe it. I'm so happy for you. I need the full story. Right, you and me, drinks after work.' Her expression becomes cautious. 'David will be okay with that, won't he?'

I smirk. 'He'd probably encourage it. But should we really go out on a Monday?'

'Of course. We have major catching up to do. We're leaving here at five pm sharp.'

'Okay, I'm in.'

'I'd better dash. Good luck with Wesley.' She goes to open my office door when she stops. 'Oh, I have to warn you. Wesley was a complete shit last week.'

'Tell me something I don't know.'

'No, even more than he normally is. He got Stacey to do all his PA work to cover your absence, but then he starting telling everyone how good she is. She's basically been taking over your job.'

'What? So that's why I've got no emails.'

'I suppose it doesn't matter now you're leaving, but watch yourself, Loppy. She's been worming her way in and he's been lapping it up.'

'What a little bitch.' I squeeze the letter in my hand. 'I need to go and see him.'

'Best of luck.'

I head down to Wesley's office. Straight away I see that Stacey is in there with him and it really riles me. I'm back now, she's not having my job. Not before I leave, anyway. I open the door, without knocking, and step in.

'I thought you'd like to know that I'm back.' They both turn to look at me, gobsmacked.

'Loppy, how are you? You look well,' Wesley says.

'Much better, thank you.'

'Good.'

'I hear my job has been in safe hands while I've been off.' I turn my attention to Stacey and try hard not to flash her too much of a dirty look.

'Yes, Stacey has been a fantastic help.'

'But I'm back now.'

'Yes,' Wesley nods.

'What would you like me to do?'

Wesley turns to Stacey and they share a secret look. It can't mean anything good. 'Stacey's on top of everything for the minute.' *I bet she is.* 'You could make us a coffee, though.'

'Us?' I'm hoping he doesn't mean what I think he means.

'Yes. Stacey takes it the same way I do.'

I feel a bolt of rage electrify me, which doubles in impact when Stacey smugly adds, 'Thank you, Loppy.'

I remind myself of my resignation letter that is now curled up in my increasingly sweaty hands. 'Can I grab some time with you this morning, Wesley?'

He shakes his head, as if it's a major inconvenience.

'Wesley has the Infriltech people in today,' Stacey informs me. Of course. They've approached Wesley for a merger. He seemed really excited about it before I was off.

'You'll have to wait, Loppy,' Wesley says.

'I need just five minutes of your time.'

'And we need a cup of coffee,' he orders, glaring at me.

I stomp off, deliberately leaving his door open, and charge into the kitchen. I grab two mugs from the cupboard, but I'm too angry to think.

I can't do this. This is so humiliating. I leave the kitchen and make a beeline for Siobhan's office. She looks up from her computer, bewildered.

'That bastard! He's only asked me to make him and Stacey a cup of coffee. She's in there now. I'm not his PA anymore, I'm like hers now. I've dropped down the hierarchy to be the assistant of the junior assistant. What's that about?'

'Loppy, calm down. I've never seen you like this.'

'It's because I'm off my medication. I'm not being sedated anymore.' I can't stop the words.

'Sedated?'

'I'll fill you in later.' I had decided that there would be limits to what I'd tell Siobhan, but at the moment I feel so pumped up I'm ready to let it all go.

Siobhan nods in the direction of her window and we watch Stacey walking by. 'I can't say I've been impressed with how she's been all over Wesley in the past week.'

'I thought she was nice. She's too young to be so manipulative.'

'She's too young to be sleeping with Wesley. Isn't he old enough to be her dad?'

We both pull disgusted faces and I try not to conjure up any unwanted images. 'I'm sure he's not complaining,' I say.

The voices of some visitors grab our attention and we look out as Stacey leads three people by. I know they're from Infriltech and I know they're going directly to Wesley's office.

Her eyes meet mine and she stops. She pokes her head through the doorway. 'It will be coffee for all of us now, if you don't mind?' she smiles, then she leads the visitors onwards.

Another bolt of anger rages through me.

'I know,' is all Siobhan can say as she witnesses my whole body tense up. She gives me a hug. 'Think positively. You're leaving anyway. At least this will make it easier.'

'That's not the point. I've got a degree. I had a fantastic job. I'm more than just a fucking coffee maker. He can't treat me like this! Why does everyone always think they can push me around?' Fuelled by more anger than I've ever felt before, I storm out of Siobhan's office and march down to find Stacey sitting with Wesley's guests, poised with her notepad.

My fingers start to burn and I take a few deep breaths to try and control the light.

Suddenly I have a flash of memories. I look around the office and the years of being ignored and treated like a second class citizen - the ugly PA - all hurtle to the forefront of my mind. I recall how, when I changed my appearance, I became flavour of the month, only to be completely cast aside again when I didn't want to sleep with him. It's obvious who around here has slept with him. They should be ashamed of themselves.

All of the disgusting treatment rumbles inside of me. I've put up with so much from this place. It hurts, it actually hurts.

Then I see red. It's like I'm not even thinking anymore. I just know that I don't want another minute of this hell, let alone another four weeks.

I take a deep breath and I take charge. I walk steadily towards the kitchen and I hit the fire alarm right by the door.

I casually make my way outside and I wait for everyone else. I move down the street a little so the wailing of the alarm isn't too overwhelming. It's still audible but not drowning anymore.

Slowly, as if they know there's not a real fire, my colleagues and the other people in the building all head out and join me, right in the middle of Birmingham. Towards the back of the stream of bodies I see Wesley and Stacey escorting their guests. They make their way onto the street and I know this is my moment.

My fingers are still burning and it's time to let it go.

I cast out my hand and I beam four circles of light directly above Wesley's head. It's so bright, everyone else stands back, but Wesley is stuck in his dazzling spotlight.

'You see him there!' I shout and all the eyes in the immediate area turn to me. I focus on the two men and one woman from Infriltech. 'Believe it or not, I'm this disgusting man's PA.'

'Loppy!' Wesley shouts. I know he wants me to shut up, but the bright light is keeping him in check.

'But I won't be joining you today because I didn't sleep with him.'

'Loppy, what are you talking about?' Wesley's outrage is convincing, but I have more to say.

'He didn't speak to me when I wore baggy jumpers, but the day I showed a bit of cleavage, that's when he asked me to go to Europe with him. I was the best thing since sliced bread for a few weeks. Until he felt my leg in his office and asked me to have a fling with him. I think I was well within my rights to say no, but since then he's cast me aside like I don't even exist.'

The three visitors all turn to Wesley. They're a bit confused by my outburst, but I can see I've got their attention.

'That is not what happened and you know it,' Wesley argues, but the light is making it impossible for him to even gauge who's around him.

'No, Wesley's interpretation would be that I was in the process of leaving my husband and he assumed it meant I was fair game. What he doesn't know is that I'm going back to a man I was engaged to years ago, before my husband tricked me into marrying him.'

I hear a gasp and I know it's from Siobhan. We're going to need lots of wine at some point.

'Look around you. Eighty percent of his workforce is

female. He's a filthy lech who's slept with virtually every member of staff. Ask them if you don't believe me. And if one should turn him down, which they shouldn't even have to do in the first place, then he basically pushes them out. Is that the sort of man you want to do business with? I know he's a clever bloke with a great product, but at what cost? Because one day that perverted man over there is going to be facing a hell of a sexual harassment charge, and it's going to eat his company alive.'

'Loppy, stop this now. Stop these lies.'

I walk towards the bastard and I show him my letter, in its now gloriously crumpled state. 'You see this? This was my resignation letter giving my four weeks' notice. But you know what, Wesley, I think I'll leave right now. I think I'll head back up to my office, clear out my things, and then head right down to London to be with a man who actually treats people with respect. And if you have a problem with it, I can always speak to my lawyer about that proposition in your office.'

'Lies, all lies. You don't need to worry about working your notice. You're fired!'

'You sad, pathetic little man. And you really are little.'

I tear up the letter and throw it at his feet. Everyone around me is in complete silence. I'm sure it's partly because of the strange, brilliant light that's completely surrounding and blinding my former boss, but it must also be because of my stand-out speech.

No one knows what to do and I just turn around confidently and head towards Siobhan. 'I think I'm going to London now. Can we go for that drink really soon?'

I can see the smile ready to burst on her lips, but she's keeping composed. It's too awkward a moment. 'You'd better make it soon. And you'd better keep in touch.'

'I promise.'

I hug her tightly. She's the only friend I've got but I couldn't wish for any more.

I step back into the building, ignoring the siren still

screeching. I know I have enough time to pack up my desk before the light around Wesley's head fades away. It never lasts.

I collect up anything that's important to me and I take one last look around. I can't believe I'm finally leaving. I can't believe this is it.

I close the door to my office and take a deep breath. My new life is just about to start.

24. BLACKOUT

I have about a half hour wait for my train at Birmingham New Street so I treat myself to a cup of coffee and a muffin. Even though I'm now unemployed, I'm perfectly relaxed and perfectly happy.

I casually catch my train and decide to surprise David. It all feels too big to do over the phone.

When I arrive in Rugby I take a taxi to Billy's house - feeling very grateful that he gave me a key - and I pack up my things. I text Billy quickly to explain what's happened and then I call for another taxi to take me back to the train station.

I'm ecstatic as I press the button for a single ticket to London. I can't wipe the smile from my face. As I wait for my train in the late April sun, I'm almost floating with delight.

It's quarter past two when I set foot on the Euston platform. I make my way towards the concourse, full of confidence, knowing it's just a short walk to QAR Research.

That's when I remember that silly receptionist at David's work and I grind to a halt. She's pleasant enough but stubborn to the core. I don't have an appointment to see David, and even though she's met me several times now, I can guarantee she won't let me surprise the ridiculously busy and important Director of Biomedical Sciences. I need to give him a call. It'll still be sort of a surprise.

'How did it go?' David asks as he answers his mobile.

I hesitate. How do I put it? 'Painful at first but ultimately satisfying.'

'Good. I'm proud of you. Just hang on in there, four weeks will fly by.'

'Erm... I'm not sure it matters.'

'What do you mean?'

'Where are you now?'

'Why?' I hear some concern in his voice.

'Are you in your office?'

'Yes. Why?'

'Are you up for a visitor?'

David doesn't say anything. Have I made him mad?

'I didn't exactly hand in my notice,' I explain. 'It was more like just walking out. Well, actually, it was more like making a complete spectacle and telling Wesley to shove the job and if he had a problem with it then he could talk to my lawyer about a sexual harassment charge.'

'You did what?' I can hear David's smile down the line and it makes me smile in return.

'So, I'm now in Euston ready to start my new life.'

'What are you doing, get over here!'

'I was going to surprise you, but you have to let that silly girl know who you're expecting.'

'Get over here now. I'll tell her you're coming.'

'See you in a few!'

If it wasn't for my overnight bag slapped across my back and my suitcase dragging behind me, I might be floating down the street. I feel on top of the world.

Just a fifteen minute walk later and I'm heading into the reception of QAR Research. The last few minutes have been more like a slog, it's true, but nothing is going to bring me down.

'Hello again,' I say as I reach the reception desk.

'Can I help?' the receptionist asks. I see her every time and she always asks me the same question. You'd think she'd be willing to build up some sort of a rapport with me. I'm becoming increasingly convinced that she might be a robot.

'David Royall,' I reply. 'I think you'll find he's expecting me.' She glares at me suspiciously. I can't believe she's serious. 'Penelope Fox,' I say to encourage her along.

'I'm sorry, Dr Royall isn't expecting anyone of that name.'

I look her. Is she joking? 'You know who I am.'

'You're Penelope Fox.'

'Yes.'

'And Dr Royall hasn't informed me that he's expecting you.'

'I've just spoken to him!'

'As have I. But he didn't tell me that he was expecting a Penelope Fox.'

She's got the most vacant look on her face and I want to slap her. If she's just spoken with him then surely he would have told her.

It clicks. Fox. She keeps saying Penelope Fox.

'Is he expecting a Penelope Edwards?' I ask.

'Yes he is,' she says.

'Well, that's me.'

'You said your name was Penelope Fox.'

I feel my fists clench. She's ruining my high. I really don't want to explain my life to her. David is such a pain at times. But I can't blame him for omitting the Fox. I will probably need to go back to my maiden name at some point.

I can't think about that now.

I take a deep breath. This woman is not going to get one over me. 'You know me and you know that I'm friends with David. I don't know why you're insisting on being so difficult. Either you stop playing these games or I'm going to have to call David and tell him you're preventing his visitor from seeing him. I don't think he's going to like that, do you?'

I see a small flicker in her otherwise deadpan face and I know I've won.

She picks up the phone and dials a number. 'Dr Royall, I have a Penelope Fox down here. Would that be the same Penelope you're waiting for?'

She listens and then nods before placing down the receiver. Without uttering a word, she types something into her computer.

'Please can you fill out your details and then I'll need to take a photo,' she says, handing me the longwinded form that I always have to complete. I can't believe that a modern building such as this hasn't got a slicker system for visitors.

I sigh and go through the rigmarole.

'He'll be right down,' she says as she finally hands me my visitor pass.

I smile as nicely as I can when a flash of the future sparks in my head. Just wait until I'm Penelope Royall. She'll have to treat me better then.

My moment of smugness is short-lived though, as I suddenly find myself worrying. What if David doesn't propose a second time?

'Are you sure you've got enough stuff?' David chuckles, breaking me from my taunting thoughts. He swipes himself through the barrier and into the lobby to join me.

'This is me travelling light!' I snigger back.

'I've realised I've got a meeting at three. Do you want to head back to the hotel?' David hands me the key card from his pocket.

'That's probably the easiest idea.' I take the key card from him and stuff it in my handbag.

'Leave one of your bags. I'll carry it home later.'

'Don't be silly, I've managed this far. Besides, I don't want anything to slow you down. What time will you be finishing?'

'Believe me, I won't be late tonight. I want to hear all about how you told that fuckwit to shove it. We've got some celebrating to do.'

I nod. We really do. 'It's only Monday and I feel like we've already come a long way since last week.'

David smiles warmly and kisses me. 'I'll call you when I'm leaving. Get dressed up!'

Keeping his word, David is back at the hotel for five pm, which is exceptionally early for him. He takes me out for cocktails and a fancy meal and I tell him all about Wesley and Stacey and my stunt with the fire alarm. I'm stunned I did it, but it does make us laugh.

During after-dinner drinks I ask him about what happened with Suzanne but he's cagy with the details. All he says is that everything's fine and it went just as he expected. Suzanne will apparently move on and it's all incredibly amicable. I would appear that marriages of convenience are convenient to end as well.

He starts to chat about plans for our future but something catches my eye. He's still wearing his wedding ring. It's still there on his finger. It's now the only thing I can concentrate on.

I open my mouth to ask him why but I quickly stop myself. I don't want to ruin a lovely night. I'm sure it's just a mistake.

I take a breath and remind myself that it's only been twenty-four hours since he left her. I didn't notice my wedding ring straight away. I'm sure by tomorrow it will be gone. I take another cleansing breath and put it to the back of my mind. If it's still there in a week then I'll talk to him.

By Tuesday morning I've forgotten all about it and I'm back to my elated self. I spend the whole day writing and enjoying my time as a lady of leisure.

Tuesday flies by and finally Wednesday arrives. The day we officially move in together.

David has arranged to work from home so we can pick up the keys nice and early. I'm on top of the world. We're about to start our new life together in our new apartment.

Our apartment.

We step in and I'm in awe. It's even more beautiful than I remember. It's so light and airy with masses of floor space and the cutest balcony. It's classed as a flat, technically, but it's bigger than my old house. I can't digest that this is my new home. I feel like I've tricked somebody. But it's all real.

We chose for it to be furnished to save us a lot of hassle, and David immediately sets up a work station on the kitchen table. Luckily he only checks up on things intermittently, mainly while I unpack my stuff. Generally we have a full day together. It's wonderful.

At six pm I convince him to turn off his laptop for good and I start dinner. It's the first meal I've cooked for him – to my recollection – and I opt for fajitas, knowing they're one of his favourites.

We wash the food down with some Mexican beers and then we snuggle up on our huge settee. My hand interlinks with his in our cuddly embrace when suddenly my body tenses. My finger runs over the wedding ring he's still wearing and it makes me nauseous. It's been three days.

He went back to his old home after work last night to pack up a lot of his stuff. He said he knew Suzanne wasn't going to be there. But what if she was there? What if he doesn't really want to leave her?

I know I should say something but I can't formulate the words. I'm too scared of what the answer might be. What if he isn't sure? I know he loves me, but I also sense there's something he's not telling me.

No, I'm sure it's all a mistake. I have to trust him. I just hate it being there on his finger still. I hate that he's still connected to her. I hate that he's married to someone else. Even though I also am.

I take a deep breath and stand up. I have a little stretch as if that's my reason for moving and I walk out onto the balcony. I told myself I'd give him a week before I mentioned it. I bet he hasn't even noticed. I need to give him some time. Maybe he did love her? Maybe this transition is harder for him than he expected?

I look down and see the buzz of the city below. I decide I need to enjoy this moment more. What's a ring? He's here with me and not her. I have to stop obsessing.

'It's such a beautiful evening,' I call back to David who's checking his mobile. He can't resist.

'You want to go for a walk?' he shouts in reply.

I step back into the living room. 'That sounds like a lovely idea.'

'Come on. I'll show you some of my favourite places.'

We head out into the sunny evening. It's cooled down quite a bit, but the smell of spring is all around.

We walk in the opposite direction to David's office. It's a place we've spent very little time in as he was always worried that Suzanne would see us. I'm relieved he's not worried about that anymore.

It seems to get a bit quieter as we move away from the main shops and bars, but this is where David tells me the good places are.

'Excuse me, do you have the time?' a man in a baseball cap asks. David goes to look at his watch and I have a sickening sense of déjà vu.

Just as I am about to warn him that this might be a set-up, a hand grasps me from behind.

A stinging sensation pierces my neck and I look at David with desperation.

Then everything goes black.

PART TWO

DAVID ROYALL

25. REALISATION

'It's ten to eight,' I say, glancing at my watch. I look back at the well-built man who has enquired when suddenly I see Penny being grabbed from behind.

'Hey!' I yell, but the fist across my face floors me. I try to get up as quickly as I can, but for a moment I'm a little dizzy. By the time I scramble to my feet Penny has been dragged into a car and is being driven away. In the speed of it all, I only see that it's a grey car. It could have been any make, model or size. It could have had any number plate.

I curse myself for my slow reactions before panic quickly sets in. Where's she gone? Who's taken her? What am I going to do?

My mobile starts to ring and I pray for it to stop. Not now. It's rare I think it, but not now. Please.

I feel compelled to answer, knowing how important the current project is at work. They'll just keep calling. My team knows I'll always answer my phone. I yank it out of my pocket. It's a private number. 'David Royall.'

'Don't involve the police and you'll get her back safely.' This extinguishes my breath. It's a male voice.

'Who is this?'

'We just want her blood and then we'll return her. But

only if you don't involve anyone else. Call the police and we'll bleed her dry.'

The line goes dead and I still haven't taken a breath. I don't know what to think. Of course I should go to the police. My girlfriend... whatever she is, she's been kidnapped.

His words echo in my mind. Her blood. He wants her blood. This isn't random.

I flick back to what Penny's brother had said. Penny had kept the facts about her condition to a minimum. She'd said it was too dangerous for them to know too much.

What sort of danger? Why can't I remember? It's enormously frustrating.

I need those memories back. I need to know what the green blood cells really are. It would appear that Penny's blood is of major importance to someone. I have to find out why, and then, more vitally, to whom.

At this present moment I have too little information to make a sensible decision. Taking a deep breath, I decide not to involve the police – for now. I need to pull together some facts first and determine just how real a threat that was. Although it certainly sounded real.

I head back to the apartment. I need to think. There must be a clue. Something that I can remember. My dreams gave me so many details about Penny, I know that my memories are somewhere in my head. I just need to access them.

I grab a beer to calm me and also to help numb the sting from the developing bruise on my face. I sit at the table with my notepad and pen. I need to work through this logically.

What is the first thing I remember after my accident? If I can process everything, I might be able to spot something I've missed. Something that might be useful.

I turn my mind back to my accident. I remember nothing about it at all. Everything I know is from what other people have told me. I was apparently driving in Exeter, somewhere near my brother's house. Michael knew nothing about why

I was there, though. I've never found out why I was there.

I was barely conscious for the next couple of weeks. My parents arranged for me to be moved to a private hospital in London. Only the best, they claimed. I know too well they were just throwing money at a problem. That's all they ever do. I imagine they spent a great deal of time boasting about the best possible care their son was getting.

They only visited me once. I should be grateful for that, I suppose. Business must come first.

My father is a hugely successful sales consultant who travels the world for work, always first class, and usually with my mother in tow. When you're in high demand, you get to call the shots.

They did one good thing for me, though. They provided the hospital with my personal details which enabled me to get home.

The first inconsistency strikes me. Penny's brother told us that we lived together. If that was the case then why were none of her belongings at my flat? When I got home, I never questioned that I lived alone.

Another inconsistency swiftly follows. Penny's sister had claimed that it was my fault we'd been in a car accident; that I'd been driving recklessly. She absolutely implied that we'd been in the car together. Yet the police informed me I'd been on my own. There was no one else in the car when I had my accident.

Why didn't I pick up on this at the time? I'd been too focussed on Penny's heart condition and the fact that her family had been sedating her, and now I'm left with huge gaps.

Where was Penny? She had a car crash at exactly the same time that also caused her severe amnesia. If we weren't together, then surely it had to be orchestrated. That's far too coincidental. But why would her sister lie?

This makes me scoff out loud. Her sister was neck deep in lies.

I scribble down some notes and read back what I've got

so far. All I can see is a lot of unanswered questions, but at least I'm starting to gauge a picture. If nothing else, there's one thing I know for certain now: this situation is far from straightforward.

I clearly didn't just drive my car into a lamppost for no reason whatsoever. Something or someone must have been behind it. That fills me with a mixture of both comfort and concern.

I momentarily consider calling Penny's family to probe for answers. At least to find out what really happened to Penny all those years ago. I take my phone out of my pocket, but I quickly decide against it. Not only could I not believe a word they tell me, but I'd also have to tell them that Penny's been taken. I'm not ready for that.

I sit back and swig my beer. What else do I know?

When I returned home from the hospital, I just slotted back into my life. Or at least the life I thought I'd had. My boss was very supportive. I couldn't wait to get back to work and I pretty much just picked right back up from where I'd left off. Or so I thought.

It never occurred to me that I was missing anything else. Although I do recall being bothered by an odd sense of loneliness, but I related that to the after-effects of the car crash. I guess I now know otherwise.

My mind flicks up an image of Suzanne. Suzanne. She filled the void.

Suzanne moved in next door to me a couple of months after I got out of hospital. She was an attractive, fellow workaholic. We'd both leave early in the morning, often at the same time, and we'd frequently return late in the evening around the same time.

After a few weeks, our general greetings developed into small talk, and it was pleasant. It was something other than work. The small talk then expanded into larger talk, then in-jokes and familiarities, and before I knew it a friendship had been born.

The week before Christmas I asked her to join me for a

drink. I couldn't see any reason why not.

Three glasses of mulled wine later and I invited her into my bed. Or maybe she pushed? It's hard to remember exactly how it happened.

It was nothing but a sexual relationship for a few months. She liked sex, very much. She still does. She's always been incredibly adventurous and I've never complained.

It was at a conference dinner when everything changed. She invited me along as her plus one and I met all of her colleagues. After that people started to think of us as a couple. I didn't mind, although I never saw her as my girlfriend. She was more just the woman in my life. I wanted nothing more. It all seemed quite satisfying. She stopped me feeling lonely but we both had our own space. It was perfect for me.

After about a year she pointed out that we were spending a great deal of our time together, yet we were both paying individual rent. Moving in together would make far more financial sense. I couldn't argue with her practical thinking.

Then the words just popped out of my mouth. I believed I wanted nothing more. Work had always been my priority and I'd met a woman who was happy to take second place. It seemed logical to ask her to marry me and formalise our relationship.

In hindsight, I can't help but think there was more to it. I had an itch that needed scratching and she fitted the bill. I'd been ready for marriage. I'd been in love. Those feelings were buried within me, I just wasn't conscious of them. I must have been trying to replace Penny somehow without being aware of any of it.

Oh Penny. My wonderful, observant Penny. She knew it. She asked me if Suzanne loved me but I refused to acknowledge it. I didn't want Suzanne to love me. We cared about each other and that was enough.

I need another beer. I grab one from the fridge and then sit back down with a sigh. I've tried not to think about this.

I've tried to put it behind me. Telling Suzanne I was leaving was horrendous.

When I got back home on Sunday evening she was in the kitchen cooking. Well, there was something in the oven. She's hardly domestic. I stood in the kitchen doorway watching her toss some salad.

'Darling!' she said with a beaming smile, but I couldn't move. 'How was your trip? Do you want half of my quiche?'

'Can we talk?' I asked.

'What is it?'

'I'm really sorry.'

Her smile vanished. 'What is it?'

'I've met someone.'

Her whole body tensed at that moment. I don't know why I thought I could just say it. 'What does that mean?' she asked, showing her first signs of anger.

'I've had a good time with you. We've really been there for each other. But I've met someone.'

She glared at me with her icy eyes. I didn't see that glare very often, but it never failed to shudder me. 'Who is she?'

All I could do was shake my head. She didn't need to know the details.

'You're not leaving me. We're married. It's tough.'

'Come on, Suzanne. I've fallen in love with someone.'

If looks could kill, my heart would have stopped beating then and there. 'Stop it.'

I didn't know what else I could say.

'It's just a fantasy,' she told me, quite to the point. 'Your life is with me. Cut it out now and come and have some quiche.'

'No, Suzanne. This is real. I've met someone.'

'You're married to me.' Her teeth were now gritted.

'Yes, but we both know what this marriage has been about. If you'd met someone, I wouldn't stop you.'

'Why do you keep saying someone? We have someone, we have each other.'

'But it's not love.'

'You bastard!' She hurtled the salad tongs at my head and I just about swerved out the way to miss them.

I couldn't see what the issue was. 'You know I care for you. Deeply. But this has never been love.'

'How can you say that?' She actually looked upset. That was a shock. I hadn't expected that.

'We've never said we love each other.' It was true. We'd never uttered those words. 'We were just a good fit. This has never been about love.'

'Don't give me that shit. You know I love you.'

'What?' That was another shock.

'You selfish bastard.' This time her glass, thankfully empty, was thrown towards me. I wasn't ready for it and it hit my arm before shattering on the floor near my feet.

'Suzanne! I didn't mean for this to happen.'

'I'm sure you just accidentally found yourself in bed with someone else.'

'It's not like that. I haven't just gone out and met another woman behind your back. I knew this person before. I was engaged to her before my car crash. I just couldn't remember. But we're back in each other's lives. I met her before I met you.'

'But you married me!'

'I was engaged to her.'

'You married me.' Her cold stare was cutting me in two. 'Have you slept with her? Oh God, that's why you've been avoiding me. I'm so stupid! How long have you been fucking her for?'

'It's not that simple.'

'You cheating bastard!' This time the salad bowl became a victim of her fists. It smashed to the floor with great impact. I don't mind admitting that I was getting a little scared of what she was going to do next.

'It was never my intention to hurt you.' I meant those words. But I suppose all along my actions were always going to hurt her.

'It's that slut, isn't it? What was her name? Penelope. I

knew you were fucking her when she wrote that book. I knew she was writing about you.'

'I wasn't with her then.'

'So it is her?' Despite her apparent certainty a few seconds before, she suddenly looked very surprised.

'It was her writing that book that reconnected us. Nothing happened before that. If you think about it, you brought us together.'

I knew the second I'd said it, I never should have. The rage across Suzanne's face was chilling. 'So it's all my fault that you've been cheating on me?' She moved for the first time so she was standing right in front of me, glaring into my eyes. For what seemed like an age she pinned me to the spot with her fierce stare. Finally she muttered, 'You must have loved me once?'

I was genuinely taken aback by her question. I knew that she was desperate for me to say yes, for me to give her at least something to hold on to. But I couldn't lie. That wouldn't have been fair. I owed her an honest answer. 'I've always cared for you, but there's only one woman I've ever loved. I'm very sorry. I have to be with the woman I love.'

She slapped me hard across the cheek. I don't know how it didn't leave a mark. 'Get out.'

'I am truly sorry, Suzanne.'

'Get out. I never want to see you again.'

'You have to know how sorry I am.'

She turned her back on me and, for the first time, I think she may have started to cry. That was awful. That grounded me.

I was so stupid to think she'd just accept it. But in all the years we've known each other, we've never said I love you. Why would I think that she loved me? How could she think that I loved her?

But Penny knew. How could I have missed it?

Penny. Amazing Penny.

I have to find her quickly. I can't stand the thought that anyone might be hurting her.

I review my notes. A useless list of questions and no glimmer of an answer. I can't think straight anymore.

Penny is not just the only woman I've ever loved, she is the only woman I will ever love. I can't let her down. I need to find her.

I decide to head to bed and get up early with a clearer mind. I review my notes one more time. At least with questions you can start to find answers. I have to believe there's a way to get answers.

I'm coming for you Penny. One way or another, I'm going to find you.

26. SEARCHING

I wake up on Thursday morning very tired after an extremely restless night. My concern over Penny has been aggravated even more by a sadness that I've just spent the first night in our new home alone. For the first time in years we have *our* bed and I'm not sharing it with her. Where could she be?

I grab my phone and check my emails. It's a habit, I can't help it. I scan through them but it's hard to focus. I shouldn't be focussing on work anyway. Penny is far more important. There's no way I'm going to be able to work today. I've never felt more confused and agitated.

I get up, shower and clothe and then nibble on an apple. I'm really not hungry but I know I need something. I glance at my watch. It's just after half seven. I'm sure Bernard will be there by now.

I leave the apartment and make the short walk to my work, grabbing a strong black coffee on the way. I go through the barriers and take the lift to the ninth floor. But instead of going to my office, I step in the other direction towards Bernard's office. He's our CEO.

The door's open but I knock anyway. 'Got a minute?' I ask.

He's signing some documents but he seems happy enough to be disturbed. 'Of course.'

I take a seat and throw my empty coffee cup in his bin. 'I know the timing is awful, but I need a few days off.'

For the first time he looks directly at me and his expression turns to one of concern. 'What happened?'

I can see he's referring to the shiny bruise that's swollen my left cheek, but I don't particularly want to elaborate. 'I know this is a crucial time for us,' I say, keeping the conversation on point, 'but it's a family emergency.'

'Are you all right?'

I've known Bernard for many years and I've always had a good relationship with him. I decide it would be best to give him some semblance of the truth. Although I'm going to be very selective with the facts. 'My partner has been kidnapped.'

'What? How? Do you know who's taken her?'

'She was grabbed off the street - just down the road - and taken in a car. I was there but...' I point to my bruise as if to explain how I was unable to help but I know it's not good enough. I should have done more. 'I don't think it's random,' I add.

'I'm very sorry. What are the police doing?'

I pause for a moment. 'They're doing as much as they can in the circumstances.'

'Is there anything I can do?'

'I just need some space. I need a few days. You know I'd never normally ask.'

'Of course, David. Take all the time you need. I'm guessing your notes are as meticulous as always?'

'Yes, and the team is fully up to speed. I know it will put extra pressure on everyone-'

'There will be even more pressure on them if your head is elsewhere. Go and find your wife. Keep me posted?'

His mistake is understandable but I feel a pang of regret at his use of the word "wife". It's not a concern that I'm misleading him, that's not what bothers me. He came to my wedding but I think that's the only time he's ever met Suzanne. He barely knows her. It's more that I realise how much I want him to meet Penny. I really want her to be a full part of my life. I'm burdened with such great sadness that I ever let her go. How could I forget about someone so important to me?

'I'll be on my phone if you need me,' I say as I stand up.

'Thank you, but we'll try not to bother you.'

'Can we not share the details with the team, if you don't mind?'

'Of course, I'll just say it's personal.'

'Thank you.'

I feel a great relief as I walk home. I hate to drop my team in it - this current project is massive for us - but some things are just more important and I need time to focus.

I enter the apartment and make myself another cup of coffee. I need the caffeine today. As I wait for the kettle to boil I question my decision again to not involve the police. Penny could be in grave danger but I can't get the words of the man on the phone out of my head. He'll bleed her dry. If I contacted the police and something happened to Penny I'd never be able to forgive myself. I decide to take a few more hours to see if I can remember anything before I involve the authorities.

Coffee made, I take it to the table and scan through my notes from last night. All I read is a long stream of questions with no answers.

Sighing with frustration, I sit back. If I'm going to get answers then I need to think differently. I imagine it's not my life. If I was looking to find out what someone else had been up to, what would I do? Like when I wanted to find out more about Penny after our initial meeting in that café. I didn't struggle then. What did I do?

The internet! How has this not occurred to me before? I've never actually Googled myself. It's a long shot but it's definitely worth a try.

I flip open my laptop and load up Chrome. I type in my

name but it brings up far too many results and none of them appear to be relevant. I need to narrow my search.

This time I type in "David Royall Scientific Research". There are still thousands of results but it's worth a trawl through. I find a great number of items that relate to me, like my whitepapers or details on talks I've done, but there's nothing that helps. I remember them all.

After six pages of not finding anything useful, I decide to click on images. It takes me a few minutes but then I come across a picture of myself standing next to Dr Graham Richards. He was my University lecturer when I was doing my degree. A brilliant man.

I click through to the web page and my interest spikes. This is dated about seven years ago. We're at a research event and it states we've been collaborating on a project. The details are sketchy but it definitely states that we're working together.

My path has crossed with Graham's several times since my accident but he's never mentioned anything about us working together. In fact, he's never mentioned anything about us doing anything together since I left university. Whenever we've met it's been when he's visited QAR for other purposes and we've had a quick catch up in the corridor or we've grabbed a quick cup of coffee. That's been about it. But that's enough time for him to mention that we've worked together.

I study the picture again and my heart stops. I can't believe it. There in the background, talking to another woman, is Penny. She's there.

I take a closer look and I can see she's talking to Olivia, Graham's wife. A shiver runs through me. This is a life I can't remember, but it all really happened.

Graham had to have met Penny. It's there; the picture says it all. Why has he never said a word? Now that I think about it, he even came to see me in the hospital. Why has he never mentioned Penny?

I Google Graham and find his LinkedIn page. He's still

a lecturer at Exeter University and he's still apparently living in Devon.

Devon again. Things keep coming back to Devon.

I head to the bedroom and pack a bag. I need to reconnect with Graham. I need to reconnect with my past. It's a place I thought I'd left for good, but it seems Devon is most definitely calling me back.

27. TRAVELLING

I drive out of our secure car park and head west towards the M4. I never imagined I'd ever go back to Devon, but it seems I can't escape it.

Devon is where I grew up. Just outside of Exeter to be more accurate. It's where my parents are both from, not that they spend any time there. My brother and I were both sent to boarding school from a young age and my life growing up was not exactly full of family joys. I hardly know my parents in all honesty.

From my first day at school I threw myself into an academic life, keeping myself to myself wherever possible. Michael, my brother, was far more sociable, but I just wanted to get through it. And then I learnt to enjoy it. Academia suited me.

At eighteen I got accepted into Exeter University to study Medical Sciences and I then went straight on to do my Master's degree. I was twenty-three when I finally left Devon for the first time, after gaining a place at King's College London to do my PhD.

I remember it vividly, the day I got on the train heading to London. I'd enjoyed my time at university, but I was ready to leave Devon and ready for the next stage of my life.

As I sat on the train and watched Exeter St. Davids station disappear, I remember wondering if I'd ever be back. It's very peculiar to know that I have been back. I have to have been, it was in Exeter that I had my accident. However, the last time I actually remember being in Devon is leaving that train station more than ten years ago.

I'm a little apprehensive about my return. I'm worried what I might find out. Although I'm even more worried that I won't find anything all.

It's a very long drive to Exeter. It's a tiring journey, but I daren't stop. I just need to get there. Four hours later and I finally arrive in the city centre.

I park in the first car park I come across. I never drove when I lived here so the roads are all quite unfamiliar. I didn't pass my driving test until I was studying for my PhD.

I walk into the heart of the city and I immediately note how different it seems. There are far more shops and it's very built up compared to how I remember it. But no matter how different it looks, I can't escape how much it feels like home. I didn't expect that.

Despite the fact that I'm still not hungry, I know I must eat and I grab a sandwich from Sainsbury's. I take it back to my car and nibble at it while I try to get my head into gear. I've always had a very good relationship with Graham, but making contact with him again is filling me with trepidation.

My gut is telling me that Graham is hiding something. As circumstantial as my evidence is, it's all stacking up against him.

I'm at a disadvantage, though, as I have so many blanks. This being the case, I decide it's best not to feed Graham any information and instead approach this encounter cautiously. I'll nudge him enough to give him every opportunity to admit that he knew Penny, but I won't say what I know. I figure what he doesn't tell me will be as revealing as the information he is willing to share.

When my sandwich has digested, I drive straight over to St Luke's campus where I know Graham's office is.

It only takes me a few minutes to get there and as I approach what used to be a home for me, I can't believe how much it too has changed. There seems to be so much development going on around the city. Perhaps that's a good thing, though.

As I near the campus, logic kicks in. What am I going to do? Just turn up randomly at his office door? What if he's not even there? I've been so focussed on getting here, the finer details haven't even crossed my mind.

I park up in a side road not far away and I grab my mobile from the pocket in my door. Calling him seems like a good first step. I search for the number of the Med School and I wait for it to dial.

'Can I speak to Dr Graham Richards, please?' I ask the lady who answers.

'I'll just check his line. Can I ask who's calling?'

I hesitate. 'Yes, could you tell him it's Dr David Royall, please?'

It's only a few seconds before I hear his voice. 'Dave?' This makes me squirm. I hate it when people call me Dave. It's not me at all.

'Hello Graham. How are you? It's been a long time.'

'Yes it has.' That's all he says.

'I'm back in Devon for family commitments and I thought it might be nice to catch up. Are you free?'

There is a pause and it makes my heart race. 'Right.' There's another pause and I desperately wait for him to continue. 'I have lectures this afternoon but why don't we meet at The Jolly Tavern at five? Do you remember where that is?'

The Jolly Tavern is right near where I used to live during my second and third years at university. I have no clue how to drive there, but that's what sat nav is for. 'Sounds good. See you there.'

I hang up and sigh with frustration. He's just metres away from me somewhere but he won't see me now.

No, I must be positive. At least he's here and at least he's willing to meet with me. It's only two hours to wait. It'll fly by.

As I sit in my car watching the seconds tick by, I realise I need a distraction. I find a cafe and grab a coffee, and spend a little time catching up on my emails. No matter what I do, though, time is dragging, and by four thirty I can't wait anymore. I programme my sat nav and drive straight over to The Jolly Tavern.

I park in the pub cark park and yet again I can't believe how different it is. It was a tattered old place when I last came here and now it looks like a family eatery, all refurbished and smart.

I make my way to the bar and order a shandy. Then all I can do is wait. I take a seat at a table near the door so there's no chance of me missing him and I feel every inch of me clench with anticipation.

Each minute seems to last an hour and when he finally turns up at five fifteen I nearly jump out of my seat to greet him.

'Hello,' I say shaking his hand.

'Can I get you a drink?' he asks.

'I'm all right, thank you,' I reply, signalling to my barely touched pint. I've been too agitated to drink it.

He goes to the bar and orders a pint of bitter and then he joins me at our little table.

'What happened to your face?' he asks as he sits down.

I haven't looked in a mirror since I left the house this morning, but I imagine my bruise has reached its peak by now. 'You want to see the other guy,' I joke, avoiding the subject.

'I've never seen you as a fighter.'

'Things change. I never thought I'd be back here. You know this is the first time I've been back to Devon since I left for my PhD.'

'Didn't you have your accident here?' he says, as if to challenge me.

I look into his dark eyes. He is very hard to read. He

always appears to be very casual about everything. He never dresses smartly, has floppy grey hair, and he fumbles about as if he's clumsy. But he's far from the man he appears to be. He's incredibly intelligent, always sharply focused, and he's massively well-respected in my field. Alongside lecturing he's been involved in some ground-breaking studies. I was lucky to have met him. I hope I can still feel that way.

I recall when he visited me in hospital. It was after my parents had moved me to London. I can't remember what we spoke about, but I know he couldn't have mentioned Penny. I would have remembered that.

'So I'm told,' I respond to him, shrugging as if to prove my laidback attitude. 'I've never found out what I was doing here. It was good of you to come and see me in hospital. Very good of you. Did I ever thank you for that?'

'It's the least I could do. I was shocked when I heard the news. As you know, Bernard told me about it. I'm glad you're okay, though. Well it certainly hasn't done you any harm. You're quite the star at QAR now.'

'Did we see each other when I was in Devon last time?' I probe.

'I had no idea you were even here. Not like this time.'

'I can't explain to you how strange it is to lose your memory. It's been incredibly frustrating. I might have worked hard for QAR, but I owe them a lot. Bernard supported me tremendously during that time. So you knew Bernard before my accident? Have you done a lot of work with QAR over the years?'

'No,' he says quite to the point. 'Just more recently.'

'Oh.'

'You work in the private sector, Dave. I'm all about the Government grants.' He smirks and takes a gulp of his pint.

'Of course. Please forgive me. I've had this quite often over the years when I've met up with old friends. I've forgotten significant details about their lives. I've also forgotten many of the things that we've done together. I don't want to offend you. Please do tell me if there's anything I need to remember.'

'There's not much to tell,' he says, and I try not to show my vexation. 'My life is pretty much the same. I'm still with Olivia. Very happily under the thumb,' he chuckles.

'Olivia!' His mention of Olivia brings me back to that picture on Google. Penny was definitely speaking to Olivia. 'At least I can be sure I haven't seen her since I was studying my Master's.'

'I appreciate memory loss,' he grins. 'I'm fifty-eight this year. Things definitely aren't as clear as they used to be.'

I nod and then try to push my point. 'Olivia used to make those wonderful pies. How she's doing?'

'Very well, thank you.'

We sit in silence for a minute and sip at our drinks. I know he's being evasive. He must be keeping something from me. I don't know what else I can ask to incite a useful answer, though. If I mention the picture I'm worried what his reaction will be. I hate to think it, but if he is involved in Penny's disappearance, anywhere along the line, I can't afford to piss him off.

'How's your wife?' he suddenly asks me.

His question makes me nauseous. I take a sip of my drink to delay my answer. I need to think logically. I know for sure that he's never met Suzanne and other than the fact that I'm married, I don't recall ever giving him any details.

I go to answer when I see him staring at my hand. I still have my wedding ring on. I'd totally forgotten about that. 'She's fine.'

'She's in the world of publishing I believe?'

'A literary agent,' I confirm, as he confirms to me that he's been discussing me with my peers.

'And very attractive I hear.'

'I suppose.'

'Good for you,' he says, and then the conversation dries up again.

He had to have met Penny. She was there, in that picture.

He must have known about her existence at the very least.

An idea comes to me.

'Everyone was shocked when I announced I was getting married. Apparently my team assumed I was gay. They said I'd always appeared to show very little interest in women.' None of that is true, at least not to my knowledge. I don't have a particularly friendly relationship with any member of my team. We're there to do a job and I like to keep things professional.

'I always preferred to think of you as being married to science.' He grins and I try to force a grin back but this is riling me. That had to be the time for him to mention Penny.

I need to be more straightforward with my questioning. I pull a puzzled face. 'Something's just come back to me. Didn't someone tell me that we'd worked together on a project a couple of years before my accident? Yes, I'm sure. Didn't we write a research paper together or something?'

Graham shakes his head. 'We've never written a research paper together.'

This is tormenting. 'Oh right. Maybe it wasn't you then. It might have been a different Graham.'

'It's a common name.'

He's lying. I'm certain that he's hiding something now. Every inch of me is warning me from asking him directly, though. There's something sinister about his behaviour and I'm worried what it will cost me – and Penny – if I push too hard. It's safer if he doesn't know that I suspect him of anything.

'Tell me about your wife,' he says. I'm very cautious about where this conversation is going.

I take another delaying sip of my drink but I know I have to be honest. I can't let him trip me up. 'Truthfully, we've recently separated.'

He again glances at my wedding ring. 'I'm sorry to hear that.'

'I've met someone else,' I say. 'It's a better relationship.'

'Two women in your life!' he smiles. 'We were all wrong

about you.'

Now's my chance. This is it. I have to say it. 'Well apparently there were three.' His face doesn't flinch. 'I don't remember any of it, but I've been told that I was engaged to someone before my accident. I don't know who she is and no one else seemed to know either. She never bothered to get back in touch after the accident so I've concluded that she was just some gold digger who couldn't care less.'

His expression becomes grave. 'That's awful. Who told you that?'

I scan my brain for a logical response. 'My brother.'

I have a flash of inspiration. Maybe Michael has met Penny. He's never mentioned it, but it's a possibility. Penny is a family girl, I know she would have wanted to meet Michael. I can imagine her demanding it.

'What did he tell you?' Graham says, for the first time seeming worried. This is good.

'Not a lot. He never met her. I'd apparently just mentioned it one time. What was her name again? Betty or Penny? Something like that. I don't know. Maybe he'd got it wrong.'

'Probably,' Graham nods. 'Fiancées don't just disappear off the face of the earth, do they?'

What a liar. Where is the man that I used to know?

'Thinking about it, I probably made her up to stop Michael being the only family man,' I smirk. 'I always have been competitive.'

'Yes,' Graham laughs. 'I bet she was gorgeous and rich and super successful.'

I pretend to laugh along as a pang of guilt punishes me. Suzanne was certainly attractive. She was also rich and successful. But there isn't one part of me that wants her. I much prefer Penny's innocent charm and natural beauty. She has an honest depth to her that puts Suzanne's superficial bravado to shame. How I miss Penny. I want more than anything to be rid of Suzanne from my life. What was I thinking?

I knock back the rest of my shandy and have one more attempt at getting an answer. 'I'm not down here for long but maybe I could drop by and see Olivia?'

For the first time I see real concern across Graham's face. This has rattled him. 'That would have been great,' he says. 'She would have loved that after all these years. But she's away.'

'Really?' I ask.

'Visiting family. Just like you.'

'Maybe next time, then.'

Graham nods and gulps down his beer.

'I'm going to have to shoot off,' I say. The only useful thing I'm getting from this conversation is the certainty that it's all lies. The best thing for me to do now is process it all and work out what to do next. 'I have to get over to Michael's,' I explain. 'Sorry we couldn't talk for longer. But next time you're in London, let's grab dinner.'

'I'd like that.'

We shake hands and say our farewells and I escape back to my car.

That was so far from the relaxed, friendly man I used to know. I dread to think how he could be connected to Penny's disappearance, but he's definitely keeping secrets and that's never a good sign.

I sit in my car and think about the ever-increasing pile of questions I have but still no answers. I need to see someone that I know I can trust. There's only one other person I can think of who may be able to give me the information I need. I start the engine and programme the sat nav. My next stop has to be my brother's house.

28. FAMILY

I pull up outside of Michael's house about fifteen minutes later. I've never been here before - well not that I can remember - but this is the address I have in my phone.

I haven't seen Michael since my wedding day. He was my best man. He was the only person I could think to ask. We're not exactly close but he was kind to me. He came to London the month before and took me out for drinks. He said it was my stag do and I couldn't have asked for anything better.

We had a really good night. We talked about our lives; we talked more than we've ever done. I thought we'd be closer after that, but when the booze had worn away and the reality of my marriage took hold, we drifted apart once again. I guess we're too far away, in both personality and miles, to form a real bond.

Michael is three years younger than me. He's the fun, centre of attention kind of person, with one hell of a brain to boot. He studied History at the University of Bristol before following in my father's footsteps and becoming a salesman. I imagine he's extremely good at it.

Michael lives with his wife, whom he'd met at university, and his three children. The only time I ever remember seeing my nephews was on my wedding day. They must be a lot taller now.

I get out of my car and walk up his drive. It's a smart semi-detached house in what looks like a new estate. It's nice; homely.

I ring on the bell. I can hear children yelling and then the lock clicks. Michael opens the door and he doesn't hide his surprise. 'David?'

We always looked very alike growing up and nothing has changed. We have the same build and features, and in fact people have often confused us for twins.

'Hello Michael.'

'Are you okay? What are you doing here?' I'm pleased to see he's not annoyed, just curious.

'I hope this isn't too much of an inconvenience. I could really do with your help.'

He looks at me strangely. I almost expect him to slam the door in my face, but he's too polite. 'Come in.'

The house is buzzing with activity. The children are screaming, the television is blaring and there are toys absolutely everywhere. It's like the polar opposite of my organised, quiet apartment.

I can smell something wonderful coming from the kitchen but I take a seat as offered in the living room. 'Can I get you a drink?' Michael asks.

'If it's not too much trouble. A coffee?'

He nods and heads into a different room, closing the door tightly behind him. I turn to find two of the kids glaring at me. I know the oldest is Jeremy, the middle one is Charlie and the youngest is Arthur, but the two staring at me are of a similar height and I have no clue which is which.

The third one comes bounding in from the room that Michael disappeared into. 'Dad says it's uncle David who has come to visit us from far away,' he announces. He's the youngest one. I can see that clearly.

'Hello,' I say. 'Have you had a good day at school?' That's the only question I can think to ask them.

They don't answer me, they all just stand there studying me curiously. 'Why is your face all bruised?' one of the older ones asks.

'David?' Harriet, Michael's wife, enters the room and her warm voice is a welcome escape from the children. I stand to greet her and she hugs me. She's such a kind woman, I've always liked her. 'This is out of the blue.'

'I know. I should have called.'

'Are you okay?' I can see her staring at my bruised cheek.

'It's a long story. If it's a bad time-'

'Family is always welcome. *You* are always welcome here. Please, we'd love you to join us for dinner. I was just about to serve up.'

'I don't want to be an inconvenience.'

'It would be a pleasure.'

I can't recall ever sitting around a table like this and enjoying a family meal. The conversation is polite and lighthearted and it's impossible not to relax. It's a relief after such a stressful day.

As the meal goes on, however, a sadness washes over me. I've never even considered children before, but I can't ignore a small yearning that suddenly tugs at my heart. Suzanne made it clear that she never wanted children and I had no issue with that. But now, sitting here around this table, I can't help but feel I'm missing something.

Penny would make a fabulous mother.

Once dinner is finished, I help to clear up and then I watch some mindless television whilst the children are put to bed.

Michael finally reappears from upstairs. He looks tired. 'I'm going to put the kettle on,' he says. 'Do you want a coffee?'

'Thank you,' I nod. I follow Michael into the kitchen and he fills the kettle up.

'What's with the surprise visit then?' he asks, now we've finally got some peace and quiet. 'I'm guessing it's related to that shiner on your face?'

I take a deep breath and decide to be honest. He's the only person I know I can be honest with and I need to talk to someone.

'This is the least of my worries,' I say, pointing to my bruise. 'Things have got... messy.'

'What things?' he asks, spooning coffee granules into two mugs.

'Do you remember my car crash years ago?'

He hesitates. 'Yes.'

I sigh. This is complicated. 'I've found out that I was engaged to someone before the crash. Someone that I couldn't remember and who was deliberately eradicated from my life.'

Michael stops what he's doing and stares at me. He doesn't say anything, though.

'Did I tell you that I was engaged before?'

He shakes his head and scoffs. 'Are you taking the piss? You never talk to me. I couldn't believe it when you had that accident just down the road. We never hear from you, you don't tell us anything, then we find out you've been just metres away from us.'

I slump down against the kitchen surface. That's another dead end.

'It especially hurts when I know you talk to other people,' he adds to my surprise. He pauses before continuing and I feel my fists clench with anticipation. 'I did hear something about an engagement.' I don't say a word, I just eagerly wait for him to elaborate. 'About a year after your accident I was in the supermarket when a lady came up to me. She was going on about how she hadn't seen me in ages.'

'Who was she?'

'I hadn't got a clue. She called me Mr Royall so for a second I was convinced that she must have known me. Then when she asked me about my fiancée it clicked that maybe she thought I was you. I asked her if she meant David Royall and she said yes and then I explained that I'm your brother.'

'But who was she?'

'She owns a B&B about a mile away. She said you were staying with her quite regularly for a few years. I have to tell you, it really pissed me off. You were a mile away. Why didn't you come and see us?'

I can't answer that question. I have absolutely no idea what I was doing. All I can say is, 'It's complicated.'

Michael rolls his eyes. 'It always is with you. You know, she asked me if you were married now. I didn't even know what to say. She knew more about you than I did. It's not good, David.' There's a tense silence between us. I know he wants me to respond, but I have no words. 'Anyway,' he continues, shaking his head, 'it was about a year later when you told me you were getting married. I put two and two together and assumed she'd been talking about Suzanne.'

'I met Suzanne after my car crash.'

'How was I supposed to know that? I only found out about *her* when you needed a best man.'

'It wasn't like that.' I'm actually hurt by that statement.

'I never know with you, David. You tell us what you want us to know. You've always been private. I get it, it's just the way you are. It's not my place to question it.'

There's another moment of tense silence. All that can be heard is Michael stirring our coffees. He pushes my mug over to me and I let what he just told me settle in my head.

This is my first lead. An actual lead. It's the most I've had yet. Someone actually knows me and Penny. 'Do you know which B&B it is?' I ask.

'Yeah, I'll sort out the address for you.'

We sip at our coffees. It all feels quite awkward until Michael says, much to my surprise, 'You know you pissed me off because I miss you, right?'

He told me something similar on my stag do, but I'd just put it down to the beer. We stare at each other and I can't think of a single thing to say.

'If you weren't with Suzanne, who was this fiancée then?'

Michael asks, but I'm not ready for the subject to be changed. I know I need to say something.

'I miss you too,' I admit. Standing with him now, I know it's true. He's the only real family I've got. I think back to our days at school. We were years apart but we always looked out for one another. Not that he needed protecting. Michael was the boy that everyone wanted to be. I always enjoyed his cocky comments. He could always make me laugh.

But then work got in the way. It's always demanded so much of my time. Or maybe I've just wanted it that way?

Michael shrugs and I have to add, 'I genuinely don't know why I was here and why I didn't visit you.' I can't be more honest than that.

I take another sip of my coffee and I know I need to share my story. It's time for me to open up.

'A couple of years ago I started dreaming about a woman,' I begin. 'She was there nearly every night and I couldn't explain it.'

'Who was she?' Michael asks.

'I didn't know. Then just before last Christmas, one morning out of the blue, Suzanne demanded that I meet her for a coffee. She told me it was an emergency. I couldn't think what emergency needed to take place in a coffee shop, but she's not a lady to be messed with. When I got there she was sitting with this woman. It was the exact same woman that I'd been dreaming about. And I mean the same in every possible way.'

'What?'

'It got even more peculiar. She'd sent Suzanne a manuscript of a novel all about me. Exactly me. It transpired that she too had been dreaming about me and she'd written me as the main character of her book. It was incredibly unnerving to read.'

I can tell Michael is intrigued. 'So, who was she?'

'I didn't know and Suzanne scared her off before I could find out. But I couldn't stop thinking about her, so I tracked her down. She had a different surname to what I thought. She'd got married. She also had a different sort of life. But I knew I loved her. It made no sense at all, but I knew I'd never felt that way about anyone.'

Michael is now leaning on the kitchen side, engrossed in my story. 'We started to have an affair.' Michael's eyebrows rise but he doesn't say a word. 'I'd say I'm not proud of it, but I never loved Suzanne and this new woman – Penny...' I pause as I think about that moment when she turned up at my work unannounced. That was a great afternoon. 'Penny was having a profound effect on me.'

'You never loved Suzanne?' Michael queries, but that really isn't a story I want to tell.

I study the mug in my hand while I choose what to say next. 'Not long after, I found out that Penny had been in a car accident too. Five years ago. And she too had suffered from amnesia. From that the truth unravelled. We found out that we'd originally met when I was twenty-four. I was doing a talk at Birmingham University and she was studying there at the time.'

'She's the one you were engaged to?'

'The love of my life.'

'What happened?'

'She's got a... she suffers from an affliction. We met because she wanted my help with understanding the science behind it. But her family misread the situation and assumed I'd been experimenting on her.' I shake my head. 'They split us up when they found out we both had amnesia. They eradicated me from her life.'

'They can't do that!'

'That's old news now. She's been kidnapped.'

This makes Michael stand up straight. 'What? By her family?'

'No. At least I don't think so. No, I really don't know what's happened to her. That's why I'm here. I've been following the leads and they've brought me back to Devon. I don't know why we were here before, staying at that B&B,

but I'm guessing the reason we never saw you was because we were caught up in something quite dangerous.'

'Dangerous?' I can see Michael is now very concerned.

'Her affliction... it's... rare. Special even. I think someone is using her for their own good and I need to find out why.'

'What are the police doing?'

'Not a lot.' I swirl round the remainder of my coffee, taking a moment to consider what I tell him. I decide I need to be honest. 'They told me if I involve the police, they'll kill Penny.'

'Bloody hell.'

'I don't know what to think, though. I remember nothing about before. How real a threat is this? I just don't know.'

'You must remember something, to be back here.'

I shake my head. 'No. As far as I recall, I've not been here since leaving for King's College. But I knew I'd had my accident here. And I found out something else.'

'What's that?'

'I Googled myself and found that I'd been working with my old lecturer from uni about seven years ago. I've seen him since but he's never mentioned it. I just met up with him.'

'What did he say?'

'Very little. I know he's lying to me. He knows something. I just don't know what, and I'm too afraid to push it. I can't risk Penny's life.'

'This is awful, David. I'm really sorry. Can I help? What are you going to do?'

'All I can do is keep following the leads as I find them. This B&B sounds like a good next move. I'll see what they can tell me. But if you remember anything from those years - anything at all - please let me know. If you find a letter or email or anything.'

Michael shakes his head and smirks. 'You, write? And you certainly don't email.' I nod. I'm an awful brother. 'So, I take it you've left Suzanne?' he asks.

I nod again. 'All I want is Penny. She's all I've ever wanted. And I know she feels the same way too. We moved in together this week.'

This saddens me greatly, but Michael smiles and clinks his mug against mine. 'Congratulations, mate. I hope this all works out and you can be happy.'

'You'd really like her. You'll have to meet her. I know she'd want to meet you.'

'As soon as you get her back, you need to come for the weekend.'

'Definitely.' And I mean it. I'm glad to be here, seeing my brother again. I really have missed him.

'You still haven't explained that corker on your face,' Michael nudges.

'I was with Penny when she was taken. They grabbed her off the street. I went to stop it but a firm right hook took care of me.'

He looks at me with pity. 'Think positively,' he says. 'You'll get her back. That lady at the B&B, she seemed to know you well. She seemed nice. You'll have Penny back before you know it. What's more important is whether I'm going to be your best man again?'

'I could think of no one better to ask,' I say, then I look at my watch with purpose. I don't want to talk about weddings. With everything going on at the minute, that's far too overwhelming for me to process.

'David, are you staying the night?' Harriet asks, joining us. She's now in her pyjamas and I feel that wave of sadness again. Penny loves her pyjamas. I think she'd wear them all day if she could.

'No, I've taken up too much of your time already,' I say. I hadn't even thought about where to stay. But I can easily sleep in my car.

'Are you booked in to a hotel?' Michael asks.

I go to speak, but nothing comes out.

'You're staying with us,' Harriet orders.

'I couldn't.'

'Don't argue with her,' Michael says. 'Do as you're told. Besides, you need family right now. Let us take care of you.'

'You look exhausted, David,' Harriet adds, rubbing my arm to comfort me. She's an amazing woman. They got married just a few months before I must have met Penny. It's one of the last significant things I remember before the blankness.

They'd only known each other for a year and were still at university, but they were very much in love. My parents threw money at it the second they announced their engagement and six months later they were getting married on the Amalfi Coast.

That was the first time I met Harriet. I don't remember meeting her again until my own wedding day, but she has a warmth about her that makes you feel like you've known her all your life. Penny would love her. They'd get on very well. Why didn't they meet before? I must try harder. I must try to be a better brother.

'Do you have room for me to stay?' I ask.

'It would have to be the settee,' Harriet replies. 'But Michael tells me it's very comfortable when he falls asleep in front of the telly almost every night.' She smirks and kisses Michael on the cheek.

'The settee is perfect. It's very kind of you.'

'Good, that's sorted then,' Michael grins. 'Right, I'll grab the iPad and show you where this B&B is for tomorrow.'

'Thank you.'

'And since you're staying, could I tempt you to a whiskey?'

Harriet rolls her eyes. 'Please say yes, David. I can't stand the stuff but he's desperate to share his prized collection with someone.'

'I collect whiskies,' Michael tells me. 'It's not an overwhelming collection, but I do have a few unusual ones. Will you join me?'

'I'd be delighted to.'

Michael does a silly dance before he jogs off to the drinks

cabinet.

'It's so good to see you, David,' Harriet says.

I smile. It's very good to be here.

29. BED & BREAKFAST

It's nearly midnight when I say goodnight to Michael and Harriet and settle under the blanket they've given me on the settee.

I'm exhausted but I can't relax. I know I won't relax until Penny is safely back with me.

I take some time to process everything that I've learnt today. Graham is obviously a liar. But what has he got to hide? I consider what his involvement could be in all of this, but my tired brain struggles to focus and I'm asleep before I know it.

It's then that my dreams catch hold of a memory.

I'm young. Just twenty-four. I'm full of an eager spirit and totally unaware of how naïve I am. I think I know the world as I'm doing my PhD. I think I'm ready for anything.

I've been invited to be a guest speaker at Birmingham University. I've been liaising with one of the Professors there and he's asked me to give a lecture relating to the research I've been doing as part of my PhD. It's the second time I've visited the university and I'm very pleased to see so many people turn up for my talk. It appears I'm making quite a name for myself and I can't deny I'm enjoying it.

The lecture goes extremely well and a couple of people

stay after to ask me some more questions.

But suddenly I can't concentrate. In the background, holding back to speak to me, is a beautiful girl. She's only young but she has an intoxicating essence about her. I can't take my eyes off her.

I wrap up the questions quickly and go over to her. 'Did you enjoy my talk?' I ask.

She smiles at me shyly and I can't help but smile back. She's incredibly sexy. 'Yes, it was good. Although I didn't understand much of it. Well, any of it really,' she replies.

'Oh?'

'I'm doing a Business Degree. I've always been rubbish at science.'

'So you joined us just for fun, then?' I ask with curiosity.

'Actually, I'm here to ask for your help.'

I know I'm not going to be able to resist helping this girl. 'With a science problem?'

'I have a friend doing this course and she told me what a huge deal you are. I don't really know who else to ask. But only if you can spare the time. I know you must be very busy.'

Flattery will get this girl everywhere. I'm increasingly fascinated by her. 'Shall we grab a beer and talk?'

She leads me off campus to a pub down the road. She says it will be quieter than the Student Union. And at three in the afternoon it is fairly quiet. She buys me a pint for my troubles and orders the same for herself, and then we find a table in the corner. I can't deny I'm both intrigued and excited by what she's going to say.

There's an awkward moment. It appears as if she doesn't know where to begin. 'Can I ask your name?' I say to break the silence. I'm also dying to know.

'Sorry. That would be useful, wouldn't it. I'm Penelope.'

'David Royall.'

'I know your name,' she smiles. 'I've read a lot about you.'

I raise my eyebrow. 'Is there a lot to read?'

'Oh yes. You've done loads. I can tell you're very clever.'

'I always have time to do more, though,' I say. 'How can I help you?'

I watch her rummage around for her words again and it gives me a chance to take her in. I've never had a girlfriend. It's not that I haven't had the opportunity. I've been on my fair share of dates and I've never been shy to share my bed. I just haven't had the time nor inclination for a full time partner. But there's something about this Penelope that's different. It's like she stops my brain thinking of anything else. I've never felt anything like it.

'Don't be freaked out,' she starts to say, immediately grabbing my attention. 'Please don't. I'm telling you this because I'm hoping you'll understand and you'll be able to give me some answers.'

She looks around to check that no one is in our proximity and then she tells me to look at her hands just below the table.

She concentrates hard and then a ball of light appears from her fingers. She bounces it around like it's a play thing and then she brushes her hands together until it fades.

I am completely lost for words. It's hard to believe what I've just witnessed. But it certainly doesn't freak me out. I'm mesmerised. 'What was that?' I ask.

'A few months ago I... It just started. I was going through a bit of a rough time and then suddenly I was shooting light all over the place. When I think about that time I get so angry and upset and it makes my fingers burn. And when I get that burn the light just appears.'

'Are you looking for my help as to what's causing it?'

'What's causing it, is it dangerous, am I dying? Can I stop it? I'm looking for any answers you could give me. Will you help me?'

I feel like the luckiest man in the world. 'I'll certainly try.'

'Oh, thank you. That's all I can ask. Thank you so much.'

I think for a moment. Where do I begin? 'When you say rough time, what do you mean?'

She looks down at her hands. 'Do you need to know?'

'If you want my help then I'll need to know everything. Understanding the catalyst is a great place to start.'

She looks up at me and I see her blush. 'Okay. Basically... I thought I was pregnant. I'm not. I wasn't. But I got a false positive on those test things and it shook me up for a while.'

'That's understandable.' I feel the rumble of jealously. 'What did the... prospective father say?' Why am I more interested in her life rather than the fact that she can emit light through her fingers?

She looks down again. 'He said there was no way I was going to university. He doesn't like it that I'm here. He's not gone to uni. He said that no mother of his children was going to university and I needed to take up my responsibilities at home. Then he proposed.'

The jealousy flares up inside of me. 'You're engaged?'

She scoffs. I like it. 'No! And I told him no then and there. Who the hell does he think he is telling me what to do? He never used to be like that. And that's when it happened. The second he tried to rule my life, my anger went off the scale. I guess I was terrified as well. I'm too young to be a mom. I was only seventeen at the time. It's like all of these emotions built up inside of me and then, out of nowhere, this flash of light shot across the room. It scared the crap out of us.'

I see sparks of light dancing on her fingertips as she speaks. 'Sorry,' she says trying to hide her hands. 'He makes me so mad. Anyway, I found out a couple of days later that I wasn't pregnant but we were now more focussed on why I was shooting light left, right and centre.'

I want to be more intrigued about the light, but I find I can't get the raging jealousy within me to calm. 'Are you still dating this man?' I ask, as if somehow it's completely relevant.

She studies her pint and I see that shyness in her again. 'I suppose, technically. But I've been at university for two months and I've not seen him. We barely even speak anymore. We just haven't exactly broken up.'

'Well, you should,' I say without meaning to.

'Should I?' she asks with a curious smile.

I shrug. 'A beautiful girl like you shouldn't waste her time on someone who doesn't appreciate her.'

She blushes again and I feel the fizz of lust.

'You're not freaked out by my bizarre ability then?' she asks.

'On the contrary, I think you're fascinating. I'd definitely like to learn more about you.' Then I make a very quick decision. The easiest decision of my life and the best decision I have ever made. 'I don't have to be back in London anytime soon. In fact I don't have anything scheduled in now until next week. Maybe I could stay for a few days and help you out? You know, study you.'

A huge grin consumes her face. 'You'd do that for me?'

'In the name of science,' I say, now not able to control my own stretched-out grin. 'Purely just for the science.'

'Of course.'

I wake up suddenly, back on the settee. My whole body is tense with a mixture of passion and sadness. That was real. It didn't just seem real, that was actually real. That's how we met and I'd forgotten all about it. Flecks of the past scatter through my brain. After that, we were apart for as little time as possible. Then the second she finished her degree, she moved to London. I remember that. I do.

But that's about it. I don't remember anything to do with her blood. I don't remember studying her in any way. All I remember is the impact she had on my life. It was incredible. She changed my life in so many ways. She still is changing it. I have to get her back.

As I rub my eyes, I catch a glimpse of my wedding band. I don't know why I'm still wearing it. I hadn't even noticed until earlier when I was with Graham. I've been so busy with everything else going on, this tiny thing has just been left there.

I sit up and sigh. What must Penny have thought? I bet

she noticed. Had she removed her ring? I can't say I'd noticed in return, but I bet she had. She's always good with the details.

I slip the ring off and tuck it in my wallet. I don't want that marriage anymore. I want it to end as quickly as possible. I want my future with Penny now. Just like I did the very first time I saw her.

I eventually fall back to sleep and I have scraps of dreams about Penny but nothing like before. The night seems to go on forever and when I finally hear Michael and his family rise, I actually feel relieved. I'm desperate to get on with the day and my search for Penny.

I join the family for cornflakes and then I let them carry on with their morning routine. I promise to keep them posted about what happens with Penny and I agree to bring her down for a visit when this nightmare is all over with. I mean it too. I really want to do that.

I drive away and start the journey towards the B&B but I see it's only eight o'clock. That might be too early. I don't want to disturb the middle of breakfast. Instead I use some time to fuel my car, and then I find a little café and grab a coffee.

I get up to date with my emails and wish away the time. This is painful.

At ten o'clock I convince myself that it's a reasonable enough time to question the B&B owner and I drive over there.

It's a beautifully kept white building at the end of a street and I'm able to park right outside the front. It looks pretty immaculate and I can see why I'd have stayed here before.

I make my way in to find a tall, well-built lady at the reception desk checking out a guest. She bids them a good day and then places her eyes on me.

'Mr Royall!' she beams with surprise, a welcoming glint in her eyes. 'Where have you been?'

I wasn't expecting such a greeting and I don't know what to say.

'Alf, Alf!' she calls behind her. 'Mr Royall's back.' She turns around to an office behind her and shakes her head. 'Oh, I don't know where he is. We wondered when we were going to see you again.'

'I'm sorry, you'll have to forgive me,' I say. 'I was in an accident and I've suffered from amnesia.'

'Oh no. Oh God, that's awful. I'm so sorry.'

'I'm trying to piece together my past and I've found myself here. I'm guessing you know me.'

'Yes, you and lovely Miss Edwards. Charming couple. Mrs Royall now I presume?' she enquires with a cheeky grin.

I feel a wave of relief to finally meet someone who knew me and Penny as a couple. 'Could you spare some time for me to ask you a few questions?'

'Of course! Anything for my favourite guest. I'll put the kettle on.'

She leads me into the small but spotless dining room and I wait for her to make us a cup of tea. I don't really like tea but I wasn't given an option and I don't care to make a fuss when I need her help as much as I do.

She brings out a pot and pours our drinks in front of me. 'Ask away then! How can I help? Tell me about your accident.'

'The truth is, I don't remember it,' I explain. 'It happened five years ago and I don't recall anything about it nor anything from the few years before. Including even knowing Penelope... Miss Edwards.'

'You forgot about her? How could that possibly happen? It sounds like you've been through quite an ordeal.'

'We were both split up after the accident.' I decide it's much easier to keep the details simple. 'It turns out we both lost our memories and somehow got separated. I've recently learnt of her existence and I'm trying to track her down.'

'Oh, how romantic!' she says, blowing on her hot tea. 'You always were such a devoted couple.'

'Could you tell me how many times we stayed here? Were we always together?'

'Oh yes. Well apart from that last time. You stayed at least two or three times a month over a couple of years. We joked that we'd put your names on the door. You see you always stayed in the same room. You liked it in room two.'

'Do you know why we were here?'

'For work. That's all you said. I thought it was weird though, if you don't mind me saying. You see you only ever stayed at the weekend. I was always curious to know what sort of work starts on a Friday night and ends on a Sunday.'

'Just the weekend?'

'Yes. Well, except for that last time.'

'You said that. What happened the last time?'

'You were alone and you were very unhappy. You said someone had hurt Miss Edwards and you'd just found out about it. You mumbled something about wanting her to be safe. It sounded very serious.'

Without even knowing the details, anger rises within me. What if someone is hurting her now? This has to all be linked. I'm getting closer, I know I am.

'Do you know what happened?'

She shakes her head. 'You didn't say much else.'

'Do you know where I worked? Was there anything else I told you?'

'Oh no. No, no, no. You barely spoke. It was Miss Edwards who would always chat to me. Sometimes, while you were at work, she'd stay here during the day and we'd get chatting. Such a lovely girl.'

'You don't know where I went?'

'It was all very secretive to tell the truth. And we don't stick our noses in where they're not wanted. We respect the privacy of our guests.'

As noble as that is, I wish she'd been a nosier lady. I search my mind for more questions but if I didn't tell her anything of importance then I can't see what help this lady will be. 'Is there anything else you can tell me that might help me find Penelope?'

She thinks for a moment, sipping her tea. 'No. You came

here together and you disappeared off together. Except for that last time. I knew you were agitated as you were speaking far more than usual. Oh yes!' She stands up with excitement. 'You'll be wanting your thingies back. Hang on.'

She disappears and I try not to get my hopes up. Is this going to be useful?

She returns a few minutes later carrying an A5 envelope. 'I kept my word, I want you to know.'

'What is this?' I ask taking it from her hands.

'It's your thingies. I've never looked at them. I promise.'

I open the blank envelope and inside I see two USB sticks. 'I gave these to you?'

'Yes. Just before you checked out that last time, you asked me to lock them in the safe. I put them in the envelope to keep them together. You said no one was ever to know they were there and you'd be back to collect them as soon as possible. I knew you'd be back one day. At least now I know why it's taken so long.'

'You've kept them all these years?' I'm genuinely astonished.

'You and Miss Edwards were our best guests. You became friends. I was happy to help. They've not left our safe since the last time you set foot in this building.'

'I can't thank you enough.' I'm desperate to leave now and find out what is on these drives. They must be vital to my quest.

'It's my pleasure. We're always here for you. I'm sure you'll find Miss Edwards again, and when you do I want you to come back and visit.'

'Of course. I promise.'

'And we want an invite to the wedding,' she winks.

I just nod and stand up. 'I'd better get going. Thank you for all your help. You've been the most helpful person I've met yet.'

'Oh, so sweet. I try.'

I pace back to my car as quickly as I can. I open my boot and pull out my laptop. Force of habit through the years, I never go anywhere without it; thankfully.

I get in my car and lock the doors. I want to start looking now but I catch the B&B lady watching me through the window and I feel terribly conspicuous.

I need to move on but I also need to see what's on these drives as quickly as possible.

30. THE STICKS

I drive on with great agitation. My head is too fuzzy for me to think of where to go. A few miles pass and my frustration is soaring.

I see a sign for a superstore up ahead and I quickly change lanes. That will do. I can easily park at a supermarket.

I drive in to the car park and head far away from the entrance, around the side where it's nice and quiet. No one will bother a parked car here.

I turn the engine off, grab my laptop and fire it up. It takes me three attempts to type in my password, my fingers are shaking with such anticipation.

I plug one of the USB sticks in and wait eagerly for it to load. Why is it taking so long?

Finally I see the contents.

I know what this is. I sigh with relief. It's here. It's all here. I knew it had to be somewhere. At last.

I open the files and I see, right before me, my research. This is all about Penny. This is everything I'd done in those lost years, trying to find out about her blood and her light ability.

A knowing smile creeps up on my lips as I learn that I

followed the same steps last time as I have done recently. All my current findings are the same. Penny's green blood cells expand when her heartbeat increases.

I skip through to a folder called Logbook. There are scanned files and Word documents in there. As I glance through them my breath extinguishes.

This is what I was working on with Graham. I'd enlisted Graham's assistance.

It seems that due to time and resource constraints, I wasn't making good progress with Penny's condition and we needed help. So I approached Graham.

I've written a diary of events. There are pages and pages of detailed notes. It's eerie that these are all my own words, but I remember none of it. I get lost in the story and I begin to get a very clear picture of those forgotten years.

It all starts off really positively with the two of us sharing the workload. But after a few months it seems that Graham begins to take control. I appear to focus more on my job whereas he's clearly making great strides with researching Penny's anomaly. I must have let him take the lead.

There are regular mentions of a purpose built lab. That's where most of the work seems to have taken place, alongside support from university resources and some of the more sophisticated equipment at QAR.

As the pages go by, I see that my input rapidly decreases. It becomes almost a full time job for Graham, whereas Penny and I just meet up with him at weekends, whenever we have the time. It's only during our visits that we get up to speed and help out where needed.

I look at the dates. Could that have been when I got my first promotion at QAR? My job, as always, must have taken priority.

I read on and find out that the samples he takes from her increase with each passing quarter. I'm writing it quite factually, but the underlying tone undoubtedly becomes more excited month by month. It's obvious that we found something big.

I go back to the other folders and open the research notes. I need to find out what the discovery was. My heart is pounding with anticipation as I scan through the documents. Her green blood cells expanded. They were definitely being affected by her heartbeat. I know all this.

Then I read it. It took two years but we found out what the green blood cells are. We found out why she's able to emit light.

I shake my head. That isn't possible. That's insane. How can that be true?

There are a few more pages so I keep reading on. Just seconds pass, though, before my eyes stop dead still. There, in black and white, I see what Graham is trying to do. I see why Penny is of such interest to him. No wonder it got dangerous.

I don't move as I try to process what I've read. I finally have the truth and it's alarming.

I can't breathe. This is far too much to take in. I need a break.

I close my laptop and exhale heavily. I shove the USB sticks in my jacket pocket, hide my laptop under the passenger seat and get out the car.

I can't believe I was so careless. How could I get blinded by our findings? Penny is all that matters. She's all that matters. I knew it the first time I met her and I know it now.

I walk around the shop aimlessly, cursing myself for my selfish behaviour. With my scientist hat on I know why I acted as I did. Of course, there's no question of the breakthroughs that this could lead to. But at what cost? The cost is too high. How could I have not seen it?

I have no clue how long I've been wandering around the aisles. My head is spinning with questions and chastisement.

I look at my watch and see that half the day has already gone. I have to pull myself together. I need to stop this. I need to find Penny. There's no question in my mind now that Graham has her and I know exactly why.

I grab a quick sandwich and a bottle of water and head

back to my car.

I open up my laptop again and pull out the two USB sticks from my jacket pocket. They look identical and I'm not sure which one I looked at before.

I assume, knowing how I work, that the second one is just a carbon copy of the first. I always like to have back-ups, so it doesn't matter which one I place in the drive.

I choose one at random and wait for it to load.

To my great surprise though, this is different. There is just one folder on this drive. All it says is David.

I open the folder to find a couple of spreadsheets, a couple of PDFs and a few Word documents, mainly with coded titles. I open one of the Word documents first and I read my notes.

A relieved smile shakes my lips and I sigh.

This is the man I know I am. This is why I kept it separate.

This is how I'm going to save the woman I love.

I flick through the other documents on the stick but they all support the one idea. That needs safe keeping. I don't need that for now. For now I need to find Penny. Then I can save her.

I swap over the USB sticks and pull up the files from before. Everything we did appears to be documented here. I must be able to work out where Penny's being kept. It has to be here.

She wouldn't be at the university, that would be far too insecure. No, I state several times that we had a purpose built lab. But where is it? Surely that would be the best place to start.

I open my sandwich, making sure to keep my strength up, as I trawl through file after file. I can't believe I wouldn't document where this place is. Especially if I knew I might need to come back to it one day.

Time seems to vanish as I flick through page after page. I'm learning loads about what we did but nothing that might lead me to Penny.

I've scoured through three quarters of the files when I finally I get my answer.

I have to read it a few times it's so unexpected. Graham hasn't developed a purpose built lab in the way I imagined. Graham has converted his shed.

And that's where I'm heading right now.

I type the address into my sat nav, get my car into gear and I'm just about to pull away when I stop. What am I going to do if Graham is there? I need to think this through. I'm not the sort of man who has a fist fight. I couldn't tackle Graham physically.

I grab my phone and decide to find out some facts.

'Hello, is Dr Graham Richards available, please?' I say as the lady at Exeter University answers.

'I'll just check his line. Can I ask who's calling?'

'Yes, it's Dr David Royall.'

I wait patiently, hopeful that he's at work today.

'I'm sorry,' she says and my heart sinks. 'He's lecturing at the minute. He won't be free until four.'

I look at the clock. It's only half past two. Some luck at last! 'Never mind. Thank you.'

I hang up and quickly restart my engine, feeling energised.

It takes me about twenty minutes to get to Graham's house. He lives in a fairly big detached house at the end of a cul-de-sac. I vaguely recall coming here before. Back in the days when I was close to Graham. Before greed ruined him.

I park directly outside the house. He said Olivia was away but I question how true that is. He couldn't afford me turning up if he has got Penny locked away here.

I step out the car and it's eerily quiet. Maybe Olivia is away. There's only one way to find out.

I'm no burglar, so I decide to knock on the door. It's the best option I have.

As I wait, my brain starts bothering me with questions. If Olivia is in, would she know about what Graham's been doing? Would she approve? He never used to talk about his work to her. She was never interested. Either way, at least I could overpower her. She's only small.

The door opens and there she is: Olivia. She has long grey hair and a welcoming face, not too dissimilar to how I remember her.

'Dave?' she says with a look of utter surprise.

I squirm at the name she calls me, but I never corrected them all those years ago, I'm not going to start now. 'Hello Olivia.'

'How are you? Fancy this! Where have you been?'

'You seem surprised that I'm here,' I say.

'Well of course I am.'

'Graham didn't tell you that I saw him yesterday?'

'What?'

'We had a drink together yesterday evening.'

She seems put out by this. 'No. He never said.'

'He told me you were away seeing family.'

'What?'

Her confusion gives me hope. 'Olivia, this isn't going to be easy. I need to talk to you. Can I come in?'

She hesitates and I can see she looks worried. 'Of course.'

I follow her into the living room. It's immaculate although a little old fashioned. I hazard a guess that it's no different to the last time I was here.

I take a seat on the flowery settee and I spot it. The French doors lead out to the spacious garden and I see at the back there's a large shed. In fact it's very large. That has to be his lab.

'What's going on?' she asks, perching herself on the corner of an armchair.

'Do you know what Graham does in his shed?'

She looks at me as if I've gone mad. 'His work.'

'Do you know what sort of work?'

'What is this about?'

'I need you to answer the question.'

'Of course I don't. I never meddle with his work. You

know that. He's told me it's highly classified. It's not my place to ask any more questions.'

I know she's telling me the truth. At least that makes things a little easier. 'I'm going to cut to the chase, Olivia, and I need you to believe me. This is going to sound crazy, but Graham isn't the man we thought he was.'

'What are you talking about?'

'I have evidence to suggest that Graham has kidnapped my... my partner... and he's keeping her here. I believe in that shed.'

Olivia looks shocked. She laughs nervously. 'Is this a joke? How can you say such things.'

'Do you remember my fiancée, Penny?'

'Yes. Of course. Before you disappeared off the face of the planet.'

'I didn't disappear. I was in a car crash and I got amnesia. Penny and I were split up and it's only been in recent months that we've found each other again.'

'I'm sorry to hear that, but I don't see what it has to do with Graham.'

'I was working with Graham on a huge project before my accident and it involved my... Penny. I have very good reason to believe that Graham has picked up where we left off and he's keeping Penny in that shed. You have to let me look.'

'Don't be ridiculous. My husband is not a kidnapper.' Olivia is getting angry now.

'The project changed him, Olivia. We found something in Penny's blood that could greatly benefit the human race. It's remarkable, I will admit, but I wasn't willing to risk her life over it.'

'And you think Graham was?'

'I know he was.'

'You need to leave.' She stands and points to the door, her finger shaking slightly with her rage.

'You have to let me look in your shed. If she's not there then I'll walk away. You can call Graham and have me arrested. But what if she is there?'

'She isn't. This is ludicrous.'

'Graham lied to me when I saw him yesterday. He told me he didn't know that I'd been engaged before. He said we'd never worked on anything together, and then he told me that you were away. Furthermore, he didn't tell you that he'd seen me. Why lie if he has nothing to hide?'

Olivia takes a deep breath. 'I'm sure he has good reason.'

'What have you got to lose by letting me look in the shed?'

'The respect of my husband.' Olivia is standing firm but I see her eyes flick out to the garden. 'Graham would never forgive me.'

'But what if I'm right? Could you live with yourself if I'm right? Look, if Penny's not there then I'll call Graham myself and I'll tell him I overpowered you. But what if she is there?'

Olivia thinks for a second. She takes another breath before snapping, 'This is preposterous! Of course he hasn't kidnapped Penny. I've never heard anything so cruel and heartless. And just to prove you wrong, I'm going to let you into the shed. Then I never want to see you again.'

She leaves the room and I wait, sighing with relief. She returns several minutes later with a set of keys. 'Come on then.'

I follow her into the garden and we walk directly towards the shed door. All of the windows have blinds across them, it's impossible to see in. I'm shaking as I wait for Olivia to open it up. She struggles for a moment as to which key will fit the lock. It's a torturous delay but eventually we hear it click.

As she opens the door my heart stops. There at the back, in a cage, is Penny. She's asleep on a mattress on the floor.

'Penny!' I dart in. 'Open this cage!'

I turn to see Olivia aghast. She doesn't move. She just stands in shock. I grab the keys from her and start trying the lock.

All of a sudden alarms blaze. I turn to Olivia with horror.

'Please don't tell the police,' she says. It's obvious she wants to cry but she remains composed.

After reading my notes I know I don't want to involve the police. My priority is to make Penny safe and end this threat once and for all. That's the best thing I can do for her. Involving the police won't help with that. It's more likely to just cause her even more problems.

I fumble with the lock some more and then I find the key that works. I fling open the cage door and grab Penny in my arms. She's completely out of it.

'Take her,' Olivia says. 'I'll deal with everything else.'

'Will you be okay? I'm so sorry.'

'The truth can never hurt so much as lies,' she utters.

I take a second to look at her. I feel awful, but I'm not the one who's wronged her. 'I'm sorry,' I whisper again, then I carry Penny out of the shed as quickly as possible.

I dash back through the house with Penny in my arms and I head straight for my car. I place her gently in the passenger seat and strap her in, before I race around to the driver's side.

Without any thought at all, I pull away, leaving the screech of the alarm far in the distance.

I don't know where I'm going, but I move, and fast. I get straight on the M5 and leave Exeter behind.

I have Penny back but there's still one more thing I need to do before she's safe.

31. THE TRUTH

We've been driving for around two hours. Penny is still out cold and my head is spinning with thoughts of what I'm going to do. I know what I need to do, but as the idea becomes more realistic, my scientific mind starts to niggle me with doubts.

I glance at Penny and I know my heart will win. I can't let her go through this anymore. We've both lost so many years of our lives and I have the power to stop anything like that ever happening again. I need to make peace with the sacrifice.

Penny sits up straight in a panic. 'No!' She sees me and immediately falls back into her seat, breathlessly. I can see her hands trembling. She grabs my arm and hugs it tightly, and I hear her sobbing.

'Are you okay?' I ask.

'You saved me.' Tears trickle down her cheeks and it breaks my heart. 'Thank you. Thank you so much. How did you find me?'

'It's a long story. Do you know who took you or why?'

'No. Some old man. I don't know. Every time I came to, he drugged me again. I wanted to fight but I couldn't. I've never been so scared.'

I can't speak I'm so angry and upset.

'Ow, my arm hurts.' She pulls up the sleeve of her cardigan to find a large plaster on the inside of her elbow. She squeaks a little as she rips it off. Underneath there are traces of needle marks and a large bruise.

I shouldn't be surprised but my anger doubles.

'They wanted my blood?' she asks.

'We have a lot to talk about. I think we need to find somewhere off the radar. We're not far from Reading. Here,' I pass her my phone from the pocket inside my door. 'Do you want to find directions to a hotel nearby? Whatever seems easiest.'

'Can't we just go to the police?'

'No, trust me Penny. We can't afford for anyone to be asking questions at the minute. There's only one way I can keep you safe. Will you trust me?'

'Okay,' she mutters after a short hesitation.

'I promise, I'm going to look after you. I'm going to make sure no one ever hurts you again.'

I lock the scientist down inside of me. My mind is made up. Nothing like this will ever happen again.

Less than an hour later, we're at a supermarket in Reading. We get some snacks and also buy some clothes for Penny. She insists that she has a pair of cosy pyjamas, too. Apparently the cosier the better. As she searches through the limited selection I can't help but smile. That's my Penny. How I've missed her.

As soon as we've paid for the items we head straight to the hotel. Before we know it we're checking in to a room at a small hotel just south of Reading.

The first thing we do is hug. We hold each other for what seems like forever, and I never want to let go.

'Sorry, I must stink,' Penny says, finally pulling away.

'Not at all.' Not that I've noticed.

'I need to wash the horror off.' She heads into the bathroom and I hear the shower turn on. I take a deep breath and get my laptop out.

I need to go over the facts again. I have a lot to tell her and I need to get my head straight.

Twenty minutes later and she reappears wrapped in a towel. I've laid out her pyjamas on the bed and she swiftly puts them on before tucking herself under the duvet. She props the pillow up slightly behind her so she can easily see me and then she rests back looking utterly beaten.

'Do you want a drink or anything?' I ask.

'Maybe just some water,' she mutters.

I grab her a glass of tap water and place it on the bedside table, then I sit down on the bed next to her. I would love to give her some time to process everything that's happened but we just don't have it.

'We need to talk,' I say.

'About what?' she asks. She looks terrified again.

'It's not bad. But it is big.' I take a second. I have no choice. I need to tell her, and it needs to be now. 'I found my notes. I know what your green blood cells are and I've found out why you can emit light.' She sits up straighter. 'I also know why you were taken.'

She doesn't say anything.

'I'm so sorry. Everything that has happened to you all comes back to your blood.'

'Go on then. What's wrong with me?'

'There's nothing wrong with you.' I shuffle on the bed to get comfortable. I don't quite know how to say it. 'We never found out why this has happened to you, but you have very special blood.'

'Special in a bad way?'

'No. Not at all. You see, your green blood cells... It appears they...' I think how to put it in layman's terms. There's no way to say this without it sounding crazy. 'They're basically... Do you know what chlorophyll is?'

'Chlorophyll? As in the stuff that knocks you out?'

'No, that's chloroform. Chlorophyll is the green pigment found in plants.'

'I have plant stuff in me?' Penny looks at me like I've gone mad.

'No, not exactly. It's unique to you but it has properties akin to chlorophyll. It's been a gift to you.'

'Akin to chlorophyll? What is that supposed to mean? And how exactly has it been a gift?'

'It really has-'

'And how does that explain my light ability?'

'It's completely explains your light ability.' I shuffle in a little closer next to her. 'Do you know what photosynthesis is?'

Penny pulls a bewildered face and I can't help but smile. 'We did that at school. It's plant stuff again, but I can't remember what it's all about.'

'Photosynthesis is the process that plants go through to make food. They convert CO2 and water into glucose and oxygen.'

'Why?'

'So we can all survive. It's a vital process.'

'Okay, but what's that got to do with me?'

'Photosynthesis could not take place without chlorophyll. It's the chlorophyll that absorbs sunlight and energises the whole process. We managed to find that in your system the green cells were doing something similar. They've been absorbing sunlight into your body. It was a ground-breaking discovery.'

Penny's whole face looks stunned with utter disbelief, but she doesn't say a word.

'The green cells have been holding on to the light in your system,' I continue. 'And they would continue to do that except there's a reaction in your body that forces them to dispel it.'

'What?'

'We managed to prove that when the blood flow increases around your body it acts as a catalyst to the green cells. They become energised in their own right.'

Penny splutters a little, but no real words are formed.

I continue, hoping I can explain it better. 'Do you remember last week when I told you your green blood cells expand when your heart rate increases?' Penny just nods in reply. 'Well, it seems that's vital to what's been happening to you. They continue to expand as your heart pumps the blood faster around your body. We found that eventually they reach breaking point, and... for lack of a better word, they explode. That's when you're able to emit light. It's the expelled energy from your expired green blood cells.' Penny is looking at me agape. 'Does that make sense?' I ask.

'No!'

'Tell me what you understand from what I said and I'll fill in the gaps. I know it's complicated. This was years of dedicated research.'

'Okay.' She swipes her hair away from her face and I can see her brain working overtime. 'I think you're telling me that I have green blood cells in me that are like plant stuff. They absorb sunlight and then carry that around my body. But when I get all anxious and stuff and my heart rate goes up, they get all excited and explode. And that's when they let go of the light and it shoots out of me.'

'Yes!' I'm so happy, I kiss her. I can't believe she wrapped her head around it. It was a simple version, but the facts nevertheless.

'What the fuck?' she snaps. I don't know what to say to that. 'Sorry. But what? How did I get plant stuff in me?'

'It's not exactly plant stuff, and we never found out where it originated from. Nor why it...' I hesitate. 'Do you remember what triggered it off in the first place?'

'No. Was it in your notes?' She looks hopeful.

I hesitate again. I have a flashback of my dream but I don't want to tell her. 'You just said it was a stressful time for you. You were doing your A Levels, about to leave for university. Our research could only assume that you'd had the green cells from birth and they grew in power over time. There's nothing to discount that theory.'

'That's really creepy. So what happens to them when

they explode? Do I have exploded bits of plant stuff in me? Will that kill me?'

I try not to smile. I hate to see her so worked up, but at the same time I love the way her brain works. 'No, when they explode, the cells die. There's nothing left of them.'

'So I won't have them forever? They'll all eventually die off?'

'No, we found that they regenerate themselves. Your green cells expand at differing rates depending on the adrenaline levels in your body. The cells that don't reach expiration point eventually return to their neutral state as your body calms. It's then that they reproduce themselves. They replenish their numbers over and over. It must have been fascinating to study.'

'That's gross. I'm overrun with nasty plant stuff that keeps growing in me?'

'Actually, it's been incredible for you. The cells have had a truly positive effect.'

'How?'

'Again, very much like chlorophyll, the green cells have detoxifying and healing properties. The light ability is just a bi-product. These cells have been keeping you healthy. That's why you never get ill. They've supercharged your immune system, helping you to fight off anything that attacks your body.' I take a deep breath. 'But that's also why you were taken. That's why our lives were ruined.'

'What do you mean?' She grows pale but I have to tell her.

'You have unique internal protection. This was a groundbreaking discovery. We realised that if we could emulate it, we could potentially use it to heal people everywhere. It could replace antibiotics. It could help to cure multiple diseases.'

'My blood?'

'We hadn't even got close to being able to use it in any practical way, but the possibility was there. It still is. And that's why you were taken.'

'They wanted to study me?'

'Study your blood.'

'Why didn't they just ask for it? It'd be amazing if I could help save the world.'

I shake my head. 'It's not that simple, Penny. Maybe it should be, but it's not.' I pause. This is the part I'd change if I could turn back time. 'I read in my notes that I was hitting dead ends with my research so I enlisted the help of my old university lecturer. The old man you saw, that was Dr Graham Richards. He was like a father to me back in the day. I thought we could trust him.'

'You know him?'

'Unfortunately. The second you were taken I received a phone call telling me that if I contacted the police they'd kill you. I couldn't take the risk so I started on a journey to find you. It led me to Devon and that's where I found I'd hidden my notes.'

'Devon?' Penny's face lights up as if she's just remembered something. 'You went to Exeter University. I wrote that in my book.'

'Yes. Why is it that we can remember certain things but not everything?'

'We only remember each other, not the events that happened around us. That's the bit we really need to know, though. Do you think this Graham hurt me before?

'The last entry I made in my notes detailed how I was on a solo mission to confront Graham and tell him I was closing down the research.'

'Closing it down?'

'He'd become obsessed. We didn't even know if your blood could actually be used in any effective way - it was still just a theory - but he was bleeding you dry. It reached a pinnacle point when you stayed with him for a week. I had to work for most of it, but when I got to Devon on the Friday you were close to death.'

'What?'

'I hadn't seen it coming. I'd been so blinded by it all.

He'd forgotten that you were a person. I wrote in my notes that he'd become so transfixed with the idea of saving the human race, he'd forgotten to look after the one person at the crux of it all. He was talking about the Nobel Prize and being famous. He'd lost himself completely. He wasn't doing it for the good of science, he was using you for the good of himself.'

'Didn't you know he was like that?'

'No,' I immediately say, but then I'm quickly not so sure. He had an ego, but we all did.

Look at what my ego did to me. I was focussed far too much on my work and climbing up the ladder. It meant I also forgot to look after the one thing that mattered. I let Penny down and it's cost us dearly.

'Do you think I could save the human race?' Penny asks with wonder in her eyes.

I take a second to consider my response. It's time for my heart to rule my head. I might be an academic genius, but I've been a lousy human being. I need to start being a better person. Choosing between science and Penny has to be a no-brainer. She's all that matters.

'It's theoretically possible, yes,' I state, being as honest as I can. 'But we're still a long way from proving we can do it practically, and the damage it's caused just this far is too a high a cost for anyone to pay. There are too few guarantees for you to have lost so much over it.'

'Can't you just study me? I want to help.' Penny's face lights up again with a recollection. 'That's what my family was talking about! You had been experimenting on me, but I wanted it. I wanted to do it for the greater good. I still do. How can I know I have blood that could cure diseases and not do anything about it?'

'It's really not that simple.'

'Couldn't you just inject my blood into someone else? Wouldn't that work?'

'We looked at transfusions, but the green cells never survived.'

'But surely-'

'Penny, I wish I could do something,' I state, grasping her hand. 'But it's become too dangerous. And I think a gift like yours will always be dangerous. Our accidents could not have just been accidents. I had my car crash in Devon and I was alone in my car. At the same time you had a car crash somewhere else in the country and we both suffered from amnesia. It can't be a coincidence.'

'You don't think my family had anything to do with it?' I'm not sure if she's accusing me of suggesting such a heinous thing or if she's actually asking me the question. Either way, I know the answer.

'No. Of course not. But I do think they made the most of it. It gave them the chance to hide you from the world. That must have been what they were doing: not just hiding you from me, but hiding you from the whole world you entered into when you met me. I believe they genuinely wanted to keep you safe. It must have only been when we reconnected that Graham was able to track you down again.'

'Are you saying that I need to leave you again? No! I'm not doing it. I'm not going back to my family; back to Lee.'

I get under the duvet and place my arm around Penny, holding her close next to me. 'No, that's not what I meant at all.' I kiss her gently on the head. 'We're together forever. Nothing is going to come between us again.'

'Then what are you saying? We hide? We leave the country?'

'No, nothing like that.' I kiss her again and take a breath. This is it. There's no other way. 'I had a plan before. I realised there was no other option, and I had a plan.'

'What sort of plan?'

'We don't have a choice. Graham will never let go. He sees you as his ticket to success. And he's obviously got some support now as he certainly wasn't there when you were taken.'

'What are you going to do?'

'I found a way to remove all the green blood cells from

your body.'

'What?'

'It's the only way. If you don't have the green cells then Graham will have no use for you. You'll be the same as everyone else. You'll get ill, yes, and you won't be able to power light from your fingers, but you'll be free. We'll be free.'

'Is that even possible? You just said the cells regenerate themselves.'

'But they have to exist to regenerate. They don't spontaneously appear, they reproduce themselves. I found out that if we increase your adrenaline levels quite significantly then it will completely eradicate all the green blood cells. Ultimately it's only because you calm down again that any survive. If we destroy them all then there will be none left to reproduce.'

'So are you planning on arguing with me until I get so mad that I can't calm down again?' she asks, looking at me like I'm ridiculous.

'No,' I say fighting the urge to smile. 'I was thinking more of injecting you with adrenaline. If we synthesise it then your body won't be able to calm down as easily. The green cells will keep on expanding until they're all gone. In essence, it's the complete opposite action to what your family has been doing to you.'

Penny shuffles. She sits on her knees on the bed and addresses me directly. 'Do you really want to get rid of all my green cells? Kill off the thing that makes me special?'

I feel awful when she says it like that. 'It's to save you. To give you your life back.'

'But what about everyone else? How selfish does that make me? My blood could change so much. Maybe I should just give myself to science.'

'No! No. Enough.' I get out of the bed and stand up. 'We tried for years to emulate the power of your blood and we didn't even get close. I dread to think how much blood Graham ended up taking from you, but it's not been enough. It's never going to be enough. This will kill you, Penny. You will be sacrificing everything for what could lead to nothing.'

'But don't we have to try?'

'We did try. For years. But we failed. I almost lost you. Twice. Please don't make me lose you again.' For the first time that I can ever remember I feel the urge to cry.

Penny grabs my arms and pulls me closer to the bed. She kisses me and for a few moments we just take each other in.

'How are you going to feel when it's all gone?' she asks. 'When you've eradicated any chance of helping people all over the world?'

'Proud,' I respond. I have no idea if that's the truth, but it's what I need to tell her. 'Proud that we gave it a go but when the stakes got too high we walked away. We tried, Penny. We saw an opportunity and we dived right in. But no one should ever be asked to give up their life for what is a long shot at best.'

'What about the greater good?'

'We tried. Besides, we have tons of data. And I'm sure Graham will still have samples. If we can't progress things from what we have then what sort of scientists are we? I will not stand back and watch you suffer unnecessarily. We need to force them to take what they've got and use that. Not use you.'

'So we've still done some good?' she asks.

'We've done everything we can and everything any sane person could ever ask of us. But now we deserve our lives back. I want to go to work and know I'm coming home to the woman I love. I want a simple life. Is that too much to ask?'

She hugs me tightly before kissing me on the lips.

'If you tell me it's the right thing to do, then we'll do it,' Penny says, firmly. 'That's good enough for me.'

I sigh with relief. This will all be over with soon.

'When do you want to do it?' she asks. 'Will it just be as simple as injecting me with some something?'

'Yes, but don't worry about it for now,' I reply. 'We'll think about it tomorrow. For now you need some rest. Let's leave early and go straight to my lab and we can take it from there. By this time tomorrow, Penny, I promise you'll be free.'

32. INJECTION

My alarm goes off at six o'clock the next morning. I immediately get up. I want us to get to the lab early and get this over with as quickly as possible. Every second that Penny still has those blood cells is a second more that she's in danger.

I walk around the bed and wake Penny up gently, letting her know that we need to leave in half an hour. Her eyes are already open and I can tell she hasn't really been sleeping. I kiss her on her head and then go into the bathroom.

I have a very quick shower, brush my teeth and then return to the bedroom. I'm surprised to find Penny fully dressed, sitting on the edge of the bed. She looks exhausted and half the woman I know her to be.

'You're eager to leave as well?' I say as I grab the jeans and T-Shirt that I laid out the night before.

'I've barely slept.'

'I'm sorry.' I too tossed and turned most of the night but I can't compare my situation to hers. She must have been through hell over the past few days.

'I had horrible dreams that plants were attacking my body. It was like *Little Shop of Horrors* meets *Evil Dead.*'

I pull up my jeans and then move over to hold her. I

don't really know what she's talking about. I don't have much time for television, but horrors and evil dead can't make for a pleasant night.

'You don't literally have bits of plant attacking your body,' I say softly, trying to soothe her nasty thoughts. 'You're the same person you were yesterday, you just know a little more about yourself today.'

'I don't feel like the same person.'

'I'm sorry.' I kiss her gently. I'm determined to take this pain away.

I finish getting dressed and we check out. We get in the car at just after six thirty and head straight towards London.

Penny is very quiet on the journey and I don't know what to say. So much has changed for her recently and we're about to deliberately alter her again today. I know it's for the best but this must be overwhelming for her. I want to ask her how she's feeling but I just can't find the words.

Being a Saturday morning, traffic isn't too bad, but it still takes us well over an hour to get back to Islington.

We park the car at our home and immediately walk on to QAR Research. We've barely stepped foot in our new apartment since we moved in, but after this morning all of that will change.

Maybe I need to use some of my annual leave after this. Work is so far from my mind at the minute. I think it might be the first time that's ever happened.

Penny grabs my hand firmly as we walk up the road. We're heading in the opposite direction from where she was taken, but I understand her agitation and I squeeze her hand back. I won't let her go.

The building of QAR Research comes into view in the distance. We're almost there. We're walking at quite a pace and I'm eager for this to be over with.

Just then a sight catches my eye. I pull Penny in against the side of a building, so we're out of view.

'What is it?' she says. I can feel her trembling.

I wish I didn't have to tell her. 'It's Graham. I just saw

him getting into a car over the road.'

'Are you sure?' she gasps.

'Yes. He's with two men. They were grabbing a coffee.'

'Did they see us?'

'No, but they're going to have to move in a minute. They shouldn't really be parking there.'

I'm right. Within a couple of minutes the car drives on. It passes us but we flatten ourselves against the wall and we think we've got away without being seen.

'We need to go. Now,' I say, pulling Penny onwards, our hands still tightly interlocked.

'Where's he going?'

'I imagine he's just finding somewhere more permanent to park.'

'How does he know we're here?'

'He can't do. But it's where I spend most of my life. It's the first place I'd look for me.'

We pace up to the doors and head in. I make a beeline straight to one of the security guards. Being a Saturday, it's only security that cover reception. It's always desperately quiet in the building at the weekend.

'I'm in a rush and I need this lady here to join me. Please just let her through.' Security is of paramount importance in our facility and no visitor should ever enter without filling in the appropriate paperwork. But I need them to let her through. Not only do we not have time for the lengthy visitor admittance process, I also don't want it documented that she's been here; or worse, is still here.

'Sorry, Dr Royall. Everyone needs to follow the correct procedure.'

'I beg of you. This is life or death. I mean it. For the sake of a few minutes, please let her through.'

'I can't Dr Royall.'

'Yes you can. What's going to happen? If you get caught then it's senior management who would have to find out. And who do you think I am? I'm telling you, let her through. I'll take full responsibility.'

The security guard glances at Penny. We're still holding hands and she looks like a quivering wreck. 'What's wrong with her?' he asks.

Thinking very quickly, I say, 'She's had some bad news and I just want her to be able to hide in my office undetected for a few hours while I work. I can't leave her on her own. Come on, look at her. I just want to give her a break. She's not going to harm anyone. And you know she's here.'

'Is it your wife?' he asks.

'The love of my life,' I reply back.

He pulls a pass out of his pocket. 'Only because it's you, Dr Royall. Only for you.' He lets her through and I follow using my own pass.

I sigh with relief as I press for the lift. We step in and Penny grabs a hold of my hand again. She's still trembling and my heart is breaking at how terrified she is.

I press for the fourth floor. 'Are we not going to your office?' she asks.

'I just need to get the adrenaline first,' I say.

We get out the lift and walk onto a balcony area and I stop. Every floor has a balcony section that looks down on reception. On this particular floor you can't pass any further without the right clearance and I realise that I will have to leave Penny here. Not only is this even more secure, but if anyone sees her it will raise a lot of questions.

'You'll need to stay here,' I say.

'Why?'

'You're not allowed in the lab. I'm really sorry.'

'I won't touch anything.'

'I'm really sorry. I'll be as fast as I can.' I kiss her swiftly on the lips and then pull my hand away.

I turn quickly and swipe my way into the lab areas. I find my way into the corridor where multiple doors lead off either side, most of them laboratories. At the end of the corridor is the storage room and that's where I know I'll find what I need.

I walk into the cool environment and don't hesitate in

grabbing a bottle of adrenaline from one shelf and a syringe and gloves from just across the room on another shelf. I don't know how I'll explain their disappearance, but that's for another day.

I turn on my heels and head straight back to Penny. I don't see another person and I'm very relieved. It would be a whole different story if it wasn't the weekend.

I press the button to let myself out the secure entrance and I expect to see Penny, but she's not there. I look around the corner and then I catch her. She's pressed in against the wall with tears in her eyes.

'What is it?' I say running to her.

'It's him,' she whispers.

'Who?' I ask, but I fear I know the answer.

'Him. The man that took me. Graham. I know it is. As soon as I saw that grey hair, I knew it was him.'

I step carefully towards the balcony and I poke my head over the railings to look down. She's right. There standing in reception, talking to one of the security guards, is Graham. He's with two well-built men and my heart starts to pound.

I turn around and press for the lift. I tap my feet, begging for it to come quickly. It finally pings and I grab Penny's hand again. 'Come on.'

I guide Penny's hand up to the button and I stretch out my finger to press for the ninth floor. I don't want to let go of her, but my other hand has the bottle and syringe in it.

The lift seems to take forever and I'm perspiring heavily as we finally get out. I take a step towards the balcony again and look down. Graham isn't in sight now. I can only make out the reception area though, the barriers are too directly below me. If he's managed to get through then I couldn't see.

I lead Penny through to my office. It's deathly quiet, as it always is at the weekend, but I still feel far too exposed.

As soon as we get into my office, I place Penny in my chair, I drop the bottle and syringe on my desk, and then I lock the door and draw all the blinds. We're now completely blocked off from anyone outside.

'Slip your cardigan off,' I say to her. She's wearing a plain navy T-Shirt underneath so I have full access to her arms. I don't want to cause her any more discomfort.

She wriggles out of her cardigan and my heart cracks further. I've never seen her looking so fragile.

'Are you okay?' I ask. I grab the chair from the other side of the desk so that I can sit next to her.

She shrugs. 'What if I get really ill and die when the green cells aren't in me anymore?'

I sigh. That's the last thing I expected to be bothering her. 'What if I get really ill and die? You'll have the same chance as me; as anyone. You'll just be normal.'

'What if I'm not, though? What if these green cells are actually keeping me alive or something?' She's starting to panic.

'They're not.'

'How do you know?'

'Because I read all my notes. I did my research on this, Penny. I promise. As soon as the green blood cells expire, the rest of your blood carries on functioning like normal. You have nothing to worry about.'

'Why is it that I'm terrified, then?'

I squeeze her hand. 'I wish we didn't have to do this. I wish you could keep this special blood. But it's too dangerous. It will end up killing you and I can't lose you. Not again. Not for good.'

'But it makes me special.'

'You're special regardless. I've known you without knowing about your blood, remember? Trust me, with or without this blood, you're the most remarkable person I've ever met.'

All of a sudden my door handle rattles. I turn to look at it and I can see someone is trying to get in.

'Dave! Dave! We know you're in there. Come on. Let's be sensible. Your girlfriend has the power to change the world.'

'Dave?' Penny notes. How well she knows me.

'We need to do this now,' I say.

'Dave! Come on, let us in.'

'Ready?' I ask. Penny takes a deep breath and I see tears form in her eyes. My heart utterly shatters as I have to witness how much this is tearing her apart. I want to stop this. I want us to be able to disappear without having to remove such an extraordinary part of her. But the danger is literally upon us and we have no choice.

'Dave! You're being careless and emotional,' Graham shouts through the door. 'But fine, we can wait here all day. There's no other way out.'

'Do it,' Penny whispers.

I look at her face one last time and watch the tears stream down her cheeks. It so painful to witness.

I must focus on my task. This is the best thing I can do for her. I quickly pop the gloves on, take the syringe out of its packaging and finally pick up the bottle of adrenaline. I open the lid and draw the liquid up into the syringe. I check it carefully before I place my eyes on Penny.

She's looking in the opposite direction, her arm just held out for me. She's has such courage.

'Dave! I'm getting bored now. Don't make me do something we'll both regret.'

'I'm so sorry, Penny,' I say. I push the needle into her and inject the fluid. It takes just seconds. After I've removed it, I press my thumb on the puncture mark and massage it gently.

Penny appears to relax. A few moments go by and nothing happens.

Then her body tenses. I take my hand away and roll back my chair an inch or two, unsure of what's going to happen next.

Suddenly Penny sits upright. Her body is not just trembling now, it's shaking. Really shaking.

Fists bang against the door of my office but I tune out

the demands of my old friend. I'm totally fixated on Penny.

She starts to turn red. Her face, her neck, her arms. I notice beads of sweat as they begin to drip down her forehead.

She glares at her hands and sparks dance across her fingertips. They become bigger and brighter and faster, and then, right before us, they turn into rays of light and shoot out across the room, rapidly and fiercely.

The second they stop, her flesh illuminates like a golden flame.

I can't breathe. What if I've made a mistake? What if I've got it wrong? The cells alone might not just expand and explode, I'm now fearful that Penny is going to burst along with them.

The colour of her skin reaches a blinding peak and she screams. It's a shrill wail that sends shudders through me. This is followed, almost instantaneously, by a blast of dazzling light that drowns my office.

I bury my head in my hands, the blaze is so ferocious. Penny is still screaming but I can't do anything. I'm hampered by the brightest light imaginable that is burning through my office. I want to help, but there's nothing I can do.

Silence. It happens so suddenly. In the same millisecond that the screaming halts, everything goes dark. I can't look. I'm too afraid to look. Everything has become eerily calm.

33. UNLOCKED

All I can hear is my own intense breathing as I slowly move my hands away. I glance across and find Penny sitting up straight with her eyes wide open. She's gasping for air.

'Are you okay? Oh my God.' She doesn't answer me. She doesn't even acknowledge me. 'Are you okay?'

She still doesn't speak. She's just panting loudly. In a panic, I grab my phone from my pocket. Do I call an ambulance?

'I remember,' she bursts out with.

'What?'

'I remember. I remember everything.' I sit back down and study her face. She looks stronger. Much stronger. Her tears have all gone and she has a vivid essence about her.

'Remember what?' I ask.

'Everything. Everything that bastard did to us. We didn't have accidental car crashes. He did it to us. He did all of this to us.'

'What are you talking about?' I feel my skin crawl as I prepare for what's next.

'Oh my God! I remember us meeting. I remember our first date. Well, it wasn't really a date. We went for a drink so I could ask for your help and you didn't go home for a week.'

I smile. I feel very lucky that I've managed to remember that too.

'We were so good together. We had an amazing life together,' she says. 'But that bastard ruined it. It wasn't my family. Okay, they definitely optimised on the situation, but it was Graham that tore us apart.'

I know what she's saying is true, but it's not easy to hear.

Penny turns in her chair. She grabs my hands and addresses me with a glistening confidence. 'He worked tirelessly trying to find out what was going on with me. Like you said, you'd got as far as you could so we asked for his help.' I can physically see her churning through a mound of memories that have unlocked themselves suddenly in her mind. 'He started out being very kind and generous. But as the potential of what we were finding grew and he saw the impact it could have on the world, it was like he went insane. It's like he forgot I was a person.'

'That's what my notes alluded to.'

'We used to go down at weekends to Devon. He used his shed as a lab. That shed I was in! That's where all the work took place; off the radar, away from inquisitive eyes. At least that's what he told us. He just wanted it for himself, though. I could see that towards the end.' She takes a second to work through her memories. 'Just like you said, he asked if I could come down for a week. He said he was close to a breakthrough and he needed uninterrupted time with me. I took a week off work but you couldn't. You've always been such a workaholic.'

I feel momentarily guilty, until her breathing quickens and a darkness appears across her face. I'm dreading what she's going to say next. 'That week he used me. He totally used me. He was bleeding me dry, and prodding and poking at me. I wasn't your lab rat, I was his.'

I squeeze Penny's hands.

'He took my phone off me. He was texting you, telling you how great everything was, pretending to be me. He must have known he was doing wrong, but he was a man obsessed.' A little smile appears on her lips. 'You're clever, though. You always have known me. You knew there was something wrong, you could sense it from the messages. You turned up a day earlier. You took a day off work! You must love me.'

'You know I do. More than anything.'

'Well, there have been times when I've felt second place to your work.'

I hate myself for what she just said. I don't want that to be the case anymore. What was I ever thinking, choosing work over her?

'But it doesn't matter, because you were there for me. I've always known you'll be there for me. And I'm so grateful for that, because when you turned up I was close to death.'

All I can do is take a deep breath. None of this should come as a surprise after what I read in my notes, but it's still hard to listen to.

'You rescued me. Just like you always do. You got me out of that place and you took me home. Back to our lovely home in London. You spent the week looking after me, but with my condition it didn't take long for me recover. It was the weekend after when you returned to Devon on your own.'

'So that's why I was alone.'

'And that's when it happened.'

Penny stops for a second. What happened? I squeeze her hands, desperate to know.

'You confronted him and he told you there was no way he could save the world with you interfering. He said your heart was leading your head and you'd lost all professionalism. He injected you with some sort of drug to make you forget. We didn't have amnesia because of the accidents, we forgot everything because he drugged us!'

'What?' I can't believe this.

'You were instantly knocked out and Graham drove you

over to a hotel. He was hoping you'd wake up convinced that you were visiting family or uni friends, but when you woke up you must have been utterly confused. You must have been trying to get to your brother's house for help. You shouldn't have been driving though, not in the state you were in. That must have been why you crashed your car.'

'They never found anything in my system. Surely they would have detected the drug?'

'I don't know, you're the scientist.'

I scan my brain to think what drug he could have used. I suppose if they weren't looking for it, it could have gone unnoticed. They'd probably be more interested in checking my alcohol levels.

'When I hadn't heard from you in a couple of days, I started to panic,' Penny continues. After exhausting all other options, I Googled Exeter news and I saw it. I read all about your car crash. I got straight on the train to come and see you.'

'You came to see me at the hospital?'

'Well, I tried. But as soon as I set foot in the hospital, Graham picked me up. I was warned not to make a fuss and they wouldn't hurt you any more. I had to go with him, I didn't have a choice. He took me back to that shed and told me all about what had happened to you. He said he was going to take my pain away. It was as if he thought I'd welcome the memory loss, but it was terrifying. Before I knew it, he'd injected me with that drug too. He said if I forget all about you then his research will be so much easier. He said it would be better for everyone and it was the only real way that he could save the world.'

This is getting desperately hard to hear now. I feel the anger raging inside of me, but I don't react.

'I'm not easy to drug, though,' Penny explains. 'My body fought it. He had to give me a second dose. I passed out for a short while after that but it really couldn't have been for long. When I woke up he wasn't watching me. He'd left me in a chair and he was busy fiddling with his test tubes and things, clearly assuming I'd be out for quite a while. I summoned up all my fear and all my anger, and it set my heart racing. I crept up behind him and blinded him with my light. Then I ran. I got through the side gate and I ran out into the road. That was it for me. The last thing I remember is hitting some car. I woke up in a hospital in Coventry.'

'Bloody hell, Penny. You could have been killed.'

I'm startled as I hear the lock in my door rattle. The key is still in the lock this side so I know no one can get in, but someone is trying.

'The bastard!' Penny says. 'He took everything from us. And now he's trying to do it all over again. What's wrong with him?'

'At least you're safe now. I'll run some tests, but you have to be free of the green cells now. That was quite a light show.'

'We're not safe. He's got samples of my blood. He'll find a way to get the cells back inside of me. He's insane. He's been brainwashed by this idea of glory. He will never stop.'

Suddenly the key shoots from the lock and across the room. Not thinking a second more, I grab my phone and dial for security.

'This is Dr Royall. Someone is trying to attack me in my office.'

'Yes, we've just been alerted to the problem. A guard is with Dr Richards now coming to find you.'

'You gave him the key?' I shout.

'Dr Richards said you needed help.'

'Dr Richards is the man who's attacking me. Get up here now!'

'What?' The guard seems utterly confused but I don't have time for explanations. 'Do I need to remind you of who you're talking to?' I state quite firmly.

'We're on our way Dr Royall.' I place the handset down just as the door clicks open. Penny and I move to the back of the room, as if we'll somehow be safer there.

'What have you been doing? Are you all right?' Graham asks as he swings open my door. You could almost believe that he's genuinely concerned.

One of the building's security guards pokes his head in. 'What's the problem, Dr Royall?' He looks small compared to Graham's sidekicks. He could easily be overpowered and I don't feel at all safe.

'It's all right,' Graham says and his colleagues push the guard back. 'Let me deal with it.'

'You should be ashamed of yourself!' Penny screams at him. She's a totally different person to the trembling wreck that was with me just minutes ago. I like it. This Penny is so much more the girl of my dreams. This is the Penny that's locked in my memories. 'I remember what you did. You made us forget about each other.'

Graham stands in the doorway and studies us both. 'Has she been taking drugs again, Dave? She does look quite a mess.' He steps over so he's closer to us. 'I have something that could help you out. Perhaps calm you down a bit. I know the right dose this time.' He smiles and drops his voice. 'You know, when you got knocked down by that car, Penny, I gave you another two doses before the ambulance arrived. It's fascinating how strong you are. Can't you see how much potential your blood holds? Why would you want to keep it to yourself?'

'You could have killed her,' I snap.

Graham shakes his head. 'Where is that brilliant man that I used to teach? You've become far too emotional. It's like you don't care about the impact her blood could have on the world. We could change everything.'

Four security guards finally appear in the doorway. 'Dr Royall?' one says, looking for clarification as to what the problem is. Graham is so well respected, I can see why they'd be confused. I certainly can't believe he's the same person I used to know.

'These men have been trying to attack us,' I reply.

The guards look at Graham strangely. 'Dr Richards?'

'Arrest them!' Penny demands. Again they look at us like we've gone mad. 'He kidnapped me! You saw me downstairs. I was hiding from him. He kidnapped me and you just let him saunter into the place.'

'What is she talking about?' the guard who let us up earlier asks.

'They're confused,' Graham says. 'But I can help them. They've been through quite an ordeal.'

'Yes, the ordeal is that Dr Richards is attacking us,' I say.

Graham turns to the guards, shaking his head. 'Do I look like I'm attacking them? They've got themselves into quite a state.'

The guards look at each other, unsure of what to do.

'Arrest him!' Penny orders again.

'Why are you still standing there?' I ask the guards. 'I'm telling you, as a director of this facility, this man has put myself and my partner in serious danger. You need to arrest him. Isn't it your job to protect me?'

The one guard nods. 'Of course, Dr Royall. Sorry.' He pushes Graham to the wall and holds him in place as the other guards follow suit and detain Graham's friends.

'This is ludicrous!' Graham yells. 'How dare you treat me like this! Just wait until Bernard finds out.'

'Check his pocket,' I say.

'Pardon?' the guard asks.

'Check his pocket,' I repeat more sternly. 'But carefully.'

The guard pats him down. Within a few seconds he seems to have found something. He reaches into Graham's inside coat pocket and pulls out four syringes. Penny gasps!

'What are these?' the guard asks.

'He was going to drug us,' Penny states.

All Graham can do is shake his head as the guards call for the police.

'Did you see Olivia last night?' I ask him.

Graham turns to me and I see a glimmer of fear in his eyes. 'No. Why? What did you do? She was out. Her sister had an emergency.'

'Really? There was no emergency when I saw her yesterday.'

'What did you do?'

I feel the stress lighten as I watch Graham squirm. He's demanding over and over that I tell him what Olivia knows, but I just don't care. He deserves nothing less. I finally have the power over him.

'You know what?' I say, cutting through his rant. This silences him. 'I've just given Penny a shot of adrenaline.'

His eyes widen as he realises what this means. 'You idiot!' he screams at me. 'Dave, you idiot!'

'And you know what else,' I say, and I know this will feel really good. 'My name is David.'

I take a deep, satisfied breath, and then I turn to Penny. I don't want to see his face anymore. He's still screaming at me, but I just happily tune him out. I want nothing more to do with that man ever again.

'I love you,' Penny says as she throws her arms around me. We stand still, holding each other, and I feel strangely complete. For the first time that I can ever remember, I feel complete.

34. HEAVEN

The next few hours seem to drag. The police eventually arrive and Graham and his sidekicks are finally taken away, but then we have to spend ages giving our statements.

We only tell the police that Penny had been kidnapped because Graham had this strange idea that she could save the world. We don't need to say anymore. It's up to them now.

After hours of waiting around and going over endless details, the police have everything they need and they leave, but neither of us can relax. All that's playing on our minds now is if it's worked. We have to find out if the green blood cells have been eradicated.

I take another sample of Penny's blood and then swiftly make my way to the lab. Without hesitation, I spin the sample in the centrifuge. It doesn't need long, just a few minutes. Although it's the longest few minutes of my life.

As I remove it, my hands are shaking with anticipation. I take a quick look, but then I start to doubt myself. Am I really seeing it right? I analyse it more carefully, just to be sure. It's quite clear, though. It can't be interpreted any other way.

I carefully take the sample back up to my office to show

Penny the evidence. Her blood is just as it should be. It's just the same as any other sample I've ever worked with. I sigh with relief as the huge weight of the last few days floats away. It's all over with.

Penny sits on my lap in my chair and we enjoy a relieved embrace. We sit quietly and let the reality settle in. No one can hurt us anymore. The drama, the fear, the years dreaming about a reality that we weren't allowed to remember; it's all gone now.

'I don't feel different, like I thought I would,' Penny says.

'You shouldn't feel different.'

'Do you think I'll miss it?'

'Maybe. Perhaps when you first get the flu. You'll probably be cursing me then. Although we don't know how your body is going to react. You haven't been avoiding illness all this time, you've been overcoming it with great ease. You might still be very strong.'

'Is it wrong that I feel sad?'

I stroke her face. 'I think it's only right. You've made a huge sacrifice. But at least you're safe. Graham wouldn't have stopped.'

'I can't believe he was going to drug us again.'

I shake my head. I dread to think what could have happened. This could have ended very differently.

'You know what,' Penny says, kissing my nose, 'I'm absolutely starving.'

As soon as she says it, I realise how hungry I am too. 'Yes, let's get some food.'

I take us out for lunch in the closest pub we can find, and I order a bottle of champagne to go with it. If there was ever a time to celebrate, it's most definitely now.

We eat and drink and talk about the last few days, sharing stories of what we've been through. I tell her about my brother and we agree to go and visit him very soon. I want to do it soon.

It's nearly four o'clock when we eventually arrive home. Exhausted, we head straight for a lie down. We curl up in each other's arms and enjoy our first time sharing our bed. It's very sad that we moved in four days ago and this is the first time we're here together.

I want to make love to her. I want to be with her properly and express my love for her without all of these other things - like wives and husbands, crazed scientists and rays of light - hanging over our heads. But as I look down at her face nestled on my chest, I can see she's asleep. I kiss her gently on the head and smile. I love her.

The next thing I know it's Sunday morning. I'm still in my clothes from yesterday. I must have been in a deep sleep. I guess I needed it.

I roll over to see Penny but she's not there. I get up to look for her and I find her filling the kettle in the kitchen.

'What time is it?' I ask, rubbing my eyes.

'Just after six. Sorry, I was getting uncomfortable. We've been out since we got home yesterday. Toast?'

'Do we have bread?'

'Of course.' She looks a little smug as she pulls out four slices of bread from a loaf in the freezer.

I grab two mugs from the cupboard and spoon in some coffee granules. 'How are you feeling?' I ask.

I turn to see a huge smile on her face. 'Like me again.'

'Yeah?'

'I remember so much. Things keep coming back to me.' She walks over and kisses me on the cheek. 'I wish you could remember too. But I'm going to fill you in. I'm going to start with how we met and work right through to when that bastard spilt us up. I'm going to tell you everything I remember.'

'Actually, I've remembered how we met.'

She takes a step back, surprised. 'How?'

'When you were gone, it came back to me in a dream. I was doing that talk and you were there. You were the sexiest woman I'd ever seen, standing there looking all naïve and inquisitive, waiting to ask me that question.'

'You like inquisitive women then?' she smirks.

'I don't think I knew what I liked until you came into my life.'

'Do you remember those first few days we spent together? We were inseparable.'

'The dream ended in the pub where we had that drink. But I had flashes that we pretty much spent all our time together after that. I think you came to London around your lectures and I came to see you as much as I could.'

'With your work, I might add,' Penny says. 'You haven't changed at all.' She smiles warmly. 'But I love you for it. I've always loved your ambition.'

I grab the kettle as it clicks off and pour water into the mugs. 'Maybe it's time for a change,' I shrug.

'What do you mean?' she asks, putting the bread in the toaster.

'The last few days have given me some perspective. Work has always been my number one but I don't want it to be like that anymore.'

Penny's silent for a moment. Finally she asks, pretending not to have a clue what the answer could possibly be, 'What do you want your number one to be then?' She's going to make me say it.

I wrap my arms around her waist and kiss her. 'Just some woman I've been seeing.'

'Really? She sounds amazing.'

I kiss her again. She has such a stirring effect on me. Even with her hair all awry and in her thick pyjamas, I still find her utterly irresistible. 'She is.'

'Aren't you lucky.'

I kiss her more passionately this time. She has no idea how lucky I feel. Not just because I found her in the first place, but I'm the luckiest man alive to be given a second chance.

My hands start to explore underneath her pyjama top as lust takes charge. I've missed her far too much. But not here. We've had sex in far too many other places. All I want now is her in our bed.

I grab her hand and lead her back to the bedroom. I gently push her down on the duvet and edge myself on top of her. 'We were supposed to christen this bed days ago,' I whisper in her ear before I kiss it.

'We'd better make up for lost time, then,' she whispers back.

I waste no time in stripping her of her pyjamas and she helps me remove my own clothes. I'm aching with desire for her now.

With so much expectation and so much prolonged desire, within minutes we're climaxing. It's like nothing I've ever felt before and I feel lucky all over again that this incredible woman is back in my life.

Breathlessly, we take each other in before our bodies slowly relax together in a loving embrace.

I close my eyes and rest my head next to hers. But the cuddle doesn't last for long before Penny sits up right, like she's been electrified with a burst of energy.

'Would you drive me home?' she says.

I feel a sharp pain strike my heart. I've done something wrong. 'You are home,' I say.

'No, don't be stupid.' She hits me playfully on the arm. 'Will you drive me back up to Rugby? My old home.'

'Why?' Then it seems obvious. 'To collect the rest of your things?'

'Well yeah, that too. But more because I want to confront my family. I've got all my memories back and I have a few things I want to say to them. And I want to do it now while I'm all fired up. They have a lot to answer for and I want to share with them a few facts myself.'

I sit up. I can see how determined she is. It's a fire in her I never saw before but it was always there in the girl of my dreams. It feels good to have my Penny back.

'No problem,' I reply. 'But I'm going to insist that we eat something first. You get that toast sorted, we'll have a shower together and then we'll get on our way.'

'We'll have a shower together?' she grins.

'Did I not mention how the shower needs christening too?' I try to say it seriously.

She shakes her head but she's smiling. 'Just like that first week we spent together. All you ever think about is sex.'

'Is that a problem?'

She jumps off the bed and I breathe in her gorgeous naked body. I feel like it's a second honeymoon period for us. She's awoken something in me and I can't wait to get to know her all over again.

'It wasn't a problem then and it's not a problem now,' she states quite to the point. 'Especially as you got the priority right: definitely toast first.'

She disappears off into the kitchen and I lie back and smile. It's been such a horrendous week, but finally I feel like I'm in heaven.

35. LOST PROPERTY

Two hours later and we make it to the car. It's been a lovely leisurely morning and I feel elated.

As we drive up north, Penny doesn't stop for breath telling me stories about our past. It's all a bit overwhelming, but the memories are still coming back to her and she's very excited. I find it hard to take everything in. She's giving me far much information. It's also quite unnerving to have forgotten it all. But it's nice to see Penny happy.

It takes just under two hours to get to Rugby. Penny phoned everyone in her family on the way to summon them to the house. Including Lee.

I don't know how I feel about seeing him again. I suppose I could be smug that I won in the end, but I actually feel uncomfortable.

I park at the end of the drive and Penny marches up to the door. She rings on the doorbell and I stand right behind her.

Her dad answers and he lets us straight in. We head into the living room to find all of the family there, all staring at us. I feel like a misbehaving animal at the zoo.

'Thank you all for coming,' Penny nods, confidence oozing out of her. She is standing tall in front of her family who are all sitting down with anticipation, like she's about to make an important announcement. I stand beside her to offer my support, not that I think she needs it. She's fully in charge of this situation.

'What's this all about? What's he done to you now?' her dad asks.

'Nothing. Nothing at all.' I can tell this immediately riles Penny but she keeps composed. 'In fact, you all need to know that if it wasn't for David, I'd probably be dead. You're all a bunch of morons.' This goes down like a lead balloon and my heart sinks along with it. This isn't the opening I was expecting. Then she announces, 'I was kidnapped this week.'

Her dad stands up. He looks ready to knock me into next week. I want to back off but I stand firm. I refuse to let a man like that get the better of me.

'Oh, sit down, dad,' Penny tuts. 'None of you have a clue.'

'Why didn't you tell us?' Tammy snaps, aiming it directly at me.

'Because he knew my life was in danger and he wasn't in a position to tell anyone. He went on a one man hunt to Devon to track me down and he saved me from the man who really was trying to hurt me. It wasn't David hurting me all those years ago, it was another man. None of you could see it. You're all a bunch of idiots.'

'Stop saying things like that!' Tammy demands.

'What are you talking about? What other man?' her dad asks.

'A man now safely locked up thanks to David. You should all be grateful he's in my life.'

'Whatever,' Lee chirps up with. 'If you hadn't have met him, you wouldn't have been in danger in the first place. He's not good for you, Loppy.'

Penny turns to address Lee quite directly. 'Not good for me? You mean like you were? At least he's honest with me. At least I know where I stand with him. I'd dumped you but you let me believe that we were engaged. You married me knowing that I was in love with someone else. You couldn't even tell me that I'd had singing lessons.' She turns her head to me. 'I'd always loved to sing so I started singing lessons at uni and then I kept them going for years. I'd been in three different choirs. I'd performed *Defying Gravity* five times. No wonder it wasn't hard for me to sing.'

I don't know what the relevance to defying gravity is, but it does explain why she has such a beautiful voice.

She turns back to Lee and her body tenses up again. 'You couldn't even give me that one little thing.'

'How was he supposed to?' her dad argues. 'We needed you to remain calm at all times, not star on stage.'

'Oh yeah! Well, for your information, when I was supposedly at all those yoga classes, I'd actually joined a choir. I was singing anyway. But behind your backs because you forced me to lie to you.'

I can see this shocks everyone in the room and I keep my lips tightly shut. The fact that I was there to see her perform will most definitely not make things easier. I pray to myself that she doesn't tell them.

'You think you know it all, don't you,' Lee says. 'But you're such a silly little girl. This is why we had to protect you. He's still going to use you for your blood. He's no knight in shining armour, you just can't see it. You're the idiot.'

'Actually, Lee, I know a lot more than you think. Like I remember how I didn't leave you for David, I left you because you were trying to control me. You lot have always been trying to control me.'

'How dare you!' her dad says.

'Oh, come on.'

'We just wanted what was best for you,' her mother says.

'Unlike him,' Lee hisses.

'Again, you're completely wrong. David has made the biggest sacrifice of all.' I'm taken aback by her statement. Does she mean it? 'Even though I'm a scientific miracle,

David has removed all the weird stuff from my blood. He's got rid of my ability. He did it to make sure I'm safe. He did it for me.'

There is silence across the room. Then Tammy stands up. 'Oh Loppy,' she says. I cringe internally. I hate that name for her. She hugs Penny and I can see for a moment that Penny doesn't know what to do. 'You've lost your power?'

'Why are you looking so shocked?' Penny says, pushing Tammy away. 'You never wanted me to have my special blood. You drugged me to stop me having it. At least David was honest.'

'No, I'm happy for you, Loppy. That's such great news. That ability cost you so much.'

I see Penny tense up. I think she's ready to explode. 'Yes, and don't I bloody well know it! I get away from one drugging psychopath only to fall into the grasp of my family who also think it's okay to drug me. Do you not realise how much you've taken from me?'

'David drugged you?' her mother gasps.

I start to tense up now. Can they really not see the irony in all of this?

'David is not a psychopath!' Penny shouts. 'He's also never drugged me. And it's starting to seem that he's about the only one who bloody well hasn't! I remember it all. Oh yeah, I forgot to tell you that. I've got my memories back. I remember exactly how it was and I can see very clearly how you were all controlling me.'

'You've got your memories back?' Tammy asks with surprise.

'Yes. We didn't get amnesia because of the crashes, we had accidents because we'd been drugged to forget. Long before you stepped in, someone else was trying to keep us apart. You just finished the job for him.'

'Are you for real?' Billy asks.

'And you really did finish his work,' Penny mumbles. I see a metaphorical light bulb ping above her head. She must have remembered something new. 'Where's all my stuff?

What did you do with it?'

'What stuff?' Tammy asks.

Penny turns to me. 'After you got out of hospital, where did you go? Where were you living?'

'In Islington,' I reply and I know exactly where this is leading. I too am very eager to know the answer to this question. 'I went back to the apartment I'd been living in for years. Apparently alone.'

'But he wasn't alone, was he?' Penny says, glaring around at her family. 'What did you do? Where are my belongings that were in our home together?'

An awkward silence grasps the room. Billy is the only one who's willing speak. 'Tammy and dad took your key and went down to London while you were still in hospital,' he explains. 'They cleared out all your stuff and made it look like David lived alone.'

'When we found out that David had also lost his memory, we saw a chance,' Tammy says. 'We just wanted to protect you.'

'Well you didn't. All you did was hurt me. Don't you see?'

'Didn't you think it was a coincidence that Penny and I had both been in accidents just days apart and we'd both suffered from severe amnesia?' I ask, not able to stay quiet any longer.

'We saw it as a gift,' Tammy responds. 'It's what we'd all been praying for: a chance to get Loppy back. A chance to get her away from you.'

'And that's why you're idiots!' Penny argues. 'David is the only person who's ever been able to help me. You ruined our lives for nothing.'

'We did the best we could to protect you,' her dad states.

'No you didn't. You made me Loppy Fox. You hid away who I really am and forced me into a life that suited all of you. Well I'm not her anymore. I've never really been her. I'm Penelope Edwards. That's the real me.'

Lee stands up at this. 'You're still my wife!'

'Only on paper, Lee. Shut up. I never wanted to be your wife. You effectively tricked me into it. Believe me, a divorce is well on its way.'

Lee is ready to argue and I don't take my eyes off him. He opens his mouth but quickly backs off.

'Have you still got my stuff?' Penny asks Tammy.

Again, there's a moment of awkward silence before her dad finally says, 'We gave all your clothes away to charity.'

'Actually, not all of them. I did keep some bits,' her mom adds.

'You gave away my stuff to charity? My personal belongings?' Penny is quite rightly enraged.

'You had no use for it,' her mother justifies.

'Only because you manufactured it that way. Besides, if that's the case, why keep some bits?'

'Well you had such nice stuff. You had a lot of money between you. You with that high flying job and him working all the time. I kept some of your nice dresses and things.'

'Money?' Penny asks, her eyes widening even more. 'Where is all this money?' She glares at Lee. If looks could kill, he'd most definitely be a dead man.

'It's in a savings account. We're not thieves, Loppy,' Tammy says. I can't help but beg to differ inside, but I know it's not my place to argue right now. 'We didn't know what to do with it, but we knew you'd wonder why you had such a healthy bank account if we didn't hide it. We used some towards your wedding and kept the rest for you. We thought maybe you and Lee could have a surprise lottery win one day or something.'

'How much is in there?' Penny asks.

'How did you get access to her bank account?' I follow with.

'We found her details when we went to London,' Tammy explains. 'It wasn't hard.'

'How much money did I have?' Penny pushes. Frankly I think the fact that her family has completely abused her trust is a far more pressing issue, but I decide it's best to keep quiet.

Tammy shrugs. 'A few thousand.'

'Right, I want the details. And mom, show me these dresses.'

Penny turns to me. 'I'll wait here,' I say. Not only am I not the slightest bit interested in viewing Penny's old dresses - as sexy as I'm sure they are - but I have something else on my mind.

The girls make their way towards the stairs and I chase after Tammy. 'Tammy.' She turns around. 'Can I have a quiet word, please?'

She looks at me a little unsure but then nods. She leads me through to the kitchen.

'What do you want?' she asks.

'Where's the ring?' I say. It's been niggling at the back of my mind for days now. Every time I've talked about Penny, I've had this ache in my chest about her being my fiancée. I want her to be my fiancée.

'What ring?' she replies. I know she knows what I'm talking about, but I see how it's going to be.

'We were engaged. I might not be able to remember anything myself, but I know I would have bought Penny an engagement ring. Where is it?'

'I don't know.' Tammy shrugs nonchalantly but I don't buy it.

'If I know Penny - and I really do - she wouldn't have taken it off. She would have been wearing it when she got knocked down by that car. Where is it?'

Tammy sighs. 'We sold it.'

'Why are you doing this?'

'Are you going to propose again?' she asks rather aggressively.

'I love her, Tammy. She's the love of my life.'

'But you... You...'

'Tell me you've never seen her happier. Tell me when I first proposed that she wasn't over the moon. I can't remember it, but I'd be surprised if you could honestly tell me that Lee is a better match for her than me.'

Tammy sighs again. 'What makes you think I've got the ring?'

'Because you're her sister and I know you love her. All of the things you did were massively misjudged, but I don't doubt that somewhere along the way it was guided by love for your sister. You know how much Penny loves me. You would have known all those years ago. There is no way you could get rid of something that holds such sentimental value to your sister. Or have I got you all wrong?'

She takes a very deep breath. 'Are you going to propose again?'

I stand still and say nothing for a few moments. I know the answer. The answer is easy. I've never wanted anything more in my life. I just don't want anyone else to be the first to hear it. But I need to get that ring. I don't want to buy another one. I want Penny to have the engagement ring that I originally bought for her. It's what I wanted for her in the first place and it will mean so much more.

'I want her to be my wife. I wish we'd never gone through this and we were already married. So yes. The second I get the chance, I'm going to ask her to marry me again. Is that a problem?'

Tammy glares at me. She's the sort of woman you want on your side. I can't believe she could be my sister-in-law one day. Hopefully will be.

'Can we come to the wedding?' she asks, to my surprise.

'Why wouldn't you be at the wedding?'

'We're not exactly in Loppy's good books right now. She hates us.'

'She doesn't hate you.'

'She does. I know you can't see it, but when she left for London we were all worried sick. We were terrified of what was going to happen to her. We didn't really know you, you were always working. All we could see was a scientist interested in our sister's weird blood. When we got the chance, we tried to protect her, but it put a huge strain on the family. We thought we were doing what was best, though. Isn't that all you can ever do?'

'I understand that. And Penny will too. She's angry at the minute, and quite rightly so. She's also really hurting. But you're her family and I know how important family is to her. I promise, get me that ring and I will help Penny work through this. I won't let her disappear out of your lives.'

'You'd do that?'

'I won't just be marrying Penny, I'll be marrying into your family. That's important to me too.'

Tammy's eyes soften and it's quite a relief. 'You know, we never chatted like this before. I guess you seem okay.'

'Will you get the ring?'

Tammy studies her fingers as she contemplates my question. I wait patiently, hoping that she'll see sense. Finally she looks up at me. 'Do you really love her?' she asks.

I shake my head. 'That doesn't even touch the surface of how I feel. She's everything to me and I'm going to look after her forever. And she feels the same way about me in return. But you already know that, don't you.'

Tammy thinks for a second before telling me, 'You'd better look after her.'

'Always.'

Her whole body relaxes and I feel hopeful that she's finally giving in. 'You were right. I slipped it out of her belongings and I hid it in my bag. No one else seemed to notice. It's been in my jewellery box ever since.' She pauses, like she's working something out in her mind. 'I do know how she feels about you. It's like she lights up when she's around you. It's hard to miss. That was another reason why I was so mad when I thought you'd hurt her. But how could I get rid of my sister's engagement ring? Wait here.'

She makes her way out of the house and I wait eagerly. Billy and Julian are still in the living room and I assume everyone else is still upstairs. Feeling a little awkward, I follow Tammy's footsteps and head out onto the drive. I need the air.

I look through my emails on my phone, but I'm not really concentrating. This is a torturous wait.

I'm delighted when Tammy finally reappears about fifteen minutes' later. She walks right up to me and slyly places a ring in my hand. I pop it straight in my pocket. I'm desperate to look at it but I'm fearful that Penny might suddenly appear from nowhere.

'Thank you,' I say, meaning it sincerely.

'Don't tell anyone. I mean how sentimental I am.'

I smirk. 'Only if you don't tell a soul that I'm going to propose. Although eventually I'm going to have to tell Penny that you kept her ring for her.'

'She'll be mad!'

'She'll be touched,' I say.

'What are you doing out here?' Penny asks, stepping outside to join us.

'Just getting to know Dave better,' Tammy says. I cringe and Penny glares straight at me.

'Dave?' Penny repeats.

'Loppy and Dave,' I shrug, and we both snigger.

36. ALL THAT MATTERS

Despite the big project that my team is working on and despite how out of character it is for me - in a move I didn't even expect myself - I ask Bernard for the week off work. He's only too happy to oblige considering the fact that I was attacked in my office at the weekend. And this begins the longest spell I've had off work since the car crash. In fact the longest spell I've ever had off work when I wasn't hospitalised.

Even more out of character, it's now Tuesday and I haven't checked my laptop once. I've not even been thinking about it. I've been too consumed with planning my proposal to Penny.

I know she said yes before, and I know she's left her current husband to be with me. I'm also aware that she's moved halfway across the country and in every way she's told me that she loves me. But I can't shake this fear that she's going to say no. What do I do if she says no?

I've sent Penny out for the day. I gave her five hundred pounds and told her to go shopping. I said it was a hundred pounds for every birthday I'd missed over the years. She argued, of course, and promised to give me five birthday treats in return, but in truth it was really to get her out of the way.

Since she's left, I've been a very busy man. I made a quick and very important stop at work and then I raced around the supermarket. I've been preparing our three course meal now for about an hour, and I've just put the final candle in place right in the centre of the table. I'm about as ready as I'm ever going to be.

I take a second to make sure I haven't forgotten anything, but I try not to overthink it. I can't believe I'm only thirty-four and this is the third time I'm going to propose. Although, to be fair, I've only proposed to two women and I don't remember doing it the first time.

I wonder how I did it? I'm sure Penny must have told me in her never-ending rambles about our past, but my brain reached saturation point by early Sunday afternoon. I really need her to tell me one story a day not everything in the space of a few hours. But I'm sure I'll eventually catch up.

The proposal to Suzanne was incredibly casual. In fact it was as much a surprise to me as it was to her. She suggested we live together, I figured marriage was a good idea as well. I wanted nothing more at the time. She filled the void that Penny had left behind. It seems so obvious now.

Due to the sheer spontaneity of my proposal to Suzanne, not surprisingly I hadn't bought a ring. We bought it together a few weeks later. She crippled my bank account that month, that's for sure. It seemed to matter greatly to her how much it cost. I could never understand why.

I suppose that's why I never thought she loved me. The cost of the ring seemed to mean more than what it signified. It's never like that with Penny.

I slip Penny's ring out of my pocket. It's beautiful. It's quite a large diamond but it's an unusual shape, like a flower. I've never seen a ring quite like it. It suits us. Penny and David Royall. Mr and Mrs Royall. I love the sound of that.

I hear the front door slam shut and I pop the ring quickly back in my pocket.

'That smells delicious,' Penny beams as she enters the kitchen. She's weighed down with bags.

'You spent the lot?' I ask. She pulls a face and I'm not quite sure what it means.

'Don't judge me,' she says.

'Why?' I ask, not able to stop the smile from growing on my face.

'I knew I had that money from before as well. And there are so many gorgeous shops in London.'

'How much did you spend?'

'Erm... Let's just say it's closer to the one thousand mark.'

I can't help but laugh.

'You're not mad?' she asks, quite seriously.

'Why would I be mad?'

'Because I don't have a job. I should be saving.'

'You needed a new wardrobe. Penelope Edwards and Loppy Fox do not dress in the same way.'

'I won't spend any more, I promise.'

'Will you stop worrying about money.'

'But-'

'Stop it. Just relax and enjoy yourself. That's all I want.'

'Okay.' She pauses and a small smirk grabs her lips. 'Just to make you aware, I do still have some of my old jumpers. You know, for when it's really cold.'

'Good to know,' I respond, trying not to snigger. 'For now, though, I want you to put on your most expensive dress and join me for dinner.'

'Are you wearing a suit?' she asks, suddenly clocking my shirt and tie. I had to dress up for this night.

'I knew you'd be coming home with all these fancy clothes. I didn't want to feel left out,' I say as an excuse.

'So cute.' She kisses me on the lips before heading to the bedroom with her new items.

I take out the salmon terrines that have been chilling and I plate them up ready for Penny's return. Then I light the candles and open the wine. The champagne is in the fridge, but that will have to wait until later. Hopefully.

She reappears and I stop in my tracks. She's wearing a stunning blue dress that shimmers in the candlelight. It's just to the knee and shows a lot of cleavage. It's perfectly respectful but has plenty on offer to drive my imagination wild.

'You look beautiful,' I say. I can't take my eyes off her.

She poses for a second and then joins me at the table. We tuck in to our starters and Penny immediately begins to talk me through her shopping trip. I'm trying to listen, I really am, but I'm getting increasingly nervous about the impending question.

The starters are quickly polished off and then I serve up our beef main course. As I bring the plates over I can feel my heart pounding.

'You're not hungry?' Penny asks as she watches me move my dauphinoise potatoes around my plate. I can't wait anymore. This is killing me.

'I have something on my mind,' I say.

She looks worried. 'What is it?'

I stand up and walk around the table to be next to her. I slowly edge down on one knee and pull the ring out from my pocket.

'Penelope Edwards. Love of my life. Will you marry me?'

Penny gasps. I see her lip quiver and I hope it's a good sign. 'Yes. Of course I will!' she beams. She throws her arms around me and hugs me tightly.

We kiss and then I take her hand. I place the ring on her finger and Penny gasps for a second time. Tears trickle down her face.

'This is my ring,' she says. 'It's my ring, from before.'

'You remember it?' I ask with surprise.

'How could I ever forget it.'

'Your sister kept it.'

'Oh my God!' She kisses me again. 'This is amazing. It's all like before. It's just like before.'

'The ring?' I ask, not really sure what she's referring to.

'Everything. This is how you proposed to me last time. Well, the food wasn't quite so fancy. You've definitely improved in the kitchen. But we had an intimate meal last time and this is what we're doing now. It's like it's officially the setting of our proposal.'

I don't know what to say. I had no idea. I just couldn't think of a better way to do it. 'I love you, Penny,' is all I can utter.

'I love you too, David.'

'All we need to do now is get divorced,' I smile.

'I hope we can do it quickly. I can't wait to be Mrs Royall.'

'I'm sorry you've had to wait this long.'

'It's not your fault. We just need to make sure we definitely get to the marriage bit this time.'

'Nothing's going to stand in our way this time,' I say with confidence. 'Losing you once was the biggest mistake of my life. I'm not going to let that happen again.'

I wake up at around two am. My head is foggy from all the wine and champagne, but it doesn't stop my mind from being niggled at. With all of the excitement earlier, I forgot to do something very important. I need to get it done. It's too risky for it not to be done.

I check that Penny is properly asleep. I can hear her snoring faintly and I'm quite confident.

I wrap my dressing gown around me and sneak out of the bedroom. I grab my car keys from the kitchen as quietly as I can and tiptoe over to one of the other bedrooms; the one that we're going to make into an office for me. I approach the chest of drawers that the landlord has given us and I open the top drawer.

It's where I shoved it earlier. I had to get the cooking started and I meant to come back and move it, but I forgot. It was careless of me but it's been a big night.

I place my fingers carefully on the vial and I take it out of the drawer. It's Penny's blood. Her original blood. The blood with the green cells. It's the last remaining sample and I need to make sure it's safe.

I open one of the boxes in the corner of the room that I'm yet to unpack and inside I find a small safety deposit box. I locate the very small key that's on my keyring and I open it up.

This is where I keep my passport and other important documents. It's the best I've got for now, until I can work out a plan. I'll need to freeze the sample somehow. I have a lot to figure out. But for now I just need to make sure that Penny doesn't see it.

I place the vial carefully in the box and lock it up again with a relieved sigh.

As I stand up, I feel the tug of guilt though. Should I tell Penny?

That's the last remaining sample in the world of the blood that could help the human race. I heard from Olivia that she'd cleared out Graham's shed. He won't be able to touch Penny's blood anymore. So this is it. The last remaining drops are right here.

I made a promise to Penny that I would keep her safe. And I must do that. So I'll keep this locked away and I'll keep her safe.

I tuck the safety deposit box away and I make my way to the door. As I open it, I take one last look in the corner of the room.

It could eradicate disease.

No, Penny is my number one. I never want to lose her again.

I don't want to deceive Penny, but I can't deny there's something comforting in knowing that there's still a sample of her blood that I can work on.

No! No. I mustn't think such things.

I turn away and leave the room, closing the door tightly behind me. All that matters now is Penny. My fiancée.

I head back to the bedroom and slip under the duvet next to her. I look at her sleeping. She's so beautiful.

She's all that matters now. All that matters in the world.

ABOUT THE AUTHOR

Lindsay is a British author who lives in Warwickshire with her husband and cat. She's had a lifelong passion for writing, starting off as a child when she used to write stories about the Fraggles of Fraggle Rock.

Knowing there was nothing else she'd rather study, she did her degree in writing and has now turned her favourite hobby into a career.

Lindsay is also the author of:

- The *Bird* Trilogy, a supernatural love story full of magical twists turns.

- *Emmett the Empathy Man*, a comic tale about a superhero who comes to life with disastrous results.

All of her books are available on Amazon.

IN THE BLOOD